THE EARLY LIFE OF STEPHEN HIND

THE EARLY LIFE

OF

STEPHEN HIND

Storm Jameson

HARPER & ROW

Publishers

NEW YORK

CHAPTER 1

SETTLING himself in his seat in the aeroplane, a long narrow hand on each bony knee in the posture of an Egyptian priest-king, Chatteney closed his eyes. He kept them closed when the air hostess spoke to him, and his lips, too. If, thought his secretary, he meant to sleep all the way, he could have given me the window seat, so that I saw whatever there is to see. It was his first flight, he was concealing a savage excitement, and his employer's natural and justified egoism vexed him.

His vexation did not last. He was naïvely happy, a happiness, a hard tension of his body—ridiculous. Here I am, he thought, I, Stephen Hind, on my way at last, at last. He smiled to assure himself that he knew he was ridiculous. To be in this state because he was, for the first time, travelling abroad—in luxury at that—oh, absurd. But I got myself here; I might be sweating my guts out in a provincial university, or clerking in an office, or God knows—but I'm here, anything can happen, and no doubt anything will. To me ... He smiled at the air hostess, expecting that her polite answering smile would give away a trace of unofficial interest: as it did.

When they were circling to come down at Bordeaux, Chatteney opened his eyes.

'Are we there?'

'I think so. Yes.'

'Good. Don't move until the others have gone. Then help me out.'

The young man did not need the reminder that nothing

annoyed Chatteney more than to appear fragile. He liked to seem as active in body at seventy-five as he was mentally, and took conscious pains. Once on his feet at the bottom of the gangway, he straightened his shoulders and walked briskly in the wake of the other passengers, carrying hat, passport, gloves, his white cock's-comb floating back in the warm breeze.

'The car, the car, where is the car?'

'It will be here,' his secretary said, 'I'll find it.'

He found it without trouble, a large white Citroen, and found, too, with relief, that his night-school French was understood—an omen of success. He helped the chauffeur to stow their suitcases in the boot, and gave Chatteney an arm to clamber inside. The old man's slender body weighed little more than a child's; his sleep had refreshed him, he sat bolt upright in the Citroen, looking out at the countryside, his eyes very bright, a just-perceptible smile in the ironic fold of his long thin mouth, colourless, like the skin of his face.

It was the third week of May: a late spring had delayed the trees, so that all the way across the Landes their leaves formed a rippling half-transparent skein of pale green across the vaporous blue of the sky, mile on mile of trees as straight as masts, no undergrowth to blur the outlines, at intervals a clearing with a farm, a small manor house, a barn, and an indefinable air of quiet, seclusion, enchantment.

No doubt, thought Hind, the people living in these places are devoured by envy, lust, boredom, like the characters in Mauriac's novels, but, my God, how beautiful.

As they neared Dax, his happiness rose to his throat. All his notions of a French spa had been drawn from novels, he expected he scarcely knew what—boulevards, casino, orchestras, hotels not more luxurious than any in London

2

but with a fingerprint of wit and delicacy only France knew how to give them. He scarcely glanced at the nondescript street ending in a bridge across the river, but as the Citroen turned into what must be the chief street of Dax, shabby and foreign, he saw a handsome white hotel—the Splendid. Ah, good, he thought. If ours is as pleasant. . . .

'Hotel des Bains,' the chauffeur said, smiling. He repeated it. 'You want the Hotel des Bains, eh? I'm right?'

'Do you know where it is?' Chatteney said.

'Of course I know. Last year I brought Spanish gentlemen here—and one lady.'

He took a short turning which brought them to the bank of the river, a concreted road full of gaping cracks, swept along it, and drew up sharply at a hotel as large as the Splendid, larger, facing the river across a strip of rough grass. It looked like a barracks, a rather shabby barracks, or a seminary about to be disaffected.

This is no good, Hind told himself. His shock of dismay and disappointment was as violent as his excitement had been. He walked, speechless, behind Chatteney up a flight of stairs into the lobby, where a bowing, smirking manager met them and led them quite a distance along corridors, across a large, ill-furnished hall, and by further corridors to a lift so antiquated that it moved in a series of jerks to the third floor, where he showed them into a bedroom. It was bare and clean, with mud-coloured paint, no carpet on the wooden floor, only a thin rug at the side of the bed, one chair, and a large wardrobe so grotesquely ugly that it must have been conceived as a joke.

'And the bathroom?' Chatteney asked.

'Your *cabinet de toilette*,' the manager said. He smiled brilliantly, and opened a door into a room equally cold and bare, where were a basin, a fragile table, a lavatory and a bidet.

3

'Ah,' Chatteney murmured, 'your letter did say *cabinet de toilette*, but I asked you for a bathroom, and I supposed...'

'But Monsieur has come for the treatment?'

'Yes, of course. I said so.'

'Then'—the man spread his fingers, ten short hairy spines—'you will take a bath every day, once if not twice.'

'Well—no doubt I shall manage. And my secretary—where is his room?'

It was immediately across the corridor, and faced the river. It also was bare and comfortless and mud-coloured, and it had no *cabinet de toilette*, only a basin between bed and door.

Had the young man's expectations been more modest he might not have felt the access of physical loathing he did. He went back to his employer's larger room, followed by the smiling manager, who wanted to know when Monsieur would like to see his doctor.

'When you wish,' Chatteney said. 'This evening?'

'I will telephone. He will come at six. That is in half an hour. Dinner is at half past seven. If there is anything more I can do for you, you will tell me. I hope you will be very comfortable.'

He backed out.

'I think,' Chatteney said, 'for three weeks—it can be borne.'

'Of course,' Hind said.

For his life he could not have added a word. He unpacked for them both—only to open the wardrobe in this room needed strength and immense agility to stop the whole thing collapsing forward—and stood at one side while the doctor, an elderly man the spit image of an admired English female novelist, examined Chatteney very thoroughly and told him that he could take, not

4

the mud bath, but mud packs on his arthritic joints.

'You are how old?' he asked brusquely.

'Seventy-five.'

'Your heart is the same age. The weight of a total mud bath would be too much for it. The packs, yes. I shall give instructions. After each treatment you will return to bed for two hours, or three. And you will not, please, attempt the thermal baths. I shall visit you three times each week and if you need me at other times I shall come at once.... I think you are a little cold'—he drew the blanket over Chatteney's body—'please dress.'

Naked, the lack of harmony between Chatteney's head and his body was startling. He was a little under middle height, thin and small-boned, perfectly proportioned from his shoulders to his narrow feet, and he had a large head, a quite magnificent head, but meant for another body. Curiously, the effect of the whole, when he was fully clothed, was impressive.

Turning towards the young man, the doctor said,

'And you, monsieur?'

'I am not taking the treatment,' Hind said.

The doctor looked him over, from his aquiline face with its jet-black eyebrows and long mouth to his feet, negligently crossed as he leaned against the wall—a look oddly compounded of regret and greed.

'No, I suppose not,' he said.

When he had gone, Chatteney said, smiling,

'I feel that I am back at school. It's rather a pleasant feeling. But I don't recall that my room was as bare as this—or as cold. I ought to have expected it—the terms are absurdly low.... I am reassured about the treatment—and that, after all, is why we are here.'

The hotel had only just opened for the season, but the tables set end to end in the dining-room, a vast room that

5

could well have been the canteen in a barracks, were all filled. Hiding his feelings, Hind looked round him: it was his introduction to the unbeatable dowdiness, above a certain age, of the French middle classes. Not a flicker of elegance, not a young or a pretty or a handsome face. The menu for the meal was pinned up outside the doors, in the hall, and their food—there was no choice of dish—was served to this multitude with a skill and at a speed that would have sent an English waiter or waitress reeling to bed at the end of half an hour. And it was good food, plain, well-cooked, admirable. Even in his sulky disappointment, the young man admitted this to himself. It was some little comfort.

The only one. When he had seen Chatteney into bed, he went out and prowled through the narrow shabby streets for an hour, blind to their modest charm, and without finding anything more amusing to do than order himself a drink in a small rather squalid café in a side street. When he asked for a second drink, the elderly dilapidated waiter leaned over him and said, 'You are English.' A strong musty smell of cheap wine and grease-stained cotton jacket came from him. Hind shifted his chair slightly.

'I am.'

'And alone. What a pity. We can cure that, very easily, you know, oh, very easily. If this is your first visit, if you don't know Dax, I, allow me, I can tell you....' He answered an impatient voice from another table. 'Coming, sieursdames, coming ... a picon, yes, two picons, a grog ...' and returned, vigorously scratching an armpit, to Hind. 'You may think it quiet here, too quiet, not London, not the Monico, I worked in the Monico in 1920, I was a young man, very young—ah, what a place, what women, what buttocks ...' he moved his hand, flat out, thin yellow fingers together, in rapid curves, like a snake. 'You'll see,

6

we have one or two here, I don't say superior, but you won't be disappointed, I . . .'

'Thanks,' Hind said. 'I'm not interested.'

The old fellow stared at him with malicious amusement. 'Ah, that explains, I understand. . . . I understand very well. And I'm not surprised . . . my grandson, you know, he was in London a year ago, he is training to do very well for himself, he . . . when he came home last week he told us, English girls now are all dirty and badly dressed, their hair like old mats, and their legs . . . in narrow trousers you cannot hide legs, and if they are not too straight, most legs are not straight . . . he went to bed with one of them, not off the street, a student, and he could not do anything, he left her, he was afraid to catch something . . . no, no, not so, quite otherwise . . . it was a little beastie on the pillow, it fell from her hair when he . . . so our poor Jean . . . it wouldn't happen to you here, have you noticed any girls or women in bent trousers, and dirty? No. But if you are not interested . . . I can still, I think, help you. . . .'

Exasperated by his goatish smell, Hind stood, dropping on the table what he felt sure was a foolishly extravagant tip, and left. It would be fatuous to try to tell the lewd friendly old fellow that he disliked tarts, had always disliked them, and would sooner go without a woman for a month, six months, than pick one up for a night. This had nothing to do with prudence, it went back to the circumstances of his childhood and was as rooted in him as any other physical intransigence.

Walking past the entrance to the Hotel Splendid, he meditated going in there in search of a bar, and decided against it. I should be over-charged, he reflected, and see the same gargoyles, better dressed. . . . Nothing about Dax pleased him; it had not even a faded grandeur, no lingering hint in the air that it had ever been fashionable or romantic. Three weeks here—an eternity of boredom! You spent a month's salary, he mocked himself, on buying linen trousers and shirts, and a pair of white shoes. On these dusty broken-down pavements, white shoes, my God!

At this lowest point of his disillusion he had the grace to laugh at himself. At least I'm going to get enough to eat for three weeks....

His days fell at once into a pattern. In the morning he escorted his employer downstairs to the treatment rooms in a separate building in the courtyard of the hotel. Naked under the monk's white gown given him by the management, Chatteney was the image of a corrupt old priest, secretly vowed to the devil. On their first morning, Hind misunderstood the directions given him by the lift-boy, and led him into the women's half of the building: it might have been an anteroom to Purgatory—wheelbarrows filled with the smoking bubbling grey mud, high peeling walls, a grey-robed old woman who chattered at them like an idiot, and the two attendants, ferociously Spanish-looking women in bright-red shorts and monkeyjackets, their huge sweating bare thighs and arms splashed with mud. One of these hurried them out, a hand like a navvy's grinding the flesh of Hind's arm, teeth displayed in a virile grin. The place she directed them to was no different, except that the attendants were ex-pugilists or exguards. Standing about outside the cell where, plastered with scalding mud and wrapped as tightly as a mummy in oil-cloth and blankets, Chatteney endured for the prescribed minutes, he watched the other patients shuffling in and out of their cells. The sense of his own feline reserves of suppleness and energy gave him an intoxicating pleasure. During these moments he did not believe that he would ever be a year older.

In the afternoon Chatteney walked a little—through the

8

town to the bridge, and back to the hotel along the bank of the Adour. After that he rested again, until dinner-time, and the young man was free. Free to do nothing. Towards the end of their first week, something at last happened. In his aimless stroll he had just reached the entrance to the Splendid as a car stopped at the kerb, and the woman who stepped out dropped her handbag. He picked it up and said carefully, 'Permettez-moi, Madame,' hoping that this was the right phrase to use to an elegant Frenchwoman.

Taking it from him, she spoke in English.

'Thanks. Won't you come inside for a drink?'

Amused, he followed her in and to a bar which was, at last, the sort of thing he had expected of a French spa. He looked round him once, rapidly, taking in the comfort of the place, the air with which the barman conveyed respect for his companion's elegance—and no doubt money—and his knowledge of what she would drink. 'Madame would like a dry martini.'

'A very dry double martini, Edouard.... And you?' she asked Hind.

'I should like the same.'

'Now ...' she smiled at him, and he revised his first guess at her age; she was older than he had thought, but not old, say, forty-five or six, very good-looking in a fine-boned way, and smoothly cared-for, from the hair cut and curled in the most natural way to her feet in most certainly hand-made shoes—'my name is Hyde, Colette Hyde. And yours ... ?'

'Stephen Hind.' He smiled at her with an engaging warmth.

Her glance moved over him as the elderly doctor's had done, but with a self-assurance tempered by lively interest; she might have been examining a painting. No one feature of the young man's face was perfect, it was too long, the

9

slender arched nose was too long, and the eyes set deeply below thick eyebrows were narrow, with small jet-black pupils, but the whole added up to a very unusual male beauty, seductive and disquieting. He had a lean body and the most charming of smiles. (To say that he knew all this suggests that he was a vain ass. In fact, he was neither vain nor an ass, he was simply aware of his advantages as he might have known what he had in the bank.)

'Are you taking the treatment?' she asked.

'No.'

'No, of course not. Neither am I. My husband has been taking it, and I came with him because—well, why did I come? There's nothing here—except the most dangerously radio-active mud in France. Where are you staying?'

He had been afraid she would ask him this. He said carelessly,

'The truth is—I know you are to be trusted—we are in hiding in Dax, I and Sir Henry Chatteney. I'm his secretary. He came here to take the baths and to be alone. We're at the Hotel des Bains, where there are only French. If we'd come here he'd have been recognised and ...'

'*I* recognised him,' Mrs Hyde interrupted, smiling. 'I saw him with you yesterday in the street. That, my dear boy, is why I picked you up just now.'

This, he said to himself quickly, is where you laugh. Throwing his head back, he laughed like a schoolboy. 'That explains it—I was without a clue.'

Her smile became more ironic. 'Were you?'

'I was indeed. You are not ...'

'Not obviously on the prowl. No, but very very inquisitive. I'm dying to ask you about the memoirs. You're working on them with him—of course you are. And you can't talk about them. But tell me—are they nearly finished?'

'Oh, you know about them?'

'My dear boy, who doesn't? He's been writing them for more than twenty years, on and off! I suppose that the four or five fragments *The Times* has printed—that marvellous piece about de Gaulle—are plums, but the whole thing is obviously splendid.'

'Even those fragments have been entirely rewritten since they were published. Everything has been rewritten—a dozen, fifty times. He revises, revises, revises, and I copy and re-copy. Like a trained monkey.'

'How long have you been his secretary?'

'Just over six months. I'm the third in a year.'

'He wears them out?'

'Not he, but ...' He checked himself, with a smile inviting her to admire his discretion.

'How,' she asked him, 'did you come to take it on?' She sent a sideways glance at the barman, who hurried to her. 'Two martinis, Edouard ... I told you I am inquisitive. I suppose he caught you the moment you left the university —before you had time to turn round?'

Her curiosity did not annoy him—any woman as rich, as good-looking, as elegant, was worth taking the trouble to amuse—but he had no intention of telling her about his background. It was not what he cared to tell about himself. With a sudden youthful candour, very charming, he said,

'A secretary! That's what I call myself, and what he calls me. What in fact I am is a typist. He has never used a secretary for his memoirs. It's only now, in the last three or four years, when he wants them copied, that he has allowed anyone to see them. And all I do is type and re-type pages I've already typed twenty times, and he has rewritten heaven knows how many times before that. They're finished—but every day he changes a word or a sentence, and that means retyping the whole page or the whole chapter. He must have a perfect script—only to put away.'

'Oh, it's true, is it? He really means to do that?'

'They're left to the British Museum, not to be published, not even to be shown, for fifty years after his death. At least fifty.'

She leaned towards him across the little table, so that he saw the faint lines round her mouth, below rather than in the well-massaged skin, and caught a light scent, not a flower scent, something he thought of as 'exotic', and very suited to her.

'Yes, that's what we'd heard.... Now I'll tell you who I am. My husband is Frederick Hyde—the publisher. You know the firm....'

'I could ask you who doesn't?' he said gaily.

An old and a rich firm, one of the richest and most respected in England, in the world. And Hyde himself, apart from his firm, was a rich man: his mother, now dead, had been the niece and heiress of a Rothschild.

'Well, he has tried—I've tried myself—to be allowed to buy them. I suppose that half the publishing firms in London and New York have made advances to your fastidious employer—and with as much success as we have had—that is, none. It's utterly absurd.... Tell me, has he included the scandal of 1946, the case?'

He frowned. 'What case?'

'Are you being discreet?'

'No,' he said, smiling at her. 'I don't know anything about it—any scandal at that time.'

She lifted her hand in a mocking half-salute. 'What it is to be young! How old are you?'

'Twenty-five.'

'In 1946—seventeen years ago—you were at your prep school.' She paused, as if expecting him to tell her where he had been schooled. He smiled vaguely, and she went on, 'But you might have heard your parents talking about it.'

12

The notion of his parents discussing a scandal of high life amused as much as it embarrassed him. He said lightly,

'Tell me what I missed.'

'If you really don't know ... In 1946 his wife accused another woman, Mary Duquesne, a terribly charming woman—I know her—of enticing him. She had found letters —in one of them there was a sentence about "your unendurable marriage", and about ending it "now, before we're too old"—oh, and there were others, just as compromising. There was one where she told him she had been left some money by an old admirer and asked him to come to France with her—that is, she would pay—and'—she laughed delightedly—'this is Mary Duquesne to the life—when Lady Chatteney's Counsel asked her: Why did you suggest going away to France? she smiled at him and said: But the money was only four hundred pounds, it wasn't worth saving. . . . As if that were reason enough for inviting another woman's husband to take a holiday with you.'

'And what happened?'

'Oh, in the end they came to an agreement—that neither woman would disturb or interfere with the other—I forget the ridiculous phrase. But the case lasted three days, with letters read in court, and Renée Chatteney swooning, and reporters from Paris and New York—nothing much else was happening at the moment.'

'There's nothing in the memoirs—so far as I have typed —about a Mrs Duquesne. What is she like?'

'Ah. It's difficult. . . . If I tell you that—enticement or no enticement—she is a gentleman, does that mean something? She dresses like someone's old cook, doesn't care tuppence about her looks—she must have been beautiful— she's a sloven, an elderly sloven. And I adore her.'

13

'It can't have been very pleasant for him.'

'Oh, it finished him. Completely. He was fifty-eight. No further career for him. There had been rumours that the Labour Government would offer him something—something important—Attlee was said to be fond of him. But after that terrible ridicule'—her eyes sparkled with malicious amusement—'ouf! And what really fascinates me—*why* did he stay with his wife? He was ruined, he might just as well have left her. Everyone knows she's a neurotic, and has a fiendish temper, and makes his life hell, so why, why . . . ?'

'No, that's not quite true,' Hind said.

'Not true?'

'No, forgive me. I mean it's exaggerated. She's not so bad as that.'

'My dear boy, at best she's an unattractive woman, goodness knows why that marriage lasted, why he didn't leave her thirty years ago. The only possible explanation, the only one I can imagine, is that she had the money, they're not Catholics—and even Catholics, nowadays. . . . What does she say about his memoirs?'

The young man hesitated. How much, without being indiscreet, could he tell her? He must please her, must make himself interesting, must, it was important, but not at the risk of his job.

'She hasn't been allowed to read them. Sometimes he reads a passage to her, to get her advice—she's shrewd, and she has a memory. But he won't let her see the whole thing.'

'No!' Mrs Hyde clapped her hands. 'Marvellous. I suppose he hardly dares. . . . Perhaps she actually doesn't know what everyone else knew, that he had mistresses, I don't mean just any sort of young woman, but the young Comtesse de this and the young elegant Madame de that and

14

the other when he was in Paris, and I suppose in London, when he came back to the Foreign Office. Do any of them appear? But you won't tell me that—no, you can't.'

'I can tell you that there are charming episodes, that he laughs at himself—but it's never certan that he is writing about an affair....'

'Isn't that rather a pity?'

'Only if you prefer gossip to literature,' Hind said swiftly. To take the edge off this impulsive sarcasm, he said, 'There's one frightfully bitter passage—it seems to belong to 1938 or thereabouts, when he says that he is too old to believe it when a young woman says: I love you. And it turns his blood to reflect that she may be thinking that he moves like an ageing man. . . .'

He had not offended Mrs Hyde. Looking at him with the sharpest curiosity, she said, 'We have time for one more martini . . . Edouard! . . . Let's see, 1938 was the year he resigned over Munich—and broke what was obviously going to be a brilliant diplomatic career. The most undiplomatic thing he could have done, and God only knows why he did it.'

'That's exactly as far as I've reached in my typing. And it seems to be two-thirds way through the whole.'

Mrs Hyde nodded. 'It would be—since it was his peak. I shall never understand it. Why, with success in your hand, throw it away? Why? Did he want to make a noble gesture? No, no, he's not a fool. In any case, as a gesture it was very nearly a total failure—pushed off the front page by Duff Cooper's resignation at the same time, almost on the same day. It wouldn't have made even what stir it did if he hadn't been so well known socially. I don't remember it at all well, in 1938 I was only twenty—you, my child, weren't born, or just—but I know from my mother that

15

they, the Chatteneys, entertained in the most amusing way; they knew everyone who mattered, socially and politically—in Paris, too. After he resigned, the *monde* rather dropped off, they kept their serious friends, but—of course—when he was no longer at the centre of things, the political side lost its brilliance. Naturally. That's the world. As I am sure you know.' She laughed. 'But he didn't become an extinct volcano until after the scandal—the famous enticement.'

'They don't entertain now,' Hind said dryly. 'He lives as piously as a monk. He works in the morning—every day. And in the afternoon he rests until four o'clock, then goes to the Athenaeum for three or four hours. If it's a particularly fine day he walks a few steps, perhaps to Hyde Park, and picks up a cab there. Other days I gallop out to get one for him. He comes home about eight, to dinner—a horribly ascetic meal, he eats like a sparrow, they both do. Either he dislikes guests or they can't afford it....'

'Oh, nonsense,' Mrs Hyde exclaimed. 'No one is so poor as that.... Tell me, I must leave you now, would it bore you to dine with us in London? We're flying tomorrow. But I should like to see you again.'

The young man's elation sharpened. Not that he lacked confidence in himself: he knew—knew very well, by some physical sense—when he had made contact—as though an invisible fluid, some kind of animal energy, passed from him to the other person. But this Mrs Hyde was incomparably the most exciting fish he had ever played. He gave her a warm candid smile.

'You're most kind. I should be—oh, delighted.'

'I'll ring you up. You're living with them, are you?'

'For my sins,' he said gaily.

'Then, good-bye. Don't forget my name.'

He looked her in the face, his eyes grave. 'Do you

suppose that my days are as filled with excitement as that?'
She laughed. 'Nice boy.'

He walked rapidly to his hotel, his thoughts leaping in
his head. Surprisingly, behind his happiness, he felt
momentarily sad. Was it always going to be so easy?
Something in him, younger than he was, for an instant
regretted this ease.

CHAPTER 2

THE house in Lowndes Place was not large, and the whole
of the first floor was given over to Chatteney, to his bedroom and the library in which he worked—these rooms,
the best in the house, opened into each other, and his
bookshelves, solidly and splendidly made of walnut, were
continued into the bedroom where they covered another
two walls. His wife's room was on the ground floor, with
the living- and dining-rooms. The kitchens and a cellar
were in the basement, and housekeeper and secretary
shared the top floor, two attic bedrooms, unheated. But his
room did not displease Hind; indeed at first sight he had
thought it superior to the plumply furnished bedroom he
had left: it had been arranged by Lady Chatteney as a
studio, with sofa, divan, small armchair, curtains in bold
black-and-red stripes. The narrow wardrobe between two
joists was large enough to hold his few garments. He had
never owned more than two suits and a dinner jacket, but
they were well-made, and so were his shoes, three pairs,
and his half-dozen shirts. He took the greatest care of
them. From the start of his adult life he had known clearly

what he wanted—and a certain elegance was part of it.

For a young man from his—it used to be called station in life, which implied fixity, not departures—his ambition was odd enough.

The half-cracked old Welshman who taught the sixth form in his shabby secondary school planted in him a passion for literature which swept him on the back of a scholarship into King's College in the Strand. It was seed on stony ground. In his first month there it withered and died, but he had the sense to hide his boredom and go on exercising and sharpening a naturally critical intelligence, uncommon enough to surprise, and an uncommonly good memory. One of his lecturers, a middle-aged little man oddly called Dorrit, fell mutely and visibly in love with him, and in his third year got him the offer of a student researchship. This mildly pleased him, until he realised what it meant—that he would spend the next two years collecting and card-indexing information for the benefit of a professor working on some monument of scholarship. At this moment he had a stroke of luck.

Invited to lunch by the professor, he was placed next a handsome middle-aged widow, to whom—because he liked pleasing people—he made himself charming. That same day she wrote to offer him a post as tutor-companion to her mentally deficient son of eighteen. Charmed by him though she was, she was also prudent, and asked him to give her 'a letter I can show my son's trustees'.

He ran to little Dorrit for this. Shocked, almost in tears, Dorrit said,

'But, my dear Stephen, this is a job for a young man with pleasant manners and no brains. You have a good mind, and your foot in the academic world, you have only to stay in it, and . . .'

Stephen interrupted him lightly. 'I couldn't bear to turn

18

into a third-rate don, with the beginnings of a paunch and the smell of foxed pages in my nose.'

'Like me, you mean,' Dorrit murmured.

'No, Timmie, I didn't mean that'—but he had meant it—'it just isn't what I want out of life.'

'What *do* you want?'

Smiling, the young man moved his fingers in one of the light gestures that ravished poor Dorrit. 'Oh, to know people, people who do things, to live decently, amusingly, to travel—but in comfort—in short, to be born again, into a well-off family. You know, my dear Timmie—well, you don't know but that's your own fault—I have no what you'd call creative faculty. Not a spark. I can criticise other men's creations, yes. But who the hell wants to spend his life among the sort of groping people who do that? Not I.'

'You . . .' Dorrit began. He paused, drew a hand over his face, wiping away disillusion and anguish, and said, 'How very curious. I see that I have been nursing a peacock, not an eagle.'

'Wrong again,' Stephen said sweetly, 'stupid birds, peacocks. I'm not stupid.'

Off he went, with three shirts and his one very good suit, to Mrs Ukley's comfortable house in Somerset. During five years there he not only enlarged his wardrobe—not a great deal: he was fairly, not lavishly paid—but corrected his accent, picked up the manners and gestures of the county families, her friends and neighbours, learned to ride, to help Frieda Ukley with the management of her tenant-farmers, and even, for a brief moment, considered trying to marry her.

This idea of marriage was a passing weakness, due to discomfort and mortification; he had been put in his place during dinner by a visitor who thought him too far out of it. He spent a sleepless night with his idea, and in the

morning rejected it—with horror. Not because of her age:
he was determined not to be caught by the ankle until he
was prepared to seem to be caught. He needed women—he
was sleeping with Mrs Ukley's plump good-humoured
maid—but not a shackle, not yet.

When the chance of being Chatteney's secretary came to
him, he leaped at it, expecting heaven knew what excite-
ments. His first week, his first hour, in the house in
Lowndes Place roughly disillusioned him. Only his ballast
of cool common sense kept him from throwing the job up.
Wait, he told himself, wait, and keep your eyes open.

Mrs Hyde's *I'll ring you up* was the first crack of light,
dazzling.

He breakfasted in his attic, on coffee, excellent coffee,
and hot rolls brought him by the housekeeper.

This Austrian woman, a Jew and a not very ardent
Catholic, had been the Chatteneys' servant since 1938:
shrewd, indefinably carnal, with the broad face, almost un-
lined (she was in her late fifties), and pale placid eyes of a
Flemish madonna, she served them with devotion, working
tirelessly—she was their only servant now—treated Lady
Chatteney as an equal and her husband as a tiresome god.
Secretaries she took, figuratively, into her lap as if they
were puppies.

Coming into his room the morning after their return
from Dax, she flicked Hind's cheek with her hard finger.

'You had a good time, eh? A fine party with French
girls. You look sleek. What was she like?'

'You were never more sadly off the mark,' Hind said. He
caught her hand and swung it. 'Be sorry for me, my old
Bruegel. . . .'

'To you, my boy, Frau Doktor Bruegel.'

'My dear cherished old Bruegel, I'm much too fond of
you. But you've forgotten the honey.'

'You would flirt with your own handsome face, wouldn't you, if you had nothing else. You're a devil. Sit still'—he had not moved—'I'll get your honey.'

At whatever minute between eight and nine he went to the library he found his employer already there. Chatteney started work at six, in bed, reading and revising passages that his secretary would afterwards copy for the tenth, twentieth time.

Seated, his superb head posed against a background of books, handsomely bound, every one of them, he was infinitely impressive, the shortness of his body hidden by his desk: a cashmere dressing-gown hung from his shoulders, its folds adding to the illusion of height and a sort of debonair authority.

'Ah, Stephen,' he said amiably—it was in Dax, when the young man was draping the monk's robe round his skinny old body after it had been hosed down, that he had started to use his secretary's Christian name—'I think, I really think, this is the last time you will retype this chapter.'

But he did not hand it over. He sat shuffling the typed pages, each with its added word or two in his elegantly simple writing, between his fingers. His eyes under their thick arch of flesh and overhanging eyebrows gleamed with a darting malice.

He doesn't feel certain of one sentence, Stephen thought. That's why he's going on talking.

'You know, my dear boy, I have never, all my life, had more than two keys in my hands—to unlock any door. One key for events, another for people. For people—the certainty that, in the last resort, what moves any man, any woman, the impulse underlying all the others, is his self-love. Or his self-dislike—it comes, you know, to the same thing. For events—an even simpler key. I learned very early indeed that a nation is not a society of more or less

intelligent individuals, but a low-grade invertebrate, of
gross instincts, the strongest of them its fear of being devoured by a neighbour. I don't mean that all embryonic
organisms are alike, no, no, they differ noticeably in their
needs and their powers of aggression. But all, without
exception, when they feel threatened, will resort to any
subterfuge or violence. A diplomat has no right to share
the ridiculous respect paid to intellect by persons who
think they possess it; he should be able to listen to a clever
or noble speech and hear only the jealousy, hate, fear, behind it. But alas, the closer a nation comes to developing
some tiny cell of intelligence or pity or delicacy, the more
vulnerable it is to cultures of a lower order. Politicians,
historians, statesmen, who talk about international law, international morality, are duping themselves and us—themselves because they are comically ignorant of the infantile
nature of the tribe, us because what they are talking about
has no existence. Not the most rudimentary. None, none.
There is no such thing as national, still less international,
morality. When you hear the head of a government talking about his country's moral reasons for not doing something, you'll know he is afraid to act. That's all. Even the
great powers are light-years away from becoming intelligent organisms. Even the French.' He laughed softly.
'Zealous logicians, eloquent to a fault, as cunning as bees,
and in the mass more irrational than any obstinate old
woman. I love France. That's why I can say these things. . . .
One of my colleagues in Paris once asked acidly: Is our
friend Chatteney accredited to this embassy or to the Quai
d'Orsay? That was in March 1936, when I was breaking
my heart trying to stiffen every French politician I knew
against Hitler's march into the Rhineland—and against
us. . . . Flandin, that nice nervous would-be adroit
ape. . . .'

22

'Yes,' Stephen murmured.

He had read it in previous chapters. Not only had Chatteney warned and implored in Paris, but, making an excuse of his wife's illness—imaginary—had got himself to London during the Council meetings, and invited Flandin to dine at his house with English politicians, journalists, bankers, to tell them just how desperate the moment was. But the nice nervous ape had been both too tortuous and too near weeping to turn the trick.

'A politician is forced to make a habit of noble phrases and optimistic lies. In the end they infect himself. Neville Chamberlain ... years of telling himself and the country that he was a man of peace and leader of the only party which knew how to avoid war acted on him like a tranquillising drug, so that with his own eyes shut he led the nation, blindfold, all but disarmed, its belly full of wind, to the very edge of extinction....'

He stopped abruptly.

'Here. Take it.'

He handed over the pages he had been shuffling.

Glancing through them, Stephen saw how few changes the old purist had made since the previous typing—not more than a score of words in thirty pages. It was the crucial scene of his resignation, inlaid (the only word) with portraits of the men and one woman involved, portraits, lucid and subtle, in which each word added one more revealing stroke. And they were without a trace of bitterness, even for men who had, he believed, gone out of their way to damage him. His admirations were few and reluctant—not from lack of charity. Simply he was unable to think that any of the important persons governing or misgoverning the country counted a straw as human beings. And he seemed equally unable to resent an injury.

Has he the faintest idea how arrogant his lack of re-

23

sentment is? his secretary wondered. He hasn't forgiven them: none of them seem to him worth hating. That's all.

He would have been delighted to come on a mean grudging phrase.

Copying and re-copying this book had, as Chatteney would have said, infected him. Behind Chatteney's early years he watched—with a savage rage—his own unroll. The old man had had everything, beginning with his birth in a family whose only other distinguished member had been one of Henry VIII's judges. He went to Eton just before his thirteenth birthday—at that age his secretary was already familiar with all the fusty smells of his run-down school and the shabby streets he scurried through to reach it. And so it went on: Paris, Göttingen, Cambridge, the Foreign Office and a desk with a charming view of the lake in St James's Park. All Chatteney's holidays, from the age of seven, were spent in Paris, with a gay young aunt married to a grossly rich French diplomat; he learned the language as naturally as he became a member of an aristocratic circle which had widened to take in politicians, editors, and well-heeled men of letters. A delicious account of his first mistress, a young married woman only five years his senior—he was seventeen—brought into Stephen's throat something like an uprush of bile, the sour memory of his own first adventure.... Never a check, never a false step: in 1915, by pulling strings, he beat his way into the army, he was severely wounded and spent the rest of his war in the Office of the Director of Military Operations, then at the Embassy in Washington. He married in 1916. And when, at the end of the war, he went back to the Central Department of the Foreign Office, his house in North Street became as faithful a copy of his Parisian aunt's circle as, given the heavier duller material he had to

24

work in—politicians of the right and centre, labour leaders, financiers, English writers—he could manage. In those days he and his wife had money.

Enough money to buy himself a reputation for incorruptibility and fine feelings, Stephen told himself. He ground his strong teeth....

In 1924, during the London Conference, the Chatteneys entertained Herr Stresemann three times, the second and third times at his own request. When the German said good-bye he added, with what passed on his face for a genial smile,

'*I* shan't see the second great war, my friend, but you will.'

When Chatteney was sent to Paris in 1930 as Counsellor, his wife did not go with him. She hated Paris and the French, volubly, and preferred, although she knew—she must have known—what sort of bachelor life he was living there, to stay in North Street. Why, Stephen wondered, did she feel this loathing of France? It was almost a disease— never explained....

The chapter he was typing stuck in the young man's throat. The decision to resign ... Heaven give me a tenth of that boldness and imprudence, he thought. But, my God, what a fool! Need he, because a great many other people were behaving like knaves, have behaved like an imbecile? Perhaps he thought he could afford a splendid gesture....

He suspected—how could he help it?—that something had been left out of the story. Why should so frankly ambitious a man—and one whose view of politics was wholly sceptical and icy—have broken his career for a principle? It made no sense. Either Chatteney was keeping something back, or—delicious thought!—he deceived himself about the motives for his act. Yet, what except fine

25

principles could be the motive? And how ineffably needless and silly....

As his secretary completed each page, Chatteney took from him the one he had been copying, and tore it in pieces, tiny tiny pieces, rarely more than a syllable left intact.

On his first day, seven months ago, he had innocently taken a carbon copy. To bring home to him his guilt, Chatteney burned it in front of him. There was to be no copy of his memoirs in existence except the one he meant to bury for half a century. Heaven alone knew how many many millions of words he had written and torn up since he began them. The extreme slowness with which he wrote—a whole morning spent on a sentence or in searching his library for a quotation—was partly indolence, partly the voluptuous happiness it gave him to linger over a phrase as he might, in his youth, have savoured an admirable dinner or the first days of a love affair.

It was also a vanity so exalted as to be mistaken for the depths of indifference.

Spreading his bony fingers to let the fragments fall into his wastepaper-basket, he said, smiling,

'I've always held that my first duty is to myself—to be excellent'—he used a Greek word, at which Stephen angrily guessed—'for my own pleasure. I'm ... I was ... very ambitious. Why not? I knew I was fitted for great things.' His smile became young and mocking. 'You see? What did I tell you? The one habit of mind you can't tear out of a man, the motive of motives, the key to his soul—self-love.'

Ah, thought Stephen, the old devil. He forces you to forgive him anything, any arrogance....

When he came into the dining-room Lady Chatteney

26

gave him her coldest least reassuring smile. In one of her moods, he thought carelessly. The moods of a woman of her age were only worth notice when they interfered with him in some way. He noticed her hands, narrow and blue-veined, closing and opening on the handle of her malacca cane. He could imagine these veins climbing the stick-like arms to her long slender neck where they emerged into sight, vanished and reappeared on either side of immense eyes, the last trace in her ruined face of what must have been dark good looks.

She had brought her dachshund with her. This animal, twice the size of any dachshund he had seen, with a long thick body and tapir-like head, was old and spiteful, and she spent on it the obsessed love its mother gives a sickly child. It was returned: no human companion, with interests of his own, would sit, as this animal did, hour after hour, watching her for signs of emotion, dejected when she was unhappy, rousing his heavy body to liveliness as soon as she smiled.

This room faced south, and since for once in an abominable summer the day was fine and warm, the sun pouring through closed windows made it intolerably hot. As soon as he came in Chatteney said,

'Open a window, Stephen, it's stifling in here.'

Lady Chatteney's voice halted him half-way. 'No. It makes a draught, and Simon'—she stooped to caress the animal's head—'catches cold so easily. Leave it.'

Stephen glanced at Chatteney, who made a resigned gesture, and said politely,

'Very well. But why not have left him in your room?'

'He frets.'

The food, as always, was good and very meagre. She not only ordered but often prepared lunch and dinner—she had taught herself to cook, well and simply—and it seemed

27

not to occur to her that a young man has a larger appetite than an old one. Today she had made a jellied soup and an egg dish, both excellent, but the soup was in tiny bowls and his share of the eggs left Stephen nearly as hungry as when he sat down. The service was Rockingham, very beautiful and he supposed valuable, and he handled his bowl gingerly.

The Austrian woman, moving round the table, asked, 'Don't you want a window open?'

'No,' Lady Chatteney said. 'And, Bruegel, the rolls were too hot. I don't like to burn my fingers.'

'Sorry. It shan't happen again.'

She went out, and Lady Chatteney said,

'There are moments when I wonder whether devotion really makes up for what would be impudence if it weren't so blankly unconcerned.'

'You get more than devotion out of her,' Chatteney said.

'That's true.' Her voice hardened. 'Tell me—why didn't you keep the appointment I made for you with Benham? He telephoned half an hour ago to ask why you hadn't come'—during the mornings she took all telephone calls, so that he should not be disturbed in the library—'and I had to apologise. You can't treat a consultant as if he were some little village doctor.' She turned on the secretary. 'Why didn't you remind him?'

'It's my fault,' Chatteney said, 'I forgot to tell him about the appointment. And ...' he smiled 'I forgot it myself. I can't take myself very seriously. What can he tell me that I don't know—that I'm old bones? Very old, very brittle.'

'You grumble when they ache.'

'Well, why not?'

'And it's your heart, not your bones, that Benham was to look at. I suppose you're afraid to hear the truth about it.'

28

Her clear taunting voice disturbed Simon; he got up from the floor and came to press his head against her leg.

'No, no, my darling,' she murmured, 'no, I'm not angry.'

'Except with me,' her husband said, smiling.

'If you would do the few important things I ask you to do. I never fuss without cause.... I'll make another appointment for you. And next time I shall wait in to see that you mean to go.... This morning, too, I rang up the bank and told Smith to sell half your steel shares, and to-morrow I'll see Cousin John about reinvesting. Do you agree?'

'My dear Renée, of course I agree—and since you've already arranged it....'

'But you wouldn't have done anything yourself! You would forget about it until too late—as always.'

He gave her a half-humorous half-absent smile. 'The truth is, I rely on you to look after me. You won't pretend you haven't always done it. How do you expect that I shall start doing for myself things you do so much better? You have infinitely more business sense, I should be lost without you.'

'Yes.' She bent her head, and Stephen turned his glance aside from a parting so white and polished that it might be bone rather than skin, as though the strands of grey finely waved hair sprang directly from a skull. 'Yes, I look after you. But I don't know what you're thinking, Simon tells me more about himself than you do.'

Pushing away her coffee cup, she gripped the edge of the table to stand up. Once on her feet, she moved briskly—her cane was strictly unnecessary, an elongated finger she used to point to an object she wanted moved or given to her. She pointed it now at the dachshund.

'Help him ... No, not you, Mr Hind. My husband will do it.'

Bending stiffly, Chatteney stroked the animal's back. 'Up you get, old boy.' Turning on him a malevolent glance, the old boy did not move. 'Come, get up.'

'He knows as well as I do that you have no feeling for him,' his wife said, in a curious voice, railing and triumphant. 'Come, Simon, my angel.'

Hurrying across the room, the secretary held the door open for the three of them, wife, Simon, husband, to walk through without looking at him. He waited a moment, until the door of Lady Chatteney's room closed, and Chatteney himself had climbed the stairs to his own room, where he would stretch himself stiffly on his bed, then ran silently down the stairs at the end of the narrow hall to the kitchen, to tell Bruegel that he was still ravenous. She would find something for him, if it were only a slice of cake.

Later in the afternoon, Mrs Hyde rang up. He had been waiting for this, almost but not entirely sure it would happen. He steadied his voice to answer coolly.

She invited him to dinner. 'On Friday—that is the day after tomorrow. Are you free then?'

He was too delighted and too sensible to pretend that he had other invitations. 'Yes, of course. How kind of you.'

'How are the memoirs?' she asked lightly. 'Still moving?'

'Like a snail.'

She laughed. 'Well—tell me about it when I see you. Until Friday. Good-bye.'

It is the memoirs that interest her, he thought coldly. Otherwise she would have forgotten. Or would she? We'll see.'

CHAPTER 3

Since he came to live in London he had visited his
mother once. Once only. He would not have gone near her
at all if there had been any other way of seeing his young
sister, but she refused, smiling—'No, no, it's too grand'—to
come to Lowndes Place, and the thought of meeting her in
a café annoyed him.

Today as he neared the house he felt the same impatience, pleasure, anxiety, as always—as though his sister
were holding out on him in some way. A cold wind blew
dust and fragments of paper against him. Unchanged since
his childhood, the street—within five minutes' walk of Victoria Station—had no graces, not even a tree, but the grey
dirty houses were old and solid, shabbily respectable, and it
would have taken a bomb to bring them down.

41A Marion Street was a narrow house of four storeys.
The front door stood open on the long dark passage with
its curious smell, the breath of an unwashed old woman,
persisting under all the newer smells. The single large
room on this level—let in his childhood to a Jewish tailor—
was now the storeroom of the small restaurant next door,
one of those pitiably engaging places, the walls decorated
with old chianti bottles, conches, fishermen's nets, French
railway posters, which sprang up in a post-war London sick
for foreign parts. He walked past it without a thought for
the four-year-old child sitting out air-raids on the littered
floor, huddled against his mother and utterly without fear
—she had told him she could deflect the bombs as they
fell, and he believed her implicitly. The door of the room
opened as he passed, to let out one of the two decent hard-
working queers who ran the restaurant. His arms full of

31

packages, he blundered unseeingly against Stephen and cried,

'Oh, sorry, my dear, sorry, sorry. Have I damaged you?'

'Not a bit.'

'Splendid. So glad.'

His eyes lingered almost sorrowfully on the young man's face and lean elegant body. Stephen smiled at him and ran up the dark staircase. The next floor, too, had only one large room—the room where his mother, in her active days as a medium, held a weekly séance. She and her clients called it the studio. On the other days of the week it was put to less spiritual uses. He noticed that the door had been given a fresh coat of paint, and wondered whether, inside too, it had been refurbished. It was years, at least fifteen, since he had set foot in it.

As though the smell of the newly-painted door offended him, his nostrils narrowed momentarily.

The lowest flight of the staircase, as far up as this room, was carpeted—it was too dark to see that grime had devoured pattern and colours. Above, a worn-out linoleum, full of holes, made coming down dangerous.

On the second floor a little light from a tiny window overlooking the back-yard fell across the landing. Here was his mother's room, and behind it the kitchen and a pantry. He knocked, and when she called, 'Who is it? Come in,' he opened the door and saw her sitting where she always sat now, her armchair pushed as close to the window as possible, her body in its shapeless garments overflowing it on both sides, her hair, still thick, dyed a shameless red, coiled on top of her head so that it caught the light and glittered a rusty green in the folds, the exact colour of the knuckleduster stones in the ring on one large fat white hand.

32

During the day she rarely moved from her chair. Not that she was unable to move if she wanted to—she had what she called 'a bad heart', but it was good enough for any normal use. She had always been lazy, and now that her body was so heavy could not be bothered to lift it.

Two other women were in the room, sitting close to her. They were old friends—he recognised one vaguely—of the sort he detested.

'Ah, it's you,' his mother said, with a wide smile. At sixty she still had all her teeth—like his, they were white and strong, splendid teeth. 'Don't stand there, shut the door, come in, come in.' She waved a hand at him. 'My son,' she told the other women, 'my handsome son. He's a snob, he never comes to see me, a snob. This is the second time he's been this year. Why do we have children?'

'Where is Tarry?' he asked.

'Out. Gone to fetch my medicine from the doctor's. Ah, in the old days doctors waited on us, now we wait on them and say thank-you for being treated like half-wits.... If it's her you've come for, you'll have to wait. Are you going to wait?'

Stephen hesitated. 'Yes.'

'Then sit down, sit down, You haven't come to see your mother, but no need to stand, as if your bottom is too good for my chairs.' A queer spasm, it might even have been grief, crossed her sagging cheeks. She turned to her friends and went on talking as though he were not in the room. 'Go on, go on. Tell me.'

Sitting as far from them and as near the door as he could, Stephen listened. The two women were obviously, as his mother had been until she became too old and grossly fat, professional mediums. One of them had been attending what sounded like a spiritualist holiday camp. In a low hoarse voice, broken by chuckles, she described it.

33

'Y'know, it was very well done. I had m'own place, one room, y'know, and what-not, like all the others, and there was a nice chapel, a one-storey job, with a good public address system for when the place was bung full. We had visiting ministers, y'know, spiritualists, I'll tell you about one of them—and a canteen. Mabel—you remember Mabel Gash?—ran it, but she worked, too—I mean like the rest of us. There was one trumpet medium, a chap called, oh I forget what he was called, but he was sissy, like they all are, these men mediums. You remember. I did clairvoyance and trances. Always by appointment—they put their names down in a book, y'see—and when she or he came I asked: Do you want clairvoyance or a trance? Seeing I couldn't do that many trances, I charged double for them —like they all did. Except one woman who was trying her damndest to get the canteen away from Mabel, so she was sucking up to the Board, showing off. Oh, it was like all these places, a boiling mess of intrigues and jealousy—I kept clear, you know me, I'm no snake.'

His mother said warmly, 'No, that you're not.'

'Y'know, I don't do materialisations. Never did. There was two did, the best was a young woman, you won't know her, Louise Murdoch, and she had her husband with her, and when the stuff—y'know—started to flow out of the cabinet he called people up to recognise their wives or sisters or what have you. Smart he was—never a mistake. This minister I was telling you about—he did splendid when he was in trance—my, he impressed me—but, y'know, when he walked about the platform getting messages from the Masters for people, he sweated so it was downright unpleasant, you'd think the flesh was melting off of his bones, I couldn't look at him, and I used to sneak out of the chapel, and one morning I . . .'

With an effort, Stephen stopped listening.

34

He had felt a twinge of his sick horror as a little boy when one night he woke in the dark out of a bad dream and called and called his mother and she did not come, and he got out of bed and went downstairs: she was not in her room and drawn by sounds he went down to the next floor, and pushed open the door of the studio, and saw her—in a chair in front of a circle of men and women; she was pale, the sweat running off her face in little streams, and she was moaning loudly, her eyes closed. The sweating and the moans curdled his stomach and he knew he was going to be sick. He screamed.

There was a candle in his room. Its weak light fell full minute when he was back in bed, in his room, clinging to his mother, his face laid against her firm pillowy body. This was the good mother. The other, the bad one, had gone: he cried a little, easily, and begged, 'You won't let her come back, will you? Ever, ever.'

'No,' the good mother answered, 'of course not. Little silly. You're all right, you're safe with me. Go to sleep.'

There was a candle in his room. Its weak light fell full across her smiling mouth, and he closed his eyes in a relief so overwhelming that it lifted his small body up, up, on a wave of stupefying pleasure....

On days when there was no séance, the studio was occupied for a few hours at a time by couples, a man and a woman, or, rarely, two men, who came and left again separately. How old was I, he asked himself, before I knew what the room was? His sister, four years younger than he, must nevertheless have understood something about their circumstances almost as soon as he did. She made no friends at school, or, if she did, never dreamed of bringing one home. No more did he. This solitude round them drove them together. From the time she was six or seven, he watched over her like a jealous lover or husband—never

35

telling her about his terror that she might grow up 'like that', and never free of it.

He remembered an evening—it must have been his first term at King's College—when his mother spoke carelessly about training the child as a medium. The blood plunged and beat in his head behind his eyes. He clenched his hands.

'You won't,' he said.

'Why not, for heaven's sake? She's thirteen. Just the age.'

'Because I say not,' he stammered. His hands were trembling, he wanted to let fly at her, beat her, trample on her full body, not then shapeless and quiveringly untidy.

'Why, you young cockalorum,' she cried, half angry, half laughing, 'who are you to tell me what I can and can't do with m'own daughter? I'll thank you to hold your tongue.'

What might have happened, what might he have done, if his young sister had not, at this point, said calmly,

'It's no use. I could never do anything of the sort. It's silly.'

For some reason the boy did not grasp, this cool young contempt silenced their mother. She sat for a moment, looking bewildered, then got up and stumbled out of the room.

Alone with him, his sister said in the same cool voice, smiling,

'She's silly.'

He laughed and kissed her....

The woman in the armchair was laughing. Laughter ran through her body like an undersea current, stirring up waves of flesh. He could scarcely bear to look at it. Her cheeks were pouched, fingermarked below the temples as though a thumb had been pressed into the yellow fat. She can't be much over sixty, he thought. Need she have let herself go? Why doesn't she die? ... An obscure fear brushed him, a twinge of the single nerve still fastening him to this monstrous old woman. She had been thirty-five when he was born, and he recalled a lively gay violently emotional woman, full of spontaneous bursts of laughter and rage, with large white arms and a body like a warm hard pillow—to a timid thin-skinned child safety and warmth itself. Some nights, after one of his nightmares, she took him into her bed, and he lay with his back curved into her belly—'making a cup and saucer', she called that. ... It seemed to him that he had begun to turn from this smothering warmth even before he knew that he lived in what was a discreet sort of brothel. Already, when he was a boy of ten or eleven, he had rejected her—coldly....

One of the women must have asked a question. His mother shook her head vigorously; one of its dyed locks fell on her shoulder.

'No, no, I never practise now. Gave it up years ago.'

'And that room where you ...'

'You mean the studio?' She laughed. 'I let that by the night—by the hour sometimes. You'd be surprised the types who come.'

'What types?'

'You should see my two olds. You'd split yourself. They've been coming for five years. They sit holding hands and talking—that's all. Well, what d'y'expect? And for five years!'

'How old?'

'Oh, older than God.'

Through the crackle of laughter, he heard a step on the landing, and jumped up. His sister came in.

At the sight of him, her face changed, lit by a smile of pure pleasure. As always when he had not seen her for some months, he was struck by a sense of her terrifying

37

fragility. He knew that she was not fragile. But, at twenty-one, she still had a childish body; her long legs, in the tight-fitting trousers of 1963, were as slender, straight and delicate as a flute; he could span her waist between his hands, and above it her breasts made scarcely any show under her cotton sweater. Fly-away eyebrows gave her small face its look of surprise, faintly anxious. She was not pretty, her eyes, though bright, were too narrow, her mouth too long, but she was infinitely attractive.

He waited, chafing, while she talked briefly and politely to the visitors. All the time her fingers were tucking her mother's dishevelled hair back into place and straightening the dress rucked over her great knees. At last she glanced at him. With no word said, they left the room together, and ran upstairs to the attic on the top floor where she slept. His own room had been next it: when she was a baby it was he, not their mother, who went into her when she cried at night, and talked her into lying quiet.

She was his half-sister. She had been born three years after his father's death, and who *her* father was no one knew, not even—with certainty—their mother; now and then she speculated about it carelessly ... 'With her nose it could be a young fellow I knew, an officer, such a nice boy. I'm sure I hope it was, he was good family. But he had such very blue eyes, hers are more greeny, so ... Anyway, what's it matter?'

'My God, Tarry,' he said, 'if you hadn't that moment come I was going. Those two ghastly women.'

'They're not bad, they amuse mummy,' she said calmly. 'I don't mind them.'

'They're obscene. Like this whole set-up. I wish to God I could take you away.'

'You worry too much,' she said, smiling at him sweetly. 'I'm all right here.'

38

His face twisted with disgust. 'No, it's never been all right, never since we were born. She and her friends.'

'Oh, poor old girls,' she said lightly.

'If you only knew how it torments me to think of you living in a shabby brothel.'

'Oh, it's not that. Not any longer. You're here so seldom that you don't notice. But, in fact, except for what mummy calls her "olds", an elderly couple I almost never see—I take good care not to see them—who come four or five times a week, no one uses that room now.' She hesitated and said swiftly, 'And I must say I'm glad.'

Below her calm, her precocious poise, he detected—not for the first time—an astonished fear of their mother's lechery. It was not like his feeling of distaste, it was a child's fear of the unmanageably gross, which she refused to give way to. He felt an access of tenderness and protective longing. The tenderness and the need to protect were so mixed in him that he could not tell them apart.

'Why have you never tried to get away? I would have helped you.'

'Why, what could I do? I'm not like you, I'm not clever, not worth helping. And'—her eyes narrowed in amusement—'what *would* she do if I weren't here, if I left her? I couldn't leave her.'

He reflected that although they had both reacted against their mother's habits and violently unrestrained emotions, it was in utterly different ways, he to icy dislike, Tarry to a cool pity. A pity not of her age. Where does she get it from? he wondered. Like her modesty about herself, and her candour, it was untaught. And she was as little sentimental as a young child.

'It can't go on.'

She shrugged her thin shoulders. 'What is it like—your new job?'

'Oh, deadly. No one ever comes to the house. I never meet anyone—I mean, anyone useful. Except . . .' he broke off and said teasingly, 'No, I won't tell you about it—yet. I did meet someone—not here—in Dax. I thought I'd made a frightful mistake in taking the job, but now I think I may have done the right thing, I can see a chance—just a chance.' He laughed. 'The things we'll do, my love, when I have money, we'll travel—first class—and you shall have pretty clothes and learn to ride and dance, and meet the right people. Just wait, Tarry, just wait.'

'Well, now,' she said softly, laughing at him, 'you know I don't want to know the right people. It's not one of *my* ambitions.'

He twitched her white sweater. 'This rag. You need everything.'

'Oh, I don't mind a bit about clothes,' she said gaily. 'You always did. D'you remember when you were at the university, and had that one good suit, how you used to press it every other night, and sponge it? And d'you remember the enormous white lawn handkerchief you found somewhere—years before that, when you were still at school—and the trouble we took to keep it out of sight, for fear she thought of a use for it in her séances? What became of it?'

'I don't know, but'—a look his sister rarely saw on his face, insolent and mocking, crossed it—'I'll tell you now just where I found it. I didn't find it, I stole it.'

'Stephen! Where?'

'From a man's flat.'

'What man?'

'No, no,' he cried, 'I won't tell you, I'm sorry, forget about it.'

Why did I start it? he thought, vexed. He saw himself, a thin good-looking boy, walking dreamily past Victoria

40

Station with his school satchel, and the middle-aged man—sunburned, large anxious yellowish-brown eyes like a dog's—who stopped him and after only a few words invited him to 'come and look at my books'. He went with him, knowing coldly what he was in for, but thinking that he would almost certainly be given money—and he could do with a little money. And then, in the flat, he had a violent revulsion; the man left him alone for a minute, and he bolted, snatching up as he fled the handkerchief lying on the sofa.

She did not insist. She smiled at him with an innocent complicity, as if they were still sharing childish secrets.

'I don't believe a word of it,' she murmured.

'Well, don't ... I must go.'

'Don't be months before you come again. She talks about you a lot, you know, and I—I sometimes think you've forgotten us completely.'

He gripped her thin arm. 'You know I don't forget you.'

Freeing herself gently, she said, 'All right. Go in and say good-bye to her.'

'No.'

He went away, and as always when he left her in that house, he was torn by an anguished impatience: he felt ill with it. When, when, would he be able to take her out of it for good? It was not his fault she had to be there, yet he felt a sort of guilt as well as his impotence.

And—again as always—after a few minutes he refused deliberately to go on thinking about it.

CHAPTER 4

F R O M his room, the door ajar, he heard Chatteney leaving the house to go to the Athenaeum, and Lady Chatteney's penetrating voice asking, 'Do you want Hind to get you a cab?' She speaks about me as if I were an errand boy, he thought savagely. 'No,' her husband said, 'no, I'll walk for ten minutes, and pick one up.' The door closed.

Stephen knew what would happen next. She would go into the library and search through the wastepaper-basket for fragments large enough to be worth reading. There were never more than three or four of these. Certainly Chatteney did not suspect her of this trick, but he was naturally meticulous in anything to do with the memoirs, and what he destroyed he destroyed thoroughly.

In the same way, at the same time, she kept an eye on letters and Chatteney's bills—for his hand-made cigarettes, shoes, toilet water, books.

Stephen's predecessor, the outgoing secretary, a young man with dandruff and a poor degree in philosophy, had told him that this would happen. 'Don't catch her at it, that's all. *I* did, without meaning to. It was the first nail in my coffin, but there were others. I'm warning you not to get too thick with the great man, she hates that. She can't endure anyone to be on close terms with him, he's her property and no one else must lay a finger on him or come near enough to influence him. She suspected me and she'll suspect you of trying to worm your way into his confidence, for some evil reason. She's not mad, only madly jealous. If you offend her, you'll go, however well you get on with him.'

'Thanks,' Stephen said.

He needed no warning to make himself agreeable to his employer's wife. Only a fool would act differently. He did not believe she was inaccessible to flattery, the only question was the form it should take. He had known people who were flattered by rudeness. There would be some way of handling Renée Chatteney, he had only to discover it.

She was no fool. And she was capable, in her own way, of a sublime gesture. He knew from the memoirs that, in 1938, at the very moment when her husband was talking of resigning, she had lost—no fault of hers—two-thirds of her income. Chatteney had been summoned from Paris and told that he was going to be posted to Stockholm, as ambassador. With complete calm she told him that if he decided he must resign she would do her best on their very diminished income—Chatteney himself had less than five hundred a year.

After he had decided, that same evening, they drank— her suggestion—a bottle of 1921 champagne, one of three bottles they had left of that marvellous year.

With the same gaiety, and immense good sense and no fuss, she pulled them clear of the financial crisis—he had debts, not large, but enough to embarrass them. The house in North Street sold badly—in the autumn of 1938 there were not a great many people certain that Mr Chamberlain had made it safe to live in Westminster—but she had a bargain in the much smaller house in Lowndes Place, and ran it with a fine-fingered ease which astonished her husband. He had always respected her head for business. Now he had reason to thank her, sincerely and humbly, for behaving as if their difficulties amused her.

No doubt he was acute enough to know that what delighted her was his new dependence on her....

Straining his ears to catch the barely audible sounds she would make as she came out of the library, Stephen reflected that she was very like an educated savage, or an Elizabethan politician; she joined practical ruthlessness and skills to outbursts of hysterical emotion. You could not say she had a civilised mind, but she had natural cunning, of the highest order.

He heard the door of the library close quietly, and her footsteps going down the stairs to the drawing-room. He decided to go down and talk to her.

In the doorway he checked himself quickly and stepped back. 'Oh, I'm sorry, Lady Chatteney,' he murmured, 'I didn't know you were here.'

'Come in, come in,' she said, looking at him. 'Is it cold in your room? You mustn't hesitate to switch on the fire. This frightful summer.'

He went in. At the sight of him, Simon growled and moved his long thick body in a shudder of dislike.

He knows I loathe him, Stephen thought. 'You're a handsome fellow', he said, 'why don't you like me?'

'I'm the only person he trusts,' Lady Chatteney said, smiling. 'But if you go on being polite to him ... I hope you're happy with us. If you need anything in your room, tell me, or speak to Bruegel.'

'I have never been happier. The last seven months'—he hesitated, and went on impulsively—'just imagine what it means to me to live in this house, with two people who know how one ought to live. I have never—forgive me for saying this—never known anyone like yourself, able to make a serenely lovely world for people lucky enough to live in it.' He laughed boyishly. 'I'm an interloper, of course, but—do believe me—I know my luck.'

'I think,' she said quietly, 'that it is a privilege for a young man, any young man, to work for my husband.'

'Yes, of course. And I do my best, but ...'

'But what?'

44

He made a confused gesture. 'It's difficult to explain. The —the distance between us is so great—I could never, I mean, pretend to any sort of personal relation with him. So that I can never be sure that I'm giving satisfaction, though I do really, I assure you, do all I can to—to be so useful that he won't notice me.'

He saw that he had delighted her. He was pleased—and not only because he wanted to keep his job, but because he liked, liked and needed, to be on the right side of the right people. And he liked to be approved of. He would have preferred even Simon to like him.

'How far have you reached now in the memoirs?'

'To 1938. The resignation.' He added humorously, 'For, I think and hope, the last time.'

'I hope so, too,' she said in a serious voice. 'But Sir Henry is a perfectionist—as you have discovered. I am his wife, and perhaps prejudiced, but I believe absolutely that you are copying out the greatest work of the kind ever written. And what grieves me'—her short-sighted eyes, a deep tarnished brown, peered at him with wary defiance, daring him to contradict her—'is that he means to bury them for fifty years after his death. They should be published now, now—when he can enjoy his fame.'

'Does he care about fame?' Stephen murmured.

'Yes. A little.' Suddenly she clenched her hands and hammered with them on her small bony knees. 'Mr Hind, I want to be alive to see him lifted up in the sight of all men. I can't bear him to live in obscurity when he could be praised, honoured, seen for what he is. Do you understand me?'

'Yes. Yes, I do indeed.'

'It's not at all a question of money. We're poor, but I have enough to let us go on living here if prices don't rise very much more.' It seemed to strike her at this moment that she was speaking too freely to a nobody, and she added coldly, 'Don't misunderstand me. I have only one reason for living. To serve him.'

'I, too,' Stephen said softly, 'in my obscure place.'

She sat silent. He tried to guess her thoughts from the expressions following each other across her little raddled face: hauteur, sadness, resentment. When he was not expecting it, she smiled at him.

'I'm glad you don't think of leaving us.'

Genuinely astonished, he cried,

'I shall never do that—so long as I'm any use to him. And to you.'

'Good. Do stay.'

'I hope ... You would tell me if there were anything I ought to be doing, wouldn't you? I'm not used'—he waved his hand at the room—'to this sort of house.'

Her face softened. 'My dear child!'

'How extraordinarily glad you must be,' he said diffidently, 'that after all these years the book really is all but finished.'

'I am, yes, glad.' She paused and said with frightful bitterness. 'And I have not read it—and never shall. Long after I'm dead, anyone will be able to read it, and I, I, have been refused.'

This was a really dangerous moment. If he made the wrong answer he would lose every step he had advanced in the last quarter of an hour. Yet he must say nothing that she could repeat to Chatteney in support of her craving to get her hands on the manuscript. Looking at her with his heart in his eyes, he said,

'Don't die yet, will you? There are a few people who should live for ever, because they're irreplaceable.' He smiled like an eager boy. 'Do your best.'

'Thank you,' she said, with a faint answering smile, 'how

sweet of you.... There was one thing I was going to ask you. Well, no, if we hadn't had this talk I shouldn't have dreamed of asking you—and very possibly you can't tell me. But it is important—it's one of the few things, if I were allowed to read the book, I should see farther into than anyone. Because it was I who acted and suffered, and I was absolutely right. Do you know what I'm talking about?'

'No, Lady Chatteney.'

'Ah—you haven't come to the tragedy yet ... 1946 ... you will come to it, no doubt.' Her mouth was distorted suddenly by a curious smile, cruel and sorrowful. 'All his—what shall I call them?—his female adorers. No one ever had so many. I don't know how far it went, in any particular instance—except one. But if you have ever seen a hen walking round and round a knife laid on the ground, not able to take her eyes off it, you would have seen any one of these silly women, young, middle-aged, clever, stupid —they all behaved in exactly the same way.'

She laughed. Her eyes gleamed with an excitement that the young man could only see as jealousy, sexual jealousy. It amused and a little horrified him. At over seventy, he thought. What an animal.

He gave her a grave, respectful, tender glance. 'Every great man attracts that sort of attention, and the greater he is the less it means to him. To Sir Henry—I'm certain— nothing or very little.'

She said swiftly, 'Ah, you gather that from the memoirs, do you? So much the better....'

This was the moment Simon chose to belch like a clap of thunder. She smiled and stood up, swaying a little.

'I must take my naughty child away.... I'm glad you're dining out this evening, my dear Stephen. It's very boring for you here.'

47

This was the first time she had called him by his Christian name. Smiling at her, he said,

'You know I'm not bored. What can I do to prove it?'

'Stay exactly as you are.'

He ran upstairs to his room, very satisfied with himself. That went off all right, he thought gaily.... At this moment he felt genuine liking for her.

CHAPTER 5

HE knew, in the moment of stepping into the entrance hall of the Hydes' house in Brook Street, that he had set foot in a world as yet entirely alien and unconquered. That Frederick Hyde was a very rich man—a personal fortune inherited from an American mother—he knew, but the thought of him as a publisher had misled him to expect anything but this suave luxury. A manservant moved forward to take his overcoat from him, and he thanked his stars that he had had the luck, in Harrod's sale, to pick up a good one, and could hand it over without a qualm. Not that he was wholly without qualms; Mrs Hyde had greeted him with the easiness of an old friend, and her husband, a big fleshy man—hard flesh, made smoothly insolent by a lifetime of power and good living—had said warmly, 'Delighted, delighted, glad you could come,' but a glance round the other guests, before the double doors of the dining-room were folded back and he found himself walking towards the large round table with its striking centrepiece—something ancient and Chinese, he thought vaguely—very slightly alarmed him. These people were—he repeated the words to himself to gain confidence—*gens du monde*. He had not been presented to more than half of them, but of these one had a title he recognised, another was a celebrated writer, the third a Greek millionaire at the moment in the news, and the fourth a well-heeled left-wing Member of Parliament. Yes, really the *monde*.

At the end of some twenty minutes, the excellence of the food, the handsome room, the wines, and above all the women, had refloated him. He could not have imagined elegance of this sort, unobtrusively flawless: the comparison was with Ukley Manor and its comfortable shabby rooms and women in whom it had amused him to detect a likeness to their horses or a matronly badger. This table, the glass, the chandelier, the forks and spoons, dazzled him as did the bare shoulders of the two women seated to his right and left, and as did their make-up, their cunningly-arranged hair, their clothes, their jewels: he turned his fine nose from one to the other to catch and compare the scent each used. He admired them both, fatuously and inexpressibly. But not more than, at this moment, he admired himself for having got here from 41A Marion Street —what a stretch!—and for knowing how to handle all these forks and glasses, how to speak as if he had been born in this world, its speech his mother tongue. Much that was said—the half-sentences, the Christian names— meant nothing to him, but he knew when to smile, and how.

A remote edge of his mind remained cold and lucid: all the rest was invaded, absorbed, by the conviction that no other sort of life was worth living; outside this world everything was dull, shoddy, cheap, a little disgraceful: this was where he wanted to live, these men, rich, self-assured, powerful, worldly, these deliciously smooth women, were the people he wanted to accept him—not at an occasional dinner-party, but as one of themselves.

49

He was here tonight on sufferance. It depended on himself to turn a precarious foothold into a parish.

Between the sole and the saddle of veal the conversation turned on the current scandal, a politician and a call-girl.

'How,' the celebrated novelist asked languidly, 'does a fellow like this other minor chap, what's his name, Ward, succeed in becoming a social figure?'

Mrs Hyde laughed at him. 'Why, my dear Duffy, by being himself—that is, by doing frankly things other people only think about in a, what shall I say?, a lascivious mood. That amused people—certain people.'

'But he had highly-placed, even aristocratic friends!'

'Who needed to be amused! He amused them. He was a comedian, a burlesque turn. Rather a sad comedian, I feel now, a *triste farceur*. His crash is disgraceful and ridiculous, and his late friends won't forgive him a farce that has ended badly. Or offer to help him.'

Words *not* meant for me, Stephen thought. He felt a prick of rage. Whatever else, I'm not playing in a farce.

Frederick Hyde's rather harsh voice had genial undertones. 'He's nothing at all. These fellows bob up from nowhere, and bob along for a bit, and sink. Trash. What I can't understand is a man, an educated man, successful, nearing the top of his particular ladder, tripping himself up over a young whore he might have fallen for at the university. What an ass, eh? When he had only to pick a woman in his own world, and there would have been no scandal.'

His glance rested briefly, a flicker of amusement and greed, on Stephen's right-hand neighbour, a Mrs Gide. His mistress, Stephen thought. How old is he? Sixty? And with an appetite for success, women, money, as gross as his other appetites. . . . He had never seen anyone eat and drink quite so devotedly, two mouthfuls to every one of his guests'.

'Perhaps he fell in love with her,' Mrs Gide said.

'Oh, nonsense, my dear Laura,' Hyde said pleasantly. He cocked an eyebrow at the plump young Labour politician. 'What's your verdict, Wexford?'

'He was bored. I've always thought that the devil doesn't need anything worse than boredom to trap people.'

'Do you *know* he was bored?' Mrs Hyde asked.

'No. It's my guess.'

She leaned forward, smiling at Stephen. 'Do you believe he was bored? Or wicked?'

My moment, thought Stephen. He was conscious in the same instant of his host's genially rapacious eyes and nostrils wide open on the scent of other men's mistakes and weakness, of the Greek meditatively picking his teeth, of a benevolent grin from the politician, and of a whiff of Mrs Gide's scent.

'Neither,' he said. 'Clumsy. No one asks public men to be strictly moral, but they must *seem* to be well-behaved. A moral politician—any public man—is one who sets a good example, who seems to conform. He has only to go through the motions. He needn't believe in a set of rules invented to keep the herd in order, in fact he'd be an imbecile if he did. But he really should make the gestures.'

'Bravo!' Mrs Gide cried, laughing. 'You're quite right. Isn't he?'

'Probably,' Wexford said.

'Of course he's right,' Mrs Hyde said. She smiled. 'Right, but a little dangerous.'

Her husband lowered his large bald head and said blandly,

'The really dangerous men are those who don't want to succeed. Unless I'm badly off course, our young friend does.' He looked at Stephen under heavy lids, a glance the young man held boldly. 'How d'y'get on with Chatteney?'

'Very well,' Stephen answered. He smiled. 'I'm only his copyist.'

'They say,' Mrs Hyde mocked, 'that Lady Chatteney makes one egg last for three meals. How can you bear it? Aren't you always hungry?'

'Always,' he said gaily. 'But we're within sprinting distance of good small restaurants, I have only to run like a hare after dinner to eat a second.'

To let them know that he had far too little money to buy himself an extra meal every day would be a mistake. Nothing is more boring than other people's poverty and troubles. The image of himself he intended to give—a young man amusing himself by acting as secretary to a once-celebrated and still interesting man—was the right one. He could see it reflected in the appraising glance Mrs Hyde passed over his dinner jacket and linen shirt, to rest on his long slender hands. The temptation seized him to make a witty story of Lady Chatteney's passion for her revolting dog. He resisted it—out of an obscure kindness. Not that for one moment did he admit that as his reason. I mustn't, he thought cynically, seem to have nothing to do with my time but placate her and her animal.

'Why on earth did he marry her?' Mrs Gide wondered. 'She has always—my mother knew her when she was young—been neurotic and boringly delicate. She was not even very rich! Quite a modest fortune, my mother said.'

'That's not the worst about her,' Hyde said. 'I can remember when he resigned'—he showed his strong yellow teeth in a rather brutal smile—'you don't, you were at school, it's a quarter of a century ago, I was thirty-five ... After he resigned, she alienated three-quarters of his friends by treating them right away as if they intended to drop him. And—she certainly encouraged his worst side, his appalling arrogance.'

52

'Is he vain?' the novelist asked Stephen.

'Come, come, Duffy,' Mrs Hyde cried. 'It's not fair to ask him that.'

Stephen smiled, a brilliant eager smile. He had expected to be questioned about his employer, and had rehearsed a few phrases, full of a young tactful loyalty, and pointed enough not to bore.

'That depends what you mean by vanity. He's a very great man, absolutely incorruptible, not impressed by cleverness or political platitudes or intrigues. You can say he's arrogant, but only if you mean that he would refuse to take any notice of criticism from inferiors.'

'A dictator, eh?'

'No, no,' Stephen said swiftly, 'the very opposite. He hates dictators as only an aristocrat can. That comes out in his attitude to de Gaulle ... I can talk about it because one version—it's been entirely rewritten—came out in *The Times*, so you must have read it. Strangely enough—no, it's not strange—he liked de Gaulle, and got on with him when no one else could. They're alike in being magnificently singleminded and magnificently sinuous—a contradiction in nature, a prodigy—two prodigies! And unlike just where neutrality was useful, Sir Henry all cold rationality and enjoyment of life, and the General a pious Catholic, believing in God and himself, or in himself and God, and genuinely ascetic. In short, it was a rather stately love-affair—and lasted as long as you would expect between two intelligent egoists ... About eighteen months ... The General, he says, has no intimacies, not even with the Almighty. He has replaced the anarchy of the old political parties by personal rule, by the respect paid to him. And there is a splendid passage where he says that after so many years of seeing himself as the man destined to re-create the France of the *Roi Soleil* or the First

53

Empire, de Gaulle had become *the dupe of his attitudes....*'

Stopping short, he said ingenuously, 'Do forgive me, Mrs Hyde, I'm talking far too much.'

'But we're all listening to you,' she said, smiling at him.

'Chatteney's dislike of Churchill was well advertised,' Hyde said, 'and his comments generously repeated to Churchill. There was one about Churchill's three-hatted style of writing which went home. Result: all he was given in 1940 was the job of liaison with the Free French—ludicrous.'

A strange sound betwen a hiss and a giggle came from the Greek.

'More to it than that,' he said, with a fine smile. 'I was at a dinner where Churchill said, "Chatteney? A talented fellow, but thinks he's a genius. He could be useful if he would do as he's told, but he never would. He can neither behave himself nor obey orders. I can't use him." Y'know, I liked that. A really beautiful contempt—like a splendid hate or a dangerous ambition—is very amusing to watch.'

'Just the same,' Hyde said dryly, 'Chatteney had a fine hand he could never, after 1938, play. A politician in bed with a whore, that's farce. Chatteney's ruin was tragic. Mind you, he wasn't irretrievably ruined until the famous case. That ought never to have happened to him. He has his vindictive wife to thank. Why in God's name he didn't strangle her or leave her—no, it defeats me.' Turning his sarcastic smile on the novelist, he said, 'A theme for your next novel, Duffy. I shall be delighted to publish it.'

Barely giving himself the trouble to glance at Stephen, Duffy drawled, 'May I ask you another question?'

'Is it one I can answer?'

'Are the memoirs true?'

'I don't think I'm a judge,' Stephen said coolly.

'Ah. I take it they're not.'

The fury Stephen felt sprang directly from an adolescent itching to tweak the noses of the very people he envied and respected. Noticing that Hyde was watching him with unkind curiosity, he controlled his voice.

'Since he is writing to be read—at some time—by all and sundry, he would be justified, surely, in leaving out anything that distorts the image he wants posterity to look at. It's as far from sincerity—that half-lie—as from conceit. And surely a greater writer can't help regarding everything—people, events—as his *material*, to be shaped in a way that will bring out his idea of its essential truth. I'd say that the book is a unique monument, a ... a witness to an age, to his friendships, his view of great men—and some small ones—and his own prodigiously living mind. He knows so much, he *really* knows the *haute monde* and the corridors of power—by living in them. No present-day novelist, I don't care whom you name, has done that. And, as well, he knows as much as a very great novelist about motives and feelings. He writes extremely lucidly, and yet —oh, a subtlety, interwoven meanings, graceful, a masculine grace....' He hesitated and said, half under his breath, 'A poet of the human possibility.'

Because he had been infuriated into saying what he felt, he blushed. In the same moment he imagined that Hyde had listened to him with surprise and ironic approval.

After dinner, in the drawing-room, he felt sure of it. Taking him by the arm in a hard grip, Hyde said affably,

'Young man, have you any politics?'

'None, sir. I haven't much experience, but I'd think that the percentage of competent men never varies more than a point or two, in any society. And if I'm to be ruled, I'd prefer it to be by an educated man, he'll be less anxious to show off his power.'

Hyde smiled. 'Good boy. I agree with you.... By the

way, your comments on Chatteney's book struck me. What you didn't say—couldn't, of course—is that one reason why he doesn't want to publish it now is that he feels certain posterity will admire it. He can't feel so certain of his contemporaries. And for a man who can't stand criticism, and wants fame.... I'd give an ear to publish him, y'know.'

'You would be the only right person for it,' Stephen said boldly.

'H'm. Have y'ever thought of writing?'

'No.'

'Why not?'

'If I had enough money to live on without earning, I might have wanted to write. But I shouldn't care to live by peddling my entrails.'

Striking him on the shoulder with an arm like a flail, Hyde laughed. 'Y're right.... Go and talk to my wife, she has something to say to you.'

Just as he reached her, Colette Hyde was saying,

'My dear Laura, you, anybody, can have all the servants you want, if you're prepared to pay for them. I pay mine considerably more than the market price, and I've had my housekeeper, the chef, and most of the others for at least ten years.' She broke off, to smile brilliantly at the young man. 'You have even fewer domestic troubles.'

'Except,' Mrs Gide said, 'having to sprint for your meals.' Her glance moved from his face to his concave body below the waist. 'I'm not going to leave the rescue work to Colette. You must dine with me soon. Will you?'

'I should like to,' Stephen murmured. He smiled at her, with a young naïve insolence he knew was attractive.

His success intoxicated him, he had begun to feel as he imagined a lion must feel after an easy succulent kill. If these women knew where I came from! ... With the thought of Marion Street came an image, unwanted at this moment, of his sister's smiling colourless face. He turned away from it. Wait, wait, my love, he told her urgently ... He could not—not yet—place her in this splendid world, and her image made it for a second grotesquely unreal. It made him wince to think of her in her cold bedroom while he was here, in this house, with these self-assured inimitably elegant women. Only wait, he thought again. Another year or two—or until *she* dies....

When he was leaving, on the heels of the novelist, Mrs Hyde contrived to talk to him alone.

'We want those memoirs,' she said frankly. 'I'm sure you often think of throwing up your job, but don't. Endure it until there is no more chance of laying hands on them.'

'I'll do that for you,' he said, laughing.

The absurdity of being urged not to throw himself out of work, into the street, exasperated him. He thought obscurely: One of these days I'll make someone pay for it.

Mrs Hyde laid a hand on his arm, four fingers with long pointed coral nails, as fantastically improbable as the immense stone—an emerald?—on the single strap of her dress.

'You'll come to see me again, Stephen? Ring me up.'

With a gust of pride, a little fatuous—as he was quick to tell himself—he realised that she was offering herself: it rested with him.

He was completely willing. And not purely because she would be able to help him in some way, but because he liked her. And because the thought of stripping off her dress—stripping her at the same time of the prestige of wealth—to get at the smooth cared-for body under it roused more than his easily-roused ravenously sharp senses —vanity, triumph, even a sort of anger.

He thought of kissing the hand lying on his arm, but bent and touched his cheek to it instead.

Outside, Brook Street was empty; he saw the tail light of the novelist's car disappearing at the far end. Unfriendly brute, he thought, but without resentment. To walk would air his brain, restless with excitement and the wines he had been drinking. He walked rapidly: all this quarter of London was the reflection in night and silence of his ambitions, desires, envy. A diabolical happiness filled him. He tried, smiling, to reduce it to order. Don't imagine you've done more than get a toe in the door, he warned himself: one door. You have a sahara to cross still.

His happiness, like the energy that went with it, was too lively to be put in its place. He felt it like a second self walking beside him, urging him over the ground. And what promise in the thin July air!

CHAPTER 6

THE next day it rained, as it had done almost every day of this miscalled summer: he had to go out and find a taxi to take Chatteney to the Athenaeum. When he came back with it to the house, he heard Lady Chatteney reminding her husband, as though he were a schoolboy, to be home no later than half past six.

'I want you to be ready waiting for Emily when she arrives. I shall be in the kitchen for a few minutes— Bruegel can take a soufflé out of the oven, but she can't put it in. You won't forget?'

Taking Stephen's arm to cross the wet pavement, Chatteney said patiently,

'Of course not, my dear.'

Stephen shut him into the cab and went back to say to

Lady Chatteney that since they had a guest that evening he would dine out. She was in the drawing-room, with one of her old fine linen sheets spread across her knees—she darned them herself, with exquisite neatness.

'No, no, no,' she told him, 'I want you to be here. Lady Emily Grosmont is one of my husband's oldest friends'— she smiled—'the oldest—she must be eighty-eight. There are very few people left who speak of him as Harry. He is fond of her. I suspect that—years and years ago, fifty years —in spite of being so much older than he is, she would not have been annoyed if he had seemed a little fonder. She has a weakness for great men.'

To the young man it sounded grotesque. Sacred monsters at play. 'If you are sure ...'

'I'm quite sure,' she said in an affectionate voice. 'It won't amuse you—it will be nothing like your dinner last night, with the Hydes. Did you enjoy that?' She looked up at him sharply. 'Did they speak of the memoirs?'

'Yes,' Stephen said. He seemed to hesitate. 'Frederick Hyde would like to publish them.'

'Of course!' She pointed her needle at him—a wasp about to sting. 'Listen, my friend—I hope you're my friend —they must be published. Must. While I am alive to see that it's done properly, with all the respect and honour due to a great monument. Tell me—are you or are you not on my side?'

He had not expected to be faced with this, and for a moment his head reeled.

'I'm not quite sure what you mean....'

'Yes, you are,' she said implacably, 'you know exactly what I mean, you're not an idiot. I want you to help me to convince my husband that the idea of burying them—to be dug up when we're all dead—is insane. Fatuous, cowardly!'

There was no possibility of evading this devil of an old woman. She had him against a wall. Either he made himself her ally, frankly, or she would turn against him, and before he knew where he was get rid of him as mercilessly as she had got rid of two other secretaries. No hope that Chatteney would put up any fight to keep him. Rather than have a scene he gave way to her on anything—except his memoirs. There and only there she came up against an obstinacy as rooted as her own.

Which of these two fabulous animals, he groaned, am I going to offend? He said slowly,

'If I'm to be of any use to you I mustn't lose Sir Henry's confidence. If, I mean, he thought I was conspiring with you to make him change his mind about publication, he would—very naturally—be irritated and ...'

She cut him serenely short. 'You shouldn't talk about a conspiracy.'

'I'm sorry.' He smiled at her, a young tender smile, infinitely seductive. 'I *am* on your side, you know that, but after all I'm only Sir Henry's copyist, he's not likely to ask my opinion, and I must, surely, take care not to show that I have one, still less one he would resent? You'—he looked her in the eyes—'you understand that, you understand everything.'

Smiling, looking down demurely at the sheet, she said,

'Yes, well ... we must be tactful. But I'm determined to see the book published—decently. It will mean cuts ...'

'The publisher's lawyers would read it for libel.'

Her wry pointed face hardened curiously. 'Oh, I'm not thinking about libel. I'm thinking only of his reputation—if you like, his honour and glory; I want the world to see the real man, not a tarnished distorted image. That's why it absolutely must come out now, when I can see to it. You understand, Stephen—there must be nothing in his 'memoirs about the women who have always buzzed round him like flies round a plum. I won't allow them to scribble their silly names on his monument. The mere thought is intolerable'—her lip sneered—'disgusting.'

'Yes,' he said, 'I understand.'

He thought derisively: Now we get her real motive. The one behind all the chatter about wanting him to be lifted up to enjoy his fame. Sexual jealousy pretending to be devotion. No, no, not so simple. Jealousy *and* devotion. But she will never admit to the jealousy; whatever she does in the way of vengeance must have the purest motives.... It gave him a singular pleasure to think that he had seen through her virtuous skin to the worm in her heart.

In the same moment he thought ruefully of all the light, gay, careless witty portraits of women that would be torn ruthlessly out of the manuscript.... Am I going to help her to be so insensitive and vindictive? We'll see....

From his place at the dinner-table he was able, without moving his eyeballs more than a fractional degree—a trick he had learned and practised at school—to examine Lady Emily Grosmont, feature by feature. This imposing old woman, as thin as Lady Chatteney but a foot taller, her spine as straight as a bolt, nose like a race-horse, was a little horrifying: the skin of a lizard, corrugated across the forehead and again in vertical folds on both sunken cheeks, the eyes a pale glaucous grey, like the bloom on a grape; even her lips, stretched between a network of wrinkles above and below, were deeply wrinkled. A line of strong black hairs growing along the upper lip was less grotesque than masterful. On either side of her neck the sinews were like the roots of a vine. My God, Stephen thought, to be so old—inconceivable, unspeakable.

61

The meal was more ample than usual, and with the cold chicken Bruegel placed a second bottle of white burgundy in front of Chatteney. His wife did not drink, and their guest refused to have her glass filled again, and after helping his secretary from it once he drank the rest himself. A little colour came into his face, seeping into the cavities below his cheekbones. He began a monologue—apparently for himself.

'Y'know, I'm unbelievably out of date. The gap that separates me from the young and middle-aged is infinitely wider than the one that separated me from my parents and grandfather. That was only the gap between an old and a young heart, it could be bridged by politeness. This is different, this is a dislocation in time which has worked a total dissimilarity of moral and intellectual feeling. Oh, no doubt certain basic sensations remain unaltered—death, sex—but the emotional attitude to them is so changed that no degree of politeness from a young man'—he waved a hand at his secretary—'could make me understand how he sets about dying and making love. With far less fuss, I'm sure ... And the younger writers—the very tone they write in is one I couldn't hope to imitate, even if I cared to. It's impossible, I was born in the very last decade when language was taken seriously in this country, and I was taught to respect it. Now grammar and taste are in ruins, they began to decay at the same time as the architecture, probably from the same causes. Today language has reached a stage of disorder—I'm talking about so-called imaginative writing, not about the functional sort which matches the corpse-like born-dead new buildings—of clumsiness, of incoherence, which makes me think of stale fish. Y'know, I can't help believing that a mind formed by, let's say, the eighteenth century—but you can make your own choice between the classic centuries—is less likely to be flabby than one formed by ... oh, never mind. None of it alters the fact that I'm infinitely out of date.'

Stephen said gravely,

'To be out of date—you mean, dateless. Built to last for centuries.'

His employer looked at him with a meditative irony. He takes as little interest in being praised as in praising other men, Stephen thought: his vanity goes deeper.

But Lady Emily was sharply pleased. 'You are perfectly right. No young writer is younger in spirit than Sir Henry.'

'Spirit?' Chatteney mocked. 'My dear good Emily, there are moments, even now, at my age, when the sight of a young woman walking arm in arm with a young man fills me with such rage that if I could wipe them both out by lifting a finger I'd do it, with all the pleasure in the world.'

'Oh, nonsense.'

'You don't know me.'

His wife struck the table with her small fist. 'Do you know that he still has every one of his teeth, where mine are all false? It's so unjust!'

Lady Emily treated this escape of bitterness in nursery fashion, by shaking a bony finger in the other woman's face.

'Don't be ridiculous, my poor Renée, we're as God made us. Would you like him better if he were toothless and senile?'

'I should like him to be franker. If you were his wife would you tolerate not being allowed to read his memoirs —only called in when he can't remember a name or a date? No doubt they deal with incidents in his life he prefers I shouldn't know about.'

Stephen was beginning to be exasperated by her. Can't she, even before their friends, refrain from taking him apart? God save me from a devoted wife.

63

'My dear woman,' Lady Emily said, 'frankness, what's frankness? Any clever liar can be frank.' She swung her scythe of a nose towards Chatteney. 'I trust you've told the truth about *events*—your resignation, for instance.'

'Yes, of course.'

'It was a very damp squib,' his wife said derisively, 'he was furious when Duff Cooper resigned the next day and got all the attention.'

Chatteney smiled.

'Renée!' Lady Emily said.

'What I hope to bring out,' Chatteney said calmly, 'is the quite absurdly small part played in the relations between great men—I mean the men, seldom great, who rule us—by their common efforts, hopes, sufferings, heroism and the rest of it. In almost every case, what decides them is some infinitesimal personal liking or dislike. Usually dislike. I remember spending three exhausting hours trying—without any success at all—to persuade de Gaulle not to oppose Churchill in a matter where he was clearly wrong and Churchill right. Finally de Gaulle said, "If he would only not speak what he believes to be French. Every word is an insult to the language and"—this under his breath—"to me." I gave up then, I knew it was hopeless!'

'Well, really,' his wife said, smiling, 'I suppose that what matters is what the speaker has to say, and the power he has—not whether he can jabber French like a parrot.'

Leaning across the table, Chatteney touched her hand gently. It might have been kindness, but was it? The truth is, Stephen thought sharply, he doesn't care enough about her to be angry ... There was even a streak of cruelty in his courteous handling of her. Surely any woman, intelligent or not, would find it impossible to forgive so impregnable an egotism?

He looked at their faces, Chatteney's serene, his wife's

alive with a shrunken mischief, Lady Emily's virile calm and guardsman's body. Three survivals from an age as un-imaginably remote as any you chose to name, harmless survivals, without a trace of any power they had once had, or two of them had had, to influence politics or society, meaningless, irrelevant in a world extended to infinity by the computer and on the edge of nuclear annihilation, in a society with no holds barred, no accepted morality.... A violent impatience seized him. What in God's name am I doing here, he thought furiously, shut up with these three withered ancients, smelling of age and impotence, talking, talking, in their sort of Sanskrit? ... The blood raged in his veins; he wanted to beat his head on the wall and began trying to phrase an excuse to get up and go.

Bruegel saved him. Standing in the doorway, she said curtly,

'Mr Hind, you're being telephoned to.'

The telephone was in an alcove in the narrow entrance hall. Colette Hyde's low strong voice—he imagined her smooth lips—said,

'Stephen? I want you to dine here on Monday? Are you free that evening?'

'Of course.'

'Are you at dinner now?'

'My God, yes,' he exclaimed.

'You sound a little exasperated.'

'I'm suffocating. The total age of the three people at the table—I'm not counting mine—is at least two hundred and thirty.'

'Impossible!' She laughed. 'Why don't you give them up and come here? I'm alone.'

The wall of the alcove tilted past his eyes like the white sail of a boat. 'May I?'

'I should be enchanted.'

'Very well,' he said, 'I'll come at once.'

Bruegel was crossing the hall from the kitchen staircase, with the coffee tray. Seizing her arm, he whispered, 'Tell them my mother rang me up, she's ill.'

'Is it true?'

'No.'

'And you're not afraid of being punished for your lies by her dropping dead?'

He grinned. 'No. I'm not.'

'Very well,' she said blandly. 'On your head.'

He left at once and walked some distance before he saw a taxi crawling towards him. In the instant before beckoning it, he changed his mind. He would walk to Brook Street, across the Park. She had told him she was alone; that left no room for wondering what she expected of him, and he had become paradoxically calmer and light-hearted. He felt as sure of himself as of her—and it amused him to draw out a little the time between being summoned to give two people a great deal of pleasure and the moment of giving it. The air, after the day's rain, was cold and fresh. A delicious feeling of release filled him.

'How long is it since you made love to anyone?'

'More than seven months.'

'My God, what happened?' she asked, smiling.

'I had to wait for you,' he said lightly.

'And if we hadn't met?' She traced a line round his face with the point of her nail. 'You're astonishingly good-looking, and disturbing and dangerous—not at all domesticated.'

Lifting himself on an elbow, he looked down at her, warm and smiling, her fine blonde hair dishevelled, one arm lying across her breasts—no sign there of her age: if signs there were, he had not yet noticed them.... He knew

66

from experience that his frank pleasure in his triumph was attractive. He had never been happier, his unqualified success and her skilful sensuality gave him acute satisfaction: even the knowledge that she was more than twenty years older than he was pleased him. In some way he did not trouble to think about that made him feel safe. Safe, roused, satisfied.

For the first time he had in his grasp a woman of the sort he used, when he was a schoolboy prowling past houses like this one, to see stepping out of a splendid car. What better sign and symbol of success—the beginning of success— than to be lying in bed with a Rolls-Royce?

'Must I go now?' he asked.

'No, my child. You can stay—oh, an hour. Longer if you like.'

CHAPTER 7

FROM his schooldays he had kept the habit of using the time spent in solitary walking to—his phrase—take a good look at himself. What in the anxious ambitious schoolboy had been a trick, a defensive trick to keep him from being overwhelmed by his difficulties, Marion Street, his gaily disreputable mother, was now a groove in his mind, half involuntary, half ironical.

A cold July afternoon, rain threatening from a livid sky, had emptied the Park of all but the hardiest or most desperate. Two of these, lying in each other's arms, oblivious, barely decent enough to escape trouble, reminded him of Chatteney's saying that he could not forgive the young their youth and lusts. Poor old devil, he thought, what must it be like to be old, impotent, disappointed?

What will save me from disappointment, he reflected coolly, is that *I know what I want*. I know it as if I were looking at a formula on a page, not in any vague romantic way. That's what puts me morally in the category of men like Frederick Hyde.

And not only do I know exactly what I want, but I know what means I have of my own for use when the chance offers itself. I'm not fumbling round. I know.

How soon after he left Colette that first evening was it before he began to see clearly the outline of a possible future? Not long.

Not, he told himself lightly, that I think of her as a means. Or only in the second place. I'm genuinely fond of her, I enjoy her enormously, there's everything to be said for a woman, as handsome as she still is, who will never need to make me feel responsible for her in any way. And if, by amusing her and sleeping with her, I can get into one of the best publishing firms in the world, she'll have done me a service, but not, not, a charity. I'm thoroughly fitted for the job.... His mouth twitched.... And dear Colette is less likely to act out of charity than anyone in the world....

The servant who opened the door to him said,

'Mrs Hyde expects you, sir. Will you go up?'

What does he think about it? Stephen wondered briefly. Uncertain of the right tone to take, he nodded without speaking, and walked upstairs.

She had on the second floor what was in effect a two-roomed apartment, with its own front door opening into a hall, a sitting-room, bedroom, and a bathroom which almost intimidated him by its size and luxurious comfort: until now he had supposed that bathrooms of this sort were an invention of film producers.

As he came into the sitting-room he saw that she had

68

another visitor, a woman, who seemed to be on the point of leaving. A woman ambiguously old, carelessly dressed—long dark coat hanging loosely over a garment that would not have been out of place on an old servant or the Mother Superior of a shabby order—hatless, with a head of thick greying curls, large face, eyes with the dull gleam of pitch, wide beautiful mouth: the effect was not one of ruined good looks but of a different order of beauty, not dependent on youth or freshness or a smooth skin or bodily elegance. She had no trace of these. She was splendidly warm, carelessly opulently alive—and old.

'Mary,' Colette Hyde said, 'let me introduce someone who will interest you.' She smiled maliciously. 'Stephen Hind is the latest of Chatteney's secretaries.' She turned to him. 'Mrs Duquesne, Stephen.'

Ah, he thought, the enticer. He gave her a brilliant smile. 'Secretary is a misnomer. I type for him. And fetch cabs.'

'The famous memoirs,' Colette said.

'Ah, the memoirs,' Mary Duquesne said, with a smile. The young man had never heard so enchanting a speaking voice, deep, lightly flawed, so that a second and a third note sounded in it below the first. 'Alas, I never see him. I haven't seen him for, let me think, at least fifteen years.'

'Not since the case,' her friend said.

'Colette, you're indiscreet,' Mrs Duquesne said, amused. 'You're going to embarrass Mr Hind. Yes—not since the case.' She went on serenely, 'How is he? And Renée Chatteney, how is she?'

'He seems to me frail,' Stephen said, 'but I think he may be stronger than he looks. Lady Chatteney...'

'Lady Chatteney is utterly impossible,' Colette interrupted. 'The only kind thing one can say about her is that she is mad.'

69

'No, you exaggerate,' Mrs Duquesne said lightly, almost gaily. 'I was very fond of her—and still would be if she allowed it. She and I, you know, Mr Hind, were friends when we were at school, the closest of friends, she knew all my secrets. All. One of them had to do with my passion for the son of the grocer who supplied the school. He was a thin boy with a long neck, and flaxen hair, and I was passionately in love with him. We must have been the same age—fourteen—and I assure you'—she laughed a little in her throat—'no adult love affair was ever more wildly fiercely obsessed—the only word. We kissed each other once, both of us shaking from head to foot. That was the evening it ended. We had been eyeing each other in church and exchanging letters through a foolish servant, and at last we arranged to meet; I was to get out of the laundry window on the ground floor after dark and run across the kitchen garden to the lane where he would be waiting. Of course I told Renée, and the moment I was through the window she hurried to the headmistress and warned her. Afterwards, she explained why she had done it. It was to save me from myself. She really believed it. Tears poured down her face—I had no tears, I was too desperate—when she was telling me how she had prayed and God had told her what she must do.' She laughed again, and said with reminiscent tenderness, 'Poor Renée.'

'Did you forgive her?' Stephen asked.

He felt—it was perhaps the first time in his life—an admiration in which there was no hidden thought of possible profit. Something about Mrs Duquesne, perhaps her double voice, perhaps the attitude, the stance, of her heavy careless body to life, adventure without a taint of defiance, casual acceptance of risks, the virtues of a good-humoured gambler, caught and held him. If she had been a young woman . . .

70

'Of course I forgave her!'

'But why?'

Mrs Duquesne looked at him with a warm lazy amusement. 'My dear boy, what is the use of resenting people? Life is too short and too full.'

'Your poor Renée started early to play God and spoil lives,' Colette Hyde said with contempt. 'You say she's not mad, but what was that hideous enticement case if it wasn't insanity? And the neurotic way she behaved after it—accusing their few remaining friends of being unkind or disloyal. Even his aunt in Paris, who adored him. I was there, drinking a martini with the old lady, when Renée rang her up from London and ordered her to prove her loyalty by some impossible action—to write to the Home Office and advise them to take away your passport, something of the kind. She refused, of course, and Renée said: Very well, I forbid you to try to see us again....'

Mrs Duquesne lifted her hands in a light gesture. 'You know—a neurosis is a sort of day-time nightmare. She was ill.'

'But, my darling, she did exactly the same thing years earlier, after his resignation! She quarrelled with their friends in the same way then. Anyone who didn't satisfy her that he was absolutely blindly loyal was rung up and told he had better not come to the house again.'

'In a way endearing,' Mrs Duquesne murmured.

'But insane! And it isolated him.'

Mrs Duquesne smiled slightly. 'My dear, Harry always had fewer friends than he supposed. And more enemies—who weren't altogether sorry to be given the chance to isolate him.' She turned to Stephen. 'You see them both every day. What do you admire most about him?'

What do you want me to say? he wondered. He took a

risk. Smiling at her as though he were in love with her, he said,

'The very thing you admire. Just when he seems so arrogant, so vain even, that it's intolerable, he turns and laughs at himself.'

'Ah,' she said warmly, 'you're cleverer than I thought you were.'

Pleased, he asked,

'Why had he so many enemies?'

Her careless manner banished Chatteney to a past so distant she might have been looking at a half-effaced photograph. 'Ah. He worked very hard, he knew Europe better than anyone, better than any Foreign Secretary, much better than Churchill. And he had no hesitation in saying so, and no patience with fools or opposition. If you opposed him, that proved you were a fool! And he really was stupefyingly clear-sighted and intelligent—but smaller men, and even his equals, didn't always forgive him for knowing it. I don't believe he ever in his life took the faintest trouble to conciliate or blandish anyone. And, you know, politics are made with men, not with ideas—only if you get on your side the people who matter will they, then, swallow your ideas. Men he charmed were often devoted to him, but not because he had taken any trouble with them.'

'And women?' Stephen asked, with an ingenuousness that excused his impudence.

She gave him a long glance, at once appraising and indifferent. It made him feel there was very little in him that she had not seen. It was not the glance of a judge, she was too careless, too urbane, too without moral instincts, to pass sentence on anyone.

'Women were a different matter,' she said, smiling. 'Even in an affair that was only going to last a month, he was endlessly charming, kind, generous. Really it was a

72

sign that he thought them inferior to men in every way. Even his wife—and he respected her more than any other woman. It wouldn't surprise me if she were the only one he really feels respect for.'

He had not the insolence to say: More than he respected you? but he thought it.

Colette Hyde laughed shortly. 'I know more than one woman he made terribly unhappy.'

'Oh, unhappy! Their own fault. They expected a ... a faithfulness he was utterly incapable of giving. He could be anything else you like, cruel, truthful, gentle, ungovernable, infatuated, devoted, but not faithful. If a woman he had tired of showed she was hurt, he was at first sorry, then bored and impatient.' Her voice filled with laughter. 'If I had been a man should I have been any different?'

'Oh, you would forgive him anything!'

'But why not?' Mrs Duquesne said lightly. 'I loved him, he was irresistible.'

She stood up, looking round in a vague way for gloves, a handbag.

'Oh, don't go,' Colette Hyde said.

'I must. What is the time?'

'Not quite five o'clock.'

'A friend will have been waiting for me for an hour before I get home,' Mrs Duquesne said serenely. Turning to Stephen she said, 'I am sure Harry never had such a clever secretary before.... Don't underrate his wife, she will outlive him, and if—I say: if—he hasn't put his memoirs out of her reach she will probably burn them—for the noblest reasons in the world.'

'God forbid!' Mrs Hyde cried. The two women embraced, touching a cheek to a cheek, with every air of devotion. 'I'll take you down.'

Before Stephen had quite closed the door on them, Mrs

73

Duquesne's low carrying voice reached him from the staircase.

'Your young man has style, but . . .'

The rest was inaudible. But what? he wondered, amused and a little uneasy.

When Colette returned she said,

'Well? What do you think of her?'

'I can see why you called her a gentleman. She couldn't be more a woman—but her heart is masculine enough, and I'm certain she never had the slightest wish to possess anyone, even her lovers. Chatteney can't have been the only one. Tell me about her.'

'You've fallen for her,' Colette said with a sharp smile. 'Everyone does. . . . I don't know a great deal. She's half French—a French mother. And she married a Frenchman, a charming moody selfish cavalry officer, who was no good to her. She spoiled him, of course—as she spoils everybody, including her children.'

'How old is she?'

'Sixty-nine. But ageless.'

'She makes me think of a camembert—a creamy perfectly ripe camembert, at its point of perfection, before it begins to turn brown and run away.'

'My God, how horrible!'

'No, no,' he protested, 'delicious. A camembert is a polite very generous cheese.'

'You are horrible,' she said laughing, 'but you have the right notion. She suffers from chronic generosity, which may be why she hasn't a rag to her back. She has two grown-up married daughters and a son, who all get money from her when she has it. Her widow's pension must be very small—Georges Duquesne was only a captain when he was killed—and I think she has as well a miserably small allowance from his family.'

74

'Tell me one more thing. Was it a great passion—she and Chatteney?'

She was silent for a moment, looking at him with a curious expression, mocking, friendly, a little avid. Stretching her hand out to stroke his face, she said,

'Would you recognise a great passion if you saw one, my dear? I doubt it.'

CHAPTER 8

THE dog Simon, who suffered from open windows on a hot day, on all other days needed a draught of cold air through the dining-room, and Chatteney unprotestingly moved his chair to avoid it. Vexed, his wife asked Stephen to shut the window, and at intervals throughout the meal fanned the animal with her napkin. Whenever this happened, Simon opened one yellow eye, leered at her, sighed, and fell asleep again.

We need, we need badly, the secretary thought, to go back to the idea of possession by devils. Nothing else explains her. She is possessed by a rage to possess him, which trembles on a knife edge between love and hate, and torments her since it can't devour him. There are only two positive things he could have done with such a woman if he was not prepared to leave her : one was to beat her to death, the other to let himself be possessed, body and soul. From her devil-tormented point of view, his sweet reasonableness and politeness are unforgivable. She has spent her life driving her claws into him without getting a grip on either soul or body.

In the appalling depths of her being, did she enjoy some

sort of orgasm when her fight to possess him reached one of its crises?

Bruegel brought in the coffee and set it down in front of Lady Chatteney. Handing her husband his cup, she said,

'You had something you wanted to ask me? What is it?'

'Oh, yes,' he said. 'Can you remember when in March or April of '43 I had influenza very badly? It's only important because it would help me to pin down the date of another incident.'

'I can fix it exactly,' she answered, very dryly. 'I kept the letters from one of your female adorers of that year—she wrote to me every day to ask how you were.'

'If you wouldn't mind looking them up,' he said, smiling.

'I should mind. I'll do it, of course.'

'Thank you.'

There was a moment's silence, then she said in a cold voice,

'How astonishing that even your little infidelities come in useful for this book I'm not allowed to see. Do you seriously mean to hide it away in the British Museum without my having read it?'

'We needn't talk about that now,' he said gently. 'Let me finish it first.'

'You evade, you evade, you evade. One fine day you'll say casually: I've just deposited the record of my life in a place where it will remain until you have been dead for half a century and can't defend yourself against the lies and half-truths in it that concern you.'

Now we're off, thought Stephen. He could not without awkwardness get up and go away, nor did he want to go. Not only was he intensely curious, filled by something of the excitement of watching the curtain rise on a stage set for the play's great scene, but in the last few days he had been turning over in his mind the book he might, some day, if it seemed a useful—creditable, elegant, witty—thing to do, write about his life with the great man. He sat still, looking down at his coffee cup.

'My dear Renée, nothing in it, I do assure you, can in any way vex, offend, or hurt you. I'm not writing a personal chronicle. . . .'

She cut him short. 'You are writing about yourself.'

'Yes. But not in a way that involves you.'

The look on her face was ambiguous—anger, derision, grief. 'Perhaps you have left me out altogether, and our marriage, and the harm you did me at a time when I could still be harmed by you and your egoism and deathly inability to love anyone but yourself? Have you?'

Chatteney's hand, as he set his cup down on the table, was quite steady. So was his voice, and patient and very kind. The fold of irony at the corner of his mouth seemed not directed at her.

'To talk about it now—no, no, my dear, let's leave it. If you want to, I'll talk to you later—and try to convince you that with all my crimes and my selfishness I'm not likely to have said anything worse than that I have never taken an important personal decision without asking your opinion first.'

Doesn't he really know, thought Stephen, that his gentleness infuriates her far more than sarcasm or impatience would? Obviously he doesn't—and equally obviously she is being driven over the edge by it.

Chatteney had got up to go away, which forced the young man to stand up—with some regret that the scene had been cut short. But before either man could move from the table, she said,

'Your crimes—which of your crimes? You destroyed and murdered not only my self-respect, my poor little happiness, but our child—our child. . . .'

Moving round the table as quickly as he could, her husband laid a hand on her shoulder. 'My dear Renée, *don't*. You'll hurt yourself badly, don't do it. Let me take you to your room.'

She stood up, knocking over her chair. 'He died because of your want of love.'

A voice like that must corrode her throat, Stephen thought. Startled by the chair falling—or by her voice—the dachshund had heaved his ugly body off the floor and was trying to comfort her, rubbing his head against her leg, whimpering. She began to whimper herself.

'Yes, you murdered him, too . . .'

Choking cries and sobs cut off her voice. The door opened at this moment, and Bruegel came in—perhaps she had been outside it, listening. She took the distracted woman in her arms, speaking to her with a very surprising delicacy, as to a sick child, and half led half carried her out of the room, Simon lumbering at her heels.

Chatteney had not moved. For all his adroitness, Stephen did not know what was the least clumsy thing he could do. Go away? Ask: Do you need me? He half expected that the old man would say something about the child. That there had been a child who died very young, little more than an infant, he knew already—Colette Hyde had told him. But when Chatteney did begin speaking, it was only to say calmly, almost lightly,

'I have never been able to decide whether or not I qualify as an Immoralist. Do you know what I mean? Is an Immoralist the man who feels that no one has the right to judge his actions except himself? But hasn't a rational human being—such as I believe myself to be—an instinct for what is good, valuable, civilised? What other moral code does he need than the one he makes for himself in the course of a life given up to trying to understand society, to warn people what will happen if they behave clumsily or foolishly, and—why not?—to enjoy every kind of pleasure he is fitted for? I have never wanted to over-eat....'

'If that is being immoral,' Stephen said, 'I was born without morals.'

Chatteney lifted his eyebrows over ironic eyes. 'Try not to make as many mistakes as I have made. Don't—for instance—arrange to be poor in your old age.'

Does he need money? Stephen wondered. Why? He goes nowhere, has fewer wants than a monk, and his skin-and-bone old body wouldn't stand journeys. Perhaps, if he had money, he would leave his dear Renée.... In a diffident voice he said,

'If you cared to, you could sell the memoirs for a vast sum to any reputable publisher on condition that he didn't publish for fifty years.'

'Nonsense,' Chatteney said icily. 'No commercial-minded man would be willing to lock his money up for fifty years—at least fifty. I must be certain that the book will appear without cuts or changes. In any event, I don't consider a commercial safe the proper place for it.'

His secretary blushed. 'I'm sorry.'

Melting at once, Chatteney cried,

'No, no, my dear boy, no need to be sorry. You meant to be helpful. But, you know, I can't regard my memoirs as something written for sale. To make a habit of writing for money has always struck me as a sort of debauchery, a rather poor sort. And to have written this book for money would be inexcusable. It's one thing to say: My life has been such that to record it as honestly and handsomely as possible may be of value to the future. And quite another if one says: I will now, for so much down, tell you about myself and what I have done.'

He stopped, made a sardonic face, and roared with

laughter. 'You see what forms vanity takes in the very old. After all, I don't need money. I could make good use of it—could I not!—but I don't need it. Hence I can afford to make these exalted statements about gentlemen and players in literature.'

Bruegel came in, and began clearing the table. Her broad face wore an expression of singular tranquillity and mastery, almost contemptuously affectionate. Without glancing at Chatteney, she said,

'She's in bed. I've given her the sedative the doctor left with me last time, but she didn't need it, she was *through*. She'll be all right.'

She knows as much as one of her priests about possession by devils, Stephen thought. For all her kindness to him, she intimidated him a little: he was far from confident that he had effectively charmed her.

After she had gone, Chatteney said meditatively,

'Among the few, the very few things about human beings I am sure, absolutely sure of, is that there is no possibility of communication between them at any serious level.' He hesitated, and said abruptly, 'Have you your pen? Take a note. Here'—he pulled an envelope from his pocket and handed it to the young man—'write it on that.... Years of companionship in a marriage can beget, even in a hardened egoist, an animal awareness of the other person, he comes to share physically a woman's own sense of her ageing body, her knowledge of it, her acceptance of its deformity, or her irrational anger and grief. In the same way he is aware of his own physical and *moral*'—he stressed the word—'ridiculousness. The old are comic. But no real, no deep communication is possible between two people so intimately linked on an animal level. So—as humorously as possible—all that either of them can do is to stay within touching distance, the lightest possible touch.'

What is this? Stephen asked himself. Only literature?

'I'll decide on the final form tomorrow, and where to insert it,' Chatteney said. He chuckled. 'More re-typing for you, dear boy.'

Still with a malicious smile on his thin lips, he went off to lie down—his afternoon rest before the Athenaeum.

His curiosity sent Stephen to the kitchen. Without pretending to have come for anything else—it would be waste of time—he asked,

'What is this about a murdered child?'

Bruegel looked him in the face and said calmly,

'You should know by now that a woman in a sexual rage —yes, yes, sexual: do you imagine that only young wolves have a sex?—will use anything, any fantastic lie, any knife she has at hand.'

'There *was* a child.'

'Yes, and it died. Before you were born—long before.' Her pale eyes watched him with indulgence and irony. 'Be off, my child, there's nothing for you here. Other people's hells are a bore. Run away and prepare your own.'

CHAPTER 9

WHEN he told Colette that Mrs Gide had invited him to dinner, she said smiling,

'Yes, I know. She rang me up first to ask which evening next week I was free. I have always said that dear Laura— if she had been born in that world—would have made a splendidly successful madam. You have only to look round her dining-room with a sharp eye to uncover half a dozen

intrigues, business, literary—to please Frederick, she collects well-known writers—adulterous. I don't mean that she
would not rather have invited you alone, but, knowing
what she knows, she would never, but never, fail to ask us
together.'

'What I owe you,' he said coolly.

'You owe me nothing, my darling. Except the chance to
open a few doors. I shall watch you now with the greatest
interest.'

She moved her hand upwards over his body to his cheek.
He took hold of it, and pressed his teeth rather too sharply
into a finger. 'You deserve hurting. What do you mean by
that?'

'Only that I love you as if you were a son I was launching
into the great world—as well as a very dear, very exciting
bedfellow. It adds enormously to my pleasure. I like to
manage people's lives. And I know you'll do me credit.
Otherwise, beautiful as you are, I should be a little less in
love with you.... Now you must get up, please. I have to
dress for a business-talk dinner at home with Frederick,
he's flying to New York tonight.'

Knotting his tie in front of the glass, he caught her
watching him with the half-mocking half-indulgent smile
he disliked. He said abruptly,

'Shall I tell Mrs Gide I can't come—and take you out to
dinner instead?'

'Heavens, no. You must meet people.'

'Is there a Mr Gide?'

'There was. He had the tact to die, leaving her a great
deal more money than she needs to live on.'

These people, he thought sharply, deserve to be plun-
dered....

There were more men than women in Mrs Gide's
dining-room—apart from his hostess only three: Colette,

separated from him by the width of the table, a young girl, and a middle-aged woman in a handsome black dress, with a long kind heavy face like a good-tempered mare, whose name he had failed to catch. He had been placed next the girl. On his other side was the novelist Duffy Avens, who said dryly, 'We met at the Hydes,' and thereafter turned his shoulder and talked only to his other neighbour, the kindly mare.

For the first few moments, Stephen gave the whole of his attention to the man on Colette's left, to whom she was talking with an air of intimate friendship. A tall middle-aged man, with a manner—taking the word to cover everything about him from his looks to his smile—that roused the young man's sincere envy: a good head, an agreeable intelligent face, and a smile, rarely absent from his heavily-lidded eyes, which suggested humour, ease, the habit of authority, as though he had known as a child that he would meet few people he could not talk to as an equal, or find himself in few situations where he would not be politely in control. Simply by looking at him, Stephen measured the distance he still had to go before he was better than a pretender in this world. A flood of impatience and bitterness swept over him. To escape from it, he turned to look at the girl sitting beside him.

She was, he saw now, very young indeed, and he wondered why she had been invited: she could not conceivably be one-half of any dubious intrigue. Her air of delicacy and freshness was startling in this room. She had dark hair brushed back smoothly into a coil in her neck, grey eyes, oddly flecked with black, and her unpainted mouth was full and clear. No one of her features was like his sister's, yet in some unseizable way she reminded him of Tarry. Perhaps it was only her youth and silence. Apart from smiling at him as they sat down, she had taken no notice of him, and he supposed she was too shy to start a conversation.

'Did I get your name right?' he asked her. 'Miss Stanton?'

She turned to look at him. 'Yes. Olivia Stanton. I don't know yours.'

'I'm Stephen Hind.'

'Oh. What do you do?'

'Nothing very much,' he said, smiling at her. 'Do you know Sir Henry Chatteney? I'm his secretary.'

'He's a great friend of my grandmother.' She had a thin sweet voice, a little less stiff now. 'Lady Emily Grosmont—my great-grandmother, but that takes so long to say. You may have seen her in his house, she's one of the few people who go there.'

He grinned. 'So far as I know—the only person. I admire her. No one else has the courage to treat Lady Chatteney like a fractious child, which is the right way to treat her and cuts any scene down to nursery size at once.'

He had expected that she would find this amusing enough to laugh, but all she did was give him a sidelong glance and say nothing. He would have to look for some other way into her confidence.

'Tell me now what you do?'

'I? Nothing interesting. Well, not when I'm in London.'

'Then where do you live?'

'In the country.'

'Where?'

She looked at him again with the same cool friendly distance. 'My grandmother has a house in London, but she has let it, and we live in her house in Dorset. In London I stay with a friend.'

Feeling his way, he asked, 'A friend who also does nothing?'

'She was my grandmother's cook for twenty-five years.'

This had led nowhere. Perhaps the only things she cared about were horses and dogs? He set himself to talk to her about Ukley Manor, exaggerating its charms, park, trout stream, old farms, point-to-point meetings. She listened. Now and then she asked a question, but in the end he began to feel that she was attending out of politeness, as a well-brought-up child will listen to a boring adult without fidgeting. What he had taken for shyness was a young self-possession not less baffling for being, he thought, wholly unconscious, as much part of her as her slender neck and strange eyes. As soon as he stopped talking she drew back into her silence with no sign that she had noticed his.

Towards the end of the meal, more out of pique than for any other reason, he made another effort to draw her out. 'I expect you know everybody here. Who is the man opposite us—talking to Mrs Hyde?'

'His name is Cadnam-Plessy. He's Foreign Office ... something ... I don't know what.'

'Do you know him?'

'No. Except across my grandmother's dinner-table. That is his wife at the other side of Mr Avens.'

He was tempted to ask her bluntly: What are you doing here? But he felt wryly certain that she would make some cool answer, not in the least unfriendly, but leaving him at the other side of a hedge. With relief he saw his hostess preparing to get up.

In the next room he was making his way towards Colette, intending to ask her to leave with him at the first possible moment, when he was halted by Cadnam-Plessy. Smiling pleasantly, as, the young man thought, he would smile at any subordinate, he said,

'You're Chatteney's secretary, I hear. How is he?'

'For his age, very well—I think,' he said carelessly. 'Do you know him?'

'He was my father's friend. I knew him only through listening to them talking when I was a young man—still at Cambridge. My father had an enormous respect for him, and I think regretted to the day he died that he had allowed their friendship to end badly. I'm not sure what happened. Something my poor father said or did, or failed to do, during the war, made Chatteney believe he had been let down. Even before this he had become very bitter, he had convinced himself that it was his virtues, his quite exceptional intelligence and foresight, in short his genius, which had ruined him. 'Mediocre people are afraid of me,' he told my father.... He was, is, a great man, and he over-rated his merits for the very reason that others underrated them. I have no doubt he exaggerates the importance of his resignation in 1938. What any individual does nowadays is rarely important—except the accident of a Churchill in the right place at the right moment. Chatteney's gesture had no effect—none—on the future. But can you expect a man who has ruined himself by a gesture *not* to see it as terrific?' His smile became very slightly ironical. 'It's easy when you are successful to be tactful and modest, less easy when you are a frustrated failure.'

In spite of his envy, in spite of the hornet's nest of petulant devils moving in his stomach, Stephen felt a touch of liking for this smiling self-possessed older man, supremely at ease and capable, he thought, of being amused even by his own important position, whatever it was.

'I suppose so,' he said civilly.

'Unlike Eden—and unlike our usual way with public men—Chatteney hasn't been sanctified by defeat.... It was absurd, of course, not to have used him during the war. Of all the enemies he made by being too sure of his own wisdom, and too brilliant socially, only one was fatal. And the ironical thing is that Churchill has forgotten him! Only last week someone spoke to him about Chatteney—I was there—and he scowled and said: Chatteney? Chatteney? Who the devil's he? ...' He paused, half-closing his eyes, and said,

'But you know all this, of course.'

'I don't know a great deal,' Stephen said quietly. 'Only what I learn by copying the memoirs.'

'I have no right to ask you this—don't answer if it embarrasses you—but I should very much like to know how he handles Churchill. He must, I feel, be tempted to write about him with that sort of generosity which sets a halo round the writer and leaves the—the victim in limbo.'

The temptation to try to impress the older man seized Stephen, and he could do it without being more than moderately indiscreet.

'So far as I know,' he said, smiling, 'the most generous remark comes in a comment on another man. Talking about Attlee, he says: It is only during a war that the English can endure as Prime Minister a genius; at all other times they insist on competent mediocrity: Attlee, with the exception of style, had everything necessary to be a respectable headmaster.... Something of the sort.'

'Precisely the sort of remark that made him a cloud of enemies,' Cadnam-Plessy said. 'The poor devil must have been born without any instinct for self-preservation. Add his enormous talents, and you have the complete formula for disaster....'

He was interrupted by Mrs Gide, who said sweetly,

'Tim, your wife insists on going home. Yes, I know, I know—it was a triumph to get her here at all, but....' Turning to Stephen, she said, 'Just let me say my goodbyes.... I want to ask you something. Stay where you are.'

87

She came back in less than a minute, took his arm, and said, 'How did you get on with dear Livvy?'

'Livvy?'

'Olivia Stanton. I put you next to her at dinner because you are both so absurdly enviably inexcusably young. She's charming, isn't she?'

'Yes—but so young she hasn't learned to speak.'

'That's naughty.... She's a sweet child, and when her great-grandmother dies she'll be rich—as rich as any private person can be nowadays. You know, both Emily Grosmont's sons are dead, the elder was killed in 1917—he wasn't married—and the younger died of his war wounds years later, in 1930, and *his* two boys were killed in 1944. One of them had married and Livvy is his daughter. The end of a family. End of an England. Sad, isn't it? Livvy is the last tiny bud, the heir.'

Why, he wondered dryly, is she telling me? Perhaps only for the fun of interfering.

'What would you like me to do?.'

Mrs Gide raised her eyebrows. 'Be nice to her, my dear boy. You know, she's not a fool. She's studying—of all things economics, at the School of Economics, if you know what that is. I'm sure you do, I don't.'

'She didn't tell me that.'

'Colette is looking at us,' Mrs Gide murmured. 'Perhaps I'm keeping you from her.'

On that she left him. Turning his head, he saw the girl standing, alone, at the farther side of the room. She was turning over the pages of a book lying on a table, and the thin curve of her neck as she bent forward reminded him, again, of his sister. She looked vulnerable, absurdly young, distant. An impulse he did not trouble to look at sent him across the room to her. She glanced up when he stopped beside her, and smiled at him.

'You didn't tell me you were studying economics,' he said brusquely.

She drew together eyebrows as surprised and delicate as Tarry's. 'But why should I?'

'I asked you what you did in London and you said: Nothing interesting. And you let me talk nonsense about myself.'

'I didn't know you were interested in economics.'

He looked at her with the smile which never failed him with women, young or old. 'You didn't try to find out.'

'I'm sorry,' she said calmly. 'I always wait to find out what interests people, and if they don't tell me, I'm done for.' She added, with the same directness, 'You were quite interesting about that house—what was it called?— Ukley.'

The only adroit thing he could do was to laugh, and he laughed. 'I could tell you about it again if you will have dinner with me one evening. Will you?'

To his surprise, she shook her head. 'I'm sorry. I go home on Thursday—to my grandmother's, I mean. And the three evenings I'm in London I have to work. Tonight' —she hesitated, and went on in the same cool friendly voice—'tonight was an exception. I don't know why Mrs Gide asked me, I scarcely know her, and I came because she made a fuss.... That sounds rude. It's true, though, and I'm very sorry I came.'

He had a sense that she was suppressing some feeling, perhaps of anger, but it was as fugitive as herself. She was friendly, and unapproachable.

'Then I shall never see you again?' he said.

'Why not?' She laughed at him a little roughly. 'If you really want to tell me more about your old Ukley, next time my grandmother comes to London and orders me to bring four of my friends to tea with her at her club, I'll

89

invite you. You won't enjoy it much.... And now I'm going. 'Bye.'

She walked off briskly. He stared after her for a moment, and saw that Colette was looking towards him from the other end of the room. When he joined her, she smiled at him and said mockingly,

'Not for you, my dear one.'

'What does that mean?'

'It means that whatever dear Laura's mischievous idea was, she is making an idiot of herself. And so will you be if you think of raising your eyes to Olivia Stanton. She's having an affair, very discreet, with a man more than twice her age and married. If Emily Grosmont finds out, my God!'

A flash of pure hatred for her went through him. 'How do you know?'

She shrugged her shoulders. 'I hear things, you know.'

'Perhaps it's not true.'

'Oh, it's true,' she said, laughing. 'Yes, yes, my darling. I wouldn't tell you about it, but I shouldn't enjoy seeing you run your head against a wall. Not that you were getting very far just now, were you?'

He did not answer. Touching him very lightly on the arm, she said in a low voice, 'Don't be angry with me. Let's go now, you can come back with me for a drink, and then the car can take you home to your attic. I want to talk to you. One of the things Frederick and I discussed the evening before he went to New York was his idea—mine, too— of taking you into the firm. Not yet. Eventually. He says you have an extremely good head, a good business head, and sound taste.... You may be sure I didn't contradict him! Well?'

He controlled the exhilaration that seized him. Looking at her, a glance he moved deliberately over her face with its skilful make-up effacing the nearly imperceptible lines round nose and mouth to the visible curve of breasts he knew to be roundly firm, he said under his breath,

'Yes, let's go, I want to make love to you—the talk can wait.'

CHAPTER 10

HE went, the next day, to see his mother. He went reluctantly: it was barely a month since he had seen her, and he had had no intention of going near her again for a long time. But she had been ill, what she called 'one of my attacks'—that weakness she had allowed to invade her at a time when her body began abruptly to procreate flesh in place of energy. In fact, his sister told him when she rang him up, she had had a very slight stroke, nothing to do with her heart.

'Need I come?' he asked.

'No,' she said, and in its thinness and purity her voice reminded him of Olivia Stanton's, but it was less assured. 'No need, really, she's completely recovered. To tell you the truth, she's stronger than usual, because the doctor stopped her drinking for two weeks, and that always pulls her together. All the same, I wish you'd come.'

'Very well. To see you.'

'Come anyway.'

Marion Street on a raw afternoon, the wind blowing an acid grit into his eyes and the smells of stale fish and vegetables into his nostrils, sickened him: he had the strongest impulse to turn back. Only the thought of his sister's disappointment checked it. She was waiting for him on the landing outside their mother's room, pale and heavy-eyed.

'Stay with her for an hour,' she said. 'Then I needn't hurry through my shopping.'

'Why do you let yourself get so tired?' he asked, furious.

'It's so much easier to treat her as a spoiled child,' she said, with one of her clear brilliant smiles.

His mother was in her chair, and greeted him in a voice too subdued to be altogether natural. She means me to pity her, he thought. She did not ask her how she was, she began telling him. Her eyes watched him like two cunning animals, to see the effect of her story.

'I knew I was due to pass over, it frightened me, and I began to think who would be the first person I'd see on the other side, and that got me thinking back to when I was twenty, back to the Monico and the Leicester Lounge and the Troc and Oddenino's and the old Empire, and the lights and the music and the women I knew then, and the young men, and all that swishing to and fro and strolling and laughing, and oh God, I thought, let me go to sleep and wake up young, and gay as a lark, my legs mixed up with a young fellow's legs so comfortably neither of us knows who's which, and not an ache in my body.'

She forgot that she had set out to make him sorry for her, and began to hum loudly, a deep sound like a cello, one of the tricks with which she had amused him when he was a child.

'Remember that, Stephen? That's the *Valse bleu*. No, you couldn't remember it, but d'you remember me taking you to the Café Royal with me when you were, oh, about five you must have been, you were a dear little boy, so beautiful women used to point at you in the street, and very good always, great eyes following me round all the time I was getting dressed, and asking me: May I smell you? and putting your little head between my bubs. Lily of the valley it was, from a shop in Greek Street. Only twenty years since. Lord, Lord, what life does to you, eh?'

He detested her when she reminded him of the child for whom this dilapidated creature had been the source of all warmth, safety, and pleasure. For less than a moment he saw and felt the child: the place he was sitting in twanged, droned, glittered; there was a white tablecloth and her white bared arm lying across it, his stomach felt tight, his eyelids dropped: at some moment, opening them, he saw that two officers had come to sit at the table with them, then without any transition he looked up into the laughing face of a young man who was carrying him up the staircase at home.

No doubt, he thought sharply, Tarry was born of some such casual incident.

His mother had half closed her eyes and was leaning back in her chair. She looked old and sad, disconcerted and somehow innocent. A feeling seized him that was neither pity for her nor repulsion, but both, and a very light throb of guilt—not to do with her, to do with his sister, who was supporting the concrete trouble of this ridiculous bulk of thick white flesh, sweating laziness and a childish greed from all its pores.

'If I took you there in a taxi,' he said, 'could you sit through dinner at the Café Royal this evening?'

She stared at him for a minute, her face working in a convulsion of surprise and gaiety.

'But you don't mean it!'

He had never regretted an impulse more acridly. But he said,

'I'll come for you at seven o'clock, with a cab. Now I must go'—he could not endure another minute of this room with its suffocating smell of age and lavender water—

'sit until Tarry comes back, and tell her to have you ready at seven.'

'Are you taking her, too?' she asked jealously.

'No.'

'Shall I wear a hat?'

A vermilion coil of her hair had come unpinned and was lying across her neck. He shuddered involuntarily. 'Yes, do.'

He trusted Tarry to do her best, and when he came he saw with relief and gratitude that she had contrived a gross Edwardian figure in a black silk coat and close-fitting toque. She beckoned him into the kitchen and said in a low voice,

'I was afraid you wouldn't come. I don't know what she would have done.'

'Selfish as I am,' he said, smiling at her, 'I'm not utterly devoid of scruples.'

'Don't give her too much to drink. She hasn't the head for it any longer.'

He was surprised by the show of agility with which his mother descended the stairs, holding to his arm, and launched herself, grunting, into the cab. He had ordered a table in the grill room, the only corner of the Café Royal where, like a large moth dying in the folds of a curtain, the past still clings. Looking round her in the doorway, she said loudly,

'This isn't the place.'

But she allowed herself to be led to a table and inserted somehow between it and one of the mirrors, and when, after minutes of ordering, counter-ordering, and discussion with the waiter, the meal began to be served, she ate with frank pleasure, crunching small bones of hare between her teeth, rolling the wine—she had chosen it herself, a strong burgundy—round her palate before swallowing it, cleaning the sauce off her plate with bread, patting her mouth with two fingers to excuse a belch, and laughing.

'You picked the wrong room, Stephen my dear, but never mind. The brasserie's my holy of holies, I tasted my first oyster there when I was nineteen. There was a yellow-haired old girl played the violin—Miss Haidée—and she had an sweetheart used to sit at the back of the room the whole evening, with two other old fellows, a bearded Russian sea-captain and a Swiss engineer, or was it the Russian was her sweetheart? I forget, and it doesn't signify, they must all be dead.'

He had not been able to prevent her drinking more than two-thirds of the bottle—she held her head back and her throat open and emptied the glass down it—and, watching, he saw that it had begun to affect her. I must get her away, he thought coldly.

'The brasserie you're talking about doesn't exist.'

'I know, I know. The apes tore it apart.'

With the sweet soufflé she had ordered she wanted a second bottle, and grumbled loudly when he said, 'No, you've been forbidden to drink.'

'Who forbids it?' she asked truculently. 'And why? No, I don't want any coffee, I'm fed up with this, I want to go and look what the apes did to the old brasserie.'

Since she was already struggling up from the table, knocking off it her glass and a small plate, he could only say, 'Very well, but let me pay the bill.' He was too angry with her even to feel embarrassed by the scene, and furious with himself for bringing her. If she would have the kindness to die at this minute so that he could drag her body out like the carcass of an animal, it would pay for everything. But she showed no sign of dying, and when he got her into the hall she walked stubbornly off to the right, shaking his arm from hers, and humming the *Valse bleu.*

'I know where I'm going,' she told him easily, 'I know m'way.'

But she was very soon lost. Unable to recognise anything, she stopped and looked round her with a confused smile, passing her hand uncertainly over her face.

'No, this isn't it. Here, you'—she caught the arm of a waiter standing near her—'what have they been doing here, eh? Why've you balled the place up like this? Just tell me that. Never used to be a bar out here. What have you done?'

'Now you've seen it, we'll go,' Stephen said.

Ignoring him, she let herself fall into a chair at a small table. 'Fetch me a double brandy, and double quick,' she muttered, 'before I—well, never mind, fetch it.'

The waiter glanced at Stephen. 'Bring some black coffee,' Stephen said.

He sat down himself. For the first time during this abominable evening, something tired and strangely vulnerable peered at him between her puffed eyelids. Unbidden and unwanted, the image of a laughing woman with large warm bare arms flickered in a recess of his memory. Poor old girl, let her have her brandy, he thought dryly. When it came, with the coffee, she began to talk to the waiter in an indulgent almost affectionate voice, as though he had questioned her.

'You want to know what I mean about balling up this place? You young chaps don't know you're born. Now, there was a waiter here—I mean in the brasserie—an old Dutchman, Theodor, small and very pale, as old as Adam. Where is he? Go on, boy, you must remember old Theodor.'

'Before my time, madam,' the man said, bored with her.

He went away, and before Stephen could stop her she had swallowed the whole of the brandy in a gulp. Setting the glass down, she looked round her as though from an immense distance, narrowing her eyes: one hand moved across her forehead, and down over her body to her left side.

'God, I feel old,' she said, speaking to herself rather than to Stephen, 'old as hell itself. And think of those boys I knew.' Tears of self-pity spilled down her cheeks. 'All killed. Why should *I* be afraid of dying when they ... You know what one of them used to sing?' Her voice rose, wavering, surprisingly strong. *'The best have gone before us, Only the dull are left* ... It's God's truth.'

Pressing both hands on the table, she levered herself up and would have fallen flat on her face if Stephen and a man at the nearest table had not caught her. She sagged between them. Her hat fell off, exposing her outrageous hair, and her head rolled from side to side like a broken-necked puppet. The weight of her body was dragging it from their grasp and the waiter hurried across to help them by thrusting his arms under her armpits from behind. Holding her upright, her feet jerking across the floor, they shuffled with her into the entrance hall and propped her in a chair to wait until a cab had been fetched. She had begun to recover. A malicious smile spread slowly across her face, stretching her lips out and out, an unending smile. A clown had taken possession of her. She whistled thinly, breaking off to chant,

'Here's a pretty pass. Seated on my ass ... My hat, where's my hat?'

In the taxi she slept, mouth open, bubbles of what might be laughter coming from it, and once a sentence of which Stephen caught only the words *ah, you would, would you?* spoken in a soft voice, almost young.

He kept an eye on her to see that she did not slip too far forward, but did not touch her. A cold distaste had taken

97

the place of his anger. What possessed me to bring her out? he thought briefly. I must have been out of my mind. The sooner she decides to die in one of her attacks, the better, and then . . . Thinking of Tarry, a familiar warmth welled up through his body, with all the impatience, the anxiety, that had always been part of his love for her, since their childhood, when he did for her all the things their mother left undone.

He reflected that she was the only person towards whom he felt responsibility. Others, all others, existed to be used.

Since he was an adolescent and began to classify people under two heads, those who could be useful and the negligible, he had never doubted his power to handle them to get himself the sort of satisfactions he needed as his lungs needed air.

The cab stopped at 41A Marion Street, and his mother opened her eyes. With the greatest difficulty he got her out of it and into the house, as far as the foot of the staircase. Here she stood, swaying and giggling. He did not believe that, even with Tarry's help, he could get her up, and, smiling to himself, he went next door into the little restaurant and asked the more athletic of its two owners,

'Kenneth, do you feel strong enough to help me haul my mother up to her room?'

'Oh, I'm *very* strong,' the other said eagerly. 'And as brave as a lion. Try me.'

He was better than his boast. Talking to the old woman in a coaxing voice, as to a child, he managed to get her to drag her bulk up the stairs herself. 'Come, dear, another step. Just one more teeny-weeny step. That's it. Now the next. Another little step—to please Kenneth. Clever girl! Up we go.'

Tarry must have heard their voices. She came out on to the landing and stood watching the scene with an expression on her face Stephen could not see until he was close to her. It was purely detached and kind, not at all the sort of look to be expected from a young girl. Taking the monstrous body into her arms, she said calmly,

'Thanks, Kenneth. Stephen, don't wait. I shall manage much better alone.'

CHAPTER 11

A LITTLE to his surprise, Olivia Stanton kept her promise to invite him to tea with her grandmother. Ten days after Mrs Gide's dinner-party she rang him up. 'This is Livvy Stanton. If you would really like to meet my grandmother again ...'

'I should like to see you,' he said in a quiet voice, 'and if tea with your grandmother is the only way I should like to come.'

She told him how to find Lady Emily's club near Berkeley Square, and he found when he walked into its morgue-like drawing-room that he was one of four guests, two girls, one fair, one dark, with alert smooth faces, and a very young man with the mild face of an immature goat; all three were Livvy's fellow-students at the School of Economics, all so soberly dressed and well-brushed that he suspected they had been paraded beforehand, and all a little in terror of the old woman's equine malice: it was very like being fenced inside a small field with a stallion who might or might not be harmless.

With obvious relief the three left the talk to him, and he amused himself by behaving as he imagined a well-brought-up young man, aged nineteen, born like Lady

Emily in 1875, and respectfully in love with her, might conduct himself. Some withered nerve in her brain twitched slightly, she softened, smiled, and told him a story about her grandfather who had been a page at Queen Victoria's coronation.

'That was another world,' he said.

'Another civilisation,' she corrected him, 'the one I was born into. It has died. I say: died, not vanished, because it was a living organism. A civilisation based on the family. What has taken its place is not alive; an atomised society, without security, without warmth, a chaos of fragmented mechanical relationships. Oh, I know, I know as well as you do, that in my world all was not well, there was ignorance and poverty. But the right way was not to tear that world down and replace it by anarchy. The family basis should have been extended, cherished, encouraged.' The deep grooves round her mouth and jaw formed themselves into a sardonic grimace. 'But of course the tearing-down was not an act of will. Few if any of the *responsables* in 1914 knew what they were doing. My father was in Paris that week in August, with his friend James Grimshaw of the Foreign Office, they dined in some house where the Russian ambassador was one of the guests; he kissed James on both cheeks and said: Congratulate me, c'est ma guerre.... He wasn't the only one who felt like that.... Not criminals, you know. Fools. Profoundly frivolous.'

'At least,' said Stephen gently, 'you had half a lifetime of that world.'

The stare she gave him came from a distance, the grey filmy eyeballs seeming to ice over.

'Do you imagine that reconciles me to this one?'

Her momentary excitement had flickered out. Standing up, she told Livvy, 'I'm going to rest in my room. Your friends will forgive me. Amuse yourself until dinner-time,

100

I'll come down at seven. No, no, don't take me to the lift, I know how to work it.'

As soon as her long narrow back was out of sight, the mild young goat fled.

'I think a drink,' Livvy said, and led the others out of the morgue and across a sooty courtyard into the bar.

By now, although he had mislaid their surnames and later was never able to disentangle them, Stephen had identified the fair girl as Jane and the other as Jane Mary. Both had clear high-pitched voices and the faintly rapacious air of impoverished young women on their own, depending on their male acquaintance for amusements, sexual and other. He knew the type and it bored him, but he made himself charming.

'Goodness, Livvy, I needed this,' Jane Mary said, 'I never get used to your grandmother and never shall.'

'I simply don't understand a word she says,'· the other Jane said cheerfully, 'she might be talking Greek.' She smiled lovingly at Stephen. 'You were a total godsend. Livvy, you simply must ask him every time.'

'I usually understand her,' Livvy said, 'but not with my mind.'

There's nothing to understand, Stephen thought casually. The old girl doesn't know she's dead, that's all. When she was younger, when she and her lot were still in charge and talked about society, they meant themselves—an all but closed world, open a little grudgingly to a lot of new money or a certain sort of wit.

'She's splendid,' he said, with an effect of simplicity, 'I admire her.'

The anarchy she talked about as having replaced her world was the opportunity of any clever young man who knew better than to succumb to it. His contempt for those who did succumb, the drug-addicts, the shiftless, the indifferent fornicators, was bottomless. He could scarcely remember a time when he had not known, more or less clearly, more clearly today than ever, that his job was to edge himself into a safe world, as safe in its way as Lady Emily Grosmont's, more complicated than hers had ever been because it was without benefit of religion or moral rules, but solid, rich. He was a long way from it still, but not, he had begun to think, endlessly far.

'The fact of the matter,' Jane exclaimed, 'is that we shall quite soon need anthropologists to explain these remnants of extinct tribes to us.'

Educated and fairly intelligent, Stephen reflected. On the make until they marry or decide to have marvellous free lives, on the tiles from choice. For all her comradely chatter, Livvy—whether Colette's story were true or not— was another species.

'My grandmother is not a South American savage,' she was saying.

'Goodness, Livvy, I didn't mean it like that.'

Livvy smiled at her. Visibly relieved, the other girl set herself to attract Stephen, but he felt too little interest to go through the forms. Turning to Livvy, he said,

'I must go back to my copying. Thank you for inviting me.'

'You won't want to come again,' she said carelessly.

'I'll come whenever you ask me.'

'Will you? Why?'

'I like your grandmother.'

This was not more a lie than if he said: I can admire a magnificent ruin. It amused her and she gave him a young quick smile.

Running down the steps leading to Curzon Street, he reflected that he was almost certainly wasting his time on a young woman who—even if Colette were wrong about her

—treated him with a friendly coolness far less promising than hostility.

None the less, during the next six weeks he accepted two more invitations. The same two girls were on duty on both occasions, with a different young man. It seemed that once was as often as these could face the ordeal of Lady Emily. The burden of talking to her was always left to Stephen, and he kept a dialogue of sorts going across a distance at least as great as that separating a European of 1960 from an all-but-perished tribe of Amazonian head-hunters.

The third invitation was the last he got, and after a few weeks he gave up expecting another. I've been dropped, he thought. His vanity was nettled, and, strangely, he felt regret, something to do with the unseizable way she reminded him of his sister.

He made no effort to get into touch with her. It was not worth it.

CHAPTER 12

At the end of November, with only four or five chapters to go, Chatteney began scrutinising each sentence, almost each word, under an invisible magnifying glass: page after page had to be retyped forty or fifty times, sometimes only to return at the fiftieth to its original form. His secretary reckoned that, at this rate, they had anything from two to six months' labour ahead of them.

Since he had already typed several versions of these last chapters, he knew that Chatteney ended the book in 1946, immediately before the enticement scandal, on a short paragraph to the effect that his life after this point was of interest only to himself.

The last chapter of all looked back, in a curve as peremptory as the master line in a portrait by Picasso, over the three ages he, like every man born before 1900 and still alive in 1945, had lived through. Heaven alone knew how many times it had been rewritten before Stephen saw it, nor how many more times a single altered phrase would force him to recopy the whole.

Certain long passages in these chapters he knew almost —almost—by heart. One began in an examination, at once bare and eloquent, of the end Chatteney said he had had in view from the beginning of his life—the enjoyment of fine things, whether these 'things' were travel, a line of mountains, a painting, Mozart played flawlessly, or human beings, not for the pleasure they gave but for the depth and sharpness of the passion they roused in him—and rose to the description, biting, hardy, of the many ways a love affair starts, grows, and declines into friendship or, if unwisely or clumsily conducted on either side, into boredom and flight. There might have been nothing in any of these passages to draw a line between this love and the purest egoism. But, suddenly, the old egoist had written that he knew one exception to this *natural* course of a passion, one only in his lifetime. And went on to describe a love affair which in old age became a rare *amitié passionnée*, an experience involving his whole self: mind, body, emotions. He did not put a name to the woman who had forced from him this strangely moving and delicate homage, but his secretary had no doubt, having seen her, that she was Mary Duquesne.

One other passage might or might not have to do with her—Stephen thought not. It was very short.

'The intellect is always, in the last resort, the dupe of the heart. A passion which can be subdued in the interests of ambition or prudence is not a passion.'

This dry curt phrase cancelled ironically his whole portrait of himself as a man controlled by his intellect. It sprang like a jet of acid from some depth he preferred not to look at.

During these months Stephen's relations with his employer had changed subtly. They had been friendly since Dax, but now an element of trust and affection came into the old diplomat's feeling for a young man who knew how to make himself engaging without dropping a nuance of respect.

He talked to Stephen very freely.

'I have ruined my life by mistakes any little backwoods politician would have avoided. And mark that, given the circumstances, I should make them again! The first was my inopportune detestation of Chamberlain's—not only his—lower-middle-class cowardice in 1938. And the second mistake, fatal this one, was my refusal to flatter Churchill, with the result that when he came to power in 1940 he offered to send me to Ecuador. Minister in a South American country during a war! If he could have found a more obscure tomb for me no doubt he would have chosen it. Yoking me to the Free French afterwards was his way of making his point. A great man, Churchill, but bears like the Turk no brother near the throne. . . . I admit my errors —an indelicate incontinent honesty, and a bred-in-the-bone inability to pretend to a respect I don't feel.'

'Why,' Stephen asked with charming diffidence, 'didn't you like him?'

'Dislike at first sight, dear boy—at a dinner-party in 1913. I discovered the reasons for it later. Or invented them. I don't for one instant deny his greatness or great qualities, energy, moral courage, an ambition never deflected by any weakness, any weaker passion, the capacity for grand conceptions—now and then hideously misapplied. What I couldn't stand in him was the *cabotin*. At his peak he was a comedian in the same class as Napoleon, but less ruthless, less coldly indifferent to human beings. I ought—for my own sake—to have rallied to him in the 'thirties, especially after 1938, but—I am what I am—I couldn't bring myself to rally to a man I disliked.'

He paused, and went on with an arrogance of which he seemed unconscious. 'And why didn't he rally to me? ... I will tell you why. Because he feared me, and for precisely the same reasons that mediocre men—he was not, except in this instance, mediocre—were afraid of me.'

Stephen looked him in the face. 'Surely, to talk of your having ruined your life is—forgive me—absurd?'

'No. Exact.' He laid a dried-up notably small hand on the pages his secretary had just finished retyping. 'It matters very little. Mettons que j'aie raté, this—*this*—is my monument.' A purely mischievous smile knocked twenty years off his age. 'That appalling rhetoric of his. It wouldn't surprise me if nowadays he detests me as *literary* rival.'

If, thought Stephen, he were told that the man he thinks of as his rival has completely forgotten him, would he believe it? Probably not. His colossal vanity ... Extraordinary that the same man can be an original writer, one of the great English writers, miraculously clearsighted, a sardonic analyst of himself and society, *and* as vain as a peacock....

He said firmly, 'Of course he must.'

A look of extreme bitterness crossed Chatteney's face. 'I said that I had ruined my life. But in fact I am basically indifferent to public power and glory and always have been. The last twenty years of living obscurely—in this room—have been the happiest, the most profoundly happy of all.'

Behind his lively air of interest and deference, Stephen thought mockingly: My God, does he expect me to believe him? With his monument giving him the lie on every page?

Abruptly, Chatteney went off into one of his fits of almost cruel laughter, which shook his frail body and brought a flame into his sunken eyes.

'Did you notice,' he said, 'just now, how by talking about my errors—honesty, sincerity and the rest of them—I patted myself on the back?'

He laughed again at the young man's disconcerted silence. 'I shall miss you when you leave me,' he said kindly.

Stephen waited for a question about his future. It did not come. Instead, Chatteney walked across the room to the window overlooking the small courtyard at the back of the house, with its two young plane trees, now bare. The sky behind them was a grey fleece, and in one place a veiled sun broke through it in a triple-pronged jet, too bright to look at.

'To think,' he said lightly, 'that all this will still be here when I can't see it.'

Under his surface amiability and kindness he was completely uninterested in what his secretary might be planning to do when he had no further work for him. His age —was it only his age?—set between him and other people, and even events and things, a distance he no longer wanted to cross. It was not that he had become bored, or had lost his sharpness of mind. Simply, the distance was there, isolating him. Did he, now, see—really see—any other human being in the world?

At this moment, the only creature he was trying to see was himself. He had walked over to the small antique looking-glass in a corner of the room and was peering into it with curious intentness, as though trying to force an admission from it. This was not the first time his secretary had seen him do it. He would stand there for several minutes, absorbed in whatever spectral face he was seeing through his own ruined one. This morning he was not able to go on with the game. The door opened sharply, and his wife, who never came into this room unless she had something urgent to say, caught him at it.

'I'm sorry to disturb your devotions,' she said, 'but it *is* one o'clock, you should be downstairs, and I have an American called Foster—Hudson Foster—on the telephone who wants to come and see you tomorrow. He says he wrote to you at the Athanaeum and had a reply from you telling him to ring up. Is he telling the truth?'

'I'm afraid so,' Chatteney said.

'Why didn't you tell me about it?'

Lowering his eyes like a schoolboy caught cheating, he said, 'I thought I had told you.'

'You didn't. What is it about? Am I to tell him he can come?'

'Perhaps you'd better.'

'But what does he want?' she insisted.

Chatteney shrugged his shoulders. 'He wants to buy the memoirs—for some Foundation or Institute or other. They would pay fifty thousand dollars . . . No, no, let me finish. I told him they weren't for sale, and that in any case they were not to be published for at least fifty years. He said he knew that, and was perfectly willing to give a guarantee that the manuscript would remain securely out of sight for that length of time. Some of these Foundations have so much money that . . .'

His wife cut him brutally short. 'But you must have had more than a letter from him!'

'In fact, two.'

'And you didn't tell me!' She stared at him, frowning. 'I see that you haven't turned him down,' she said dryly. 'What is it tempts you? The money?'

'I gave him no grounds for thinking I would even consider the offer,' Chatteney said. 'But, really, my dear, one doesn't refuse fifty thousand dollars without some show of politeness.'

'He's still holding the telephone,' she said, with a sarcastic smile. 'I'd better ask him to lunch tomorrow. In the meantime we must find out about him. He may be an impostor.'

'Oh, no, he's well known,' said Chatteney mildly. 'I telephoned to the American Embassy about him.'

'You did all that without telling me about it?' she said, in her harshest voice. 'You really are extraordinary.'

She turned quickly and went away. Following her downstairs, they heard her on the telephone, using the same voice, only slightly tempered, to tell the American that it would be very pleasant to see him tomorrow at half past one.

She sat through lunch without opening her mouth, except to eat as if choking on morsels of the omelette. When Chatteney got up to go to his bedroom she did not move. Stephen, still holding the door open, looked at her, and she made a fierce gesture ordering him to stay behind. He had expected it. Bruegel appeared at this moment, and she said,

'Get out, get out. Leave us alone. . . . Sit down, Stephen. Did you know about this?'

'No.'

Struggling with her agitation, she said,

'He's never been secretive about a thing of this sort. Never. Usually he wants my advice, and the only reason I can see for his not telling me about this ... this unheard-of offer, is that he actually thinks of taking it.' She was sitting stiffly upright, trembling violently with the effort she was making to seem calm. 'We must, I say must, stop it.'

Although he had his own strong reasons for wanting to get rid of the intruder—so long as the memoirs were in England and had not been buried in the Museum he could go on hoping to divert them into Frederick Hyde's powerful hard-fleshed fingers—he had the unkind curiosity to ask,

'Are you so very opposed?'

She looked at him in cold astonishment and some anger. 'Good heavens, aren't you? I thought you agreed with me that they ought to be published. Here and now. Don't you?'

'Of course I do. But—fifty thousand dollars ...'

'I should feel just as angry and upset if it were a million!' She lifted to him a face ravaged by a hurricane of bitterness and jealousy. 'To think of him making friends with this man, trusting him, confiding in him, giving the memoirs to him, letting him take them out of the country —no, no, it's intolerable. I can't bear it.'

Reflecting as he spoke, Stephen said,

'Don't you think that may be the line to take? If you suggested that *his* memoirs ought not to go to America— no more than any other unique manuscript or art treasure.... It might appeal to him. And'— he smiled charmingly—'it's true of course.

'Yes, yes, oh yes, that's the right argument, that's splendid,' she said, with energy. 'Thank God you're here. Stephen. You're the greatest help to me. I ought to have thought of that point for myself—but this has given me such a shock.... That's what you must say to him— whether it is his memoirs or a Shakespeare First Folio, the principle is the same.... You are absolutely right.'

'If Sir Henry gives me the smallest chance I'll certainly say it.'

'You must make the chance,' she cried. 'He likes you and he thinks you are intelligent and sensible. I know that.'

'I'll do anything I can.' He added in a low voice. 'For you, anything, anything I can do.'

'My dear Stephen,' she said warmly, 'my dear friend. I feel I can trust you—and that between us we can save him —you and I.'

She held out her dry claw of a hand. He kissed it.

CHAPTER 13

'No, no, give me that back,' Chatteney said. He snatched from his secretary's hand the page he had just, after making a single correction, given him to recopy. 'I'm not satisfied with it yet. I don't want to give the impression of regretting anything in my life, anything, I mean, that depended on my own will. It would be totally false. I regret nothing, nothing.'

Holding the page, he began to prowl about the room, stopping to run a finger along a line of books, to stare out of a window. His small body with its too large head made his secretary think this morning of a restless insect, a grasshopper, crackling with energy.

He came to an abrupt stop at Stephen's table, and said,

'The truth is I'm not concentrating. This fellow who is

coming to lunch, the American—what am I going to say to him? He has disturbed me.'

'In what way, sir?'

'Oh, well, you know, he tells me that the Museum has far less adequate ways, the conditions are less scientifically controlled, for storing manuscripts than a modern building such as his Foundation has built for the purpose. Controlled temperature, the right amount of dryness or humidity, how do I know which, in the air, and so on and so forth. I must say I was impressed. I spoke about it in the club to old—oh, what is the fellow's name, the physicist, Sir, Sir ... never mind—and he said the man is perfectly right—I mean Foster.'

'Did he,' Stephen asked slowly, 'say that the Museum was not properly equipped?'

'No, no, no, no. He merely said that the latest, most modern conditions will preserve a manuscript for—so far as one can use the word—eternity.' He chuckled. 'Queer how we go on hoping for eternity even after we've accepted that the word has no meaning.'

'If it simply means the longest imaginable existence, that's what one wants for this manuscript. But'—Stephen hesitated, frowning.

'But what? Go on, go on, say what you think.'

'I don't know whether I have the right to think anything at all in this ... frightfully important affair.'

'Well, I give you the right,' Chatteney said, with a sharp smile. 'I want to hear what you, a young man, think of the idea of an American sarcophagus for my mortal remains. ... I had a great-aunt when I was a boy who used to talk a great deal about her mortal garment. But she expected to be given another, less volatile.'

'I ... it seems to me wrong ... I mean unsuitable and undignified ... Forgive me for using such a word, but this

112

manuscript is part of what people call the English heritage when someone sells a great picture or a unique book to America—and even if it is a cliché it stands for something real. Really I can't see any difference between sending the manuscript of your memoirs to America and sending a Chaucer manuscript or all our Holbeins or anything else that belongs here and nowhere else.'

He had spoken gravely, reluctantly, as though driven by strong feeling to risk giving offence. His hands, clasped on the table gripping a pencil, shook a little. When Chatteney did not answer immediately, he said,

'I'm sorry. I've said too much.'

'My dear boy, not at all,' Chatteney said briskly. 'I wanted your frank opinion, anything less would have disappointed me. I'm not certain—I say: certain—that I agree with you. But we'll see, we'll see.'

Stephen's strongest hope at this moment was that Mr Hudson Foster would turn out to be an impossible fellow, loud-spoken and insupportably self-confident. Nothing of the sort. The man Bruegel showed in was a tall well-built grey-haired gentleman, wearing his slightly old-fashioned English clothes with the air of a Victorian statesman, speaking without a cat's whisker of accent unless it were a faintly Scottish whisker, and with a gesture, a small movement of large well-kept hands, which in a very agreeable way sharpened the Victorian flavour. Beside him Chatteney looked, not less distinguished or less aristocratic than usual, but painfully frailer.

Mr Foster ate sparingly of a sparing meal—Lady Chatteney had refused to make changes in it for his benefit, except to tell Bruegel to serve a good claret. This he refused.

'Thank you,' he said pleasantly, 'but I don't drink except at dinner. When I left Harvard, and joined my father in the firm, a legal firm, he inherited from his father, grandfather and great-grandfather, he told me: You will please yourself how you work, I myself have always worked slowly, long hours, eaten very little during the day and drunk water, and I believe it to be the way to stretch my energy over as many years as possible, but you do as you please.... Well, I decided to do as he did. That's thirty years ago, a long time, long enough to test any theory.'

Chatteney's smile was ironical. 'I'm seventy-five, I've been drinking claret—usually claret—at lunch and dinner for nearly sixty of those years, and when I think that an imprudent remark—too prudent—from my father might have deprived me of it, I shudder.'

Mr Foster looked at him with the deference due to an historic monument, but without a trace of awe.

'That's very interesting.'

'Other people's misspent lives always are,' Chatteney said.

His wife had been silent. She now asked carelessly,

'Is this your first visit to England, Mr Foster?'

'No, Lady Chatteney. I come every two or three years, to remind myself how much your country can still teach the world, even my own country, about dignified living. I flew here from Paris, ten days ago, after spending a week with our Ambassador—which gave me the chance to confirm my fear that France has cut itself off from the civilised world to pursue a policy of—what can I call it?—selfishness and self-indulgence in the most fatal of passions.' He lifted his fine hands. 'I am inclined to believe that the more logical a man is the more stubbornly he dupes himself about his passions. The French have persuaded themselves that what the rest of us see as egoism is harmless, even noble. They will be all the more stupefied—when the republic is actually on its death-bed—to notice that they have been crazily greedy and ambitious, and where it has led them.'

The amusement in Chatteney's glance did not spread farther than the fold at the ends of his eyes. 'The idea of a civilised world divorced from France startles me.'

Smiling, for the first time warmly, his wife said,

'I agree entirely with Mr Foster. I have never considered the French a civilised people, they over-eat, they're immoral, and I have never in my life met so many insolent rich women as in Paris.'

Mr Foster was not an insensitive man. He caught the sense of Chatteney's silence at once, and with surprising deftness turned the subject of French manners into a brief monologue on nineteenth-century painting, about which he knew a great deal. He did not come to the memoirs until he was drinking coffee in the drawing-room. Holding his gilt-and-white cup up to the light he said,

'In this country even a cup can be a masterpiece. I feel my privilege in drinking from it in this house, in your company, Lady Chatteney, and your husband's. His masterpiece is less fragile than this cup. Not fragile at all—enduring—immortal.'

'How do you know?' she said coldly.

The glance he turned on her was at once good-humoured, indulgent, and magisterial. 'I judge it by the published extracts. You won't, I'm sure, be surprised when I tell you that I have had all five of these bound up, in fine calf, six copies of each. One I kept for myself, the others are in the White House, Harvard, and three others of our universities.... I hope some time to be allowed to bear the whole manuscript in my hands to a secure place.... It would be the crown of my life.'

His earnestness, which made Chatteney move restlessly in his chair, did not soften her.

'I have no doubt my husband has written a great book. I

should be sorry to see it placed in hands that were going to carry it out of England.'

Mr Foster did not blench. He asked gently if he might have a second cup of coffee. 'One of the few things,' he said, smiling, 'which your country doesn't do as well as we do.'

'I have an Austrian housekeeper.'

'Ah,' he said, 'Austria...'

He talked about the Albertina collection in Vienna for five minutes, then got up to leave. No, he didn't want a cab, his car—'not mine, one lent me when I come to London'—was waiting. A very large black Cadillac, Stephen noticed, when he opened the front door.

Standing beside his guest in the narrow hall, Chatteney talked affably about the fog that seemed to be closing in like the breath from a million grey basements.

'It would be a pity,' Mr Foster said, 'to eliminate your fogs, they figure something in the national character, some kind of secretive patience—perhaps I don't make myself clear....' His hands, holding a pair of thick doeskin gloves, moved in a delicate circle.

'About the manuscript,' Chatteney said abruptly. 'I'll let you know.'

'Thank you,' Mr Foster said.

He smiled with surprising sweetness.

Lady Chatteney had come to the door of the drawing-room, to forestall any attempt her husband might make to escape upstairs. He gave no sign that he wanted to escape. Laying a hand on his secretary's arm, he drew Stephen with him into the room. He was in high spirits.

'Stephen, my boy, you can say that you have seen and heard the English Victorian age in its glorious noon. That confidence, that solid sense of power, only exists now in Americans like our friend, rich, serious-minded, educated, sensibly, not extravagantly cultivated. He has all the emi-

nent Victorian virtues—including one you can't call innocence, and yet... You know what they used to say about
Gladstone—that when he found a fifth ace up his sleeve he
knew that God had put it there, and so could play it without scruples.... Perhaps innocence *is* the right word.'

His wife's tongue flickered between her dry lips. 'Innocent? That man? Nonsense.'

'Then what would you call him?'

'Shrewd, calculating, double-faced, Machiavellian, a
hypocrite....'

'Exactly what they used to say about us in our great
age!' Chatteney said, delighted.

'As you like,' she said calmly. 'But if you sell him the
memoirs you'll be sorry. Or rather, you won't, because you
will have been dead for a week or two when he opens his
safe, takes them out, and publishes them to the world with
any alterations he sees fit to make.'

'Do you really think that?'

'I don't think it. I know.'

'Perhaps you're a little prejudiced,' Chatteney said. He
looked at Stephen. 'What's your opinion of him?'

'What struck me about him,' Stephen said gravely, 'was
that he said exactly what he thought would please you and
Lady Chatteney, and when something didn't have the
right effect he turned it aside like ... like a card swindler.'
He smiled. 'Perhaps that's what you meant about Gladstone. That fifth ace rather worried me.'

'I'm quite sure,' Lady Chatteney said very quietly, 'that
he would find some very good sensible noble reason for
breaking any promise he had made about the memoirs.
You'll do as you like—you always do—but if you have any
respect for my common sense in these matters you won't
touch the man.'

'My dear, I have always respected your good sense,'

Chatteney said. He seemed to reflect for a moment. Lifting his head, he said gaily, 'You're probably right. We'll turn him down.... What's the time, Stephen?'

Stephen glanced at his watch. 'Nearly four o'clock, sir.'

'Harry, you must go and lie down,' Lady Chatteney said.

'No, it's too late. I'll sit in my room for a quarter of an hour, then I shall want a cab to go to the Athanaeum.'

He walked off, erect and spry, and turned at the door to say to Stephen,

'You might draft a letter, refusing the offer very politely. I'll look at it in the morning, and we'll get it off to him.'

His wife had closed her eyes. Since they were the only point of liveliness in her face, she looked as though she had died centuries ago and been preserved under layers of dry desert sand. When she opened them, they were glittering with relief and a triumph she did not try to hide.

'Thank God. There was a moment when I thought he was going to get into that man's clutches, and all my hopes of persuading him to do the right thing with the memoirs would have vanished.... I may not be able to persuade him to publish them. But at least, at least, he has not taken them and himself away for ever, out of my reach.'

At the times when she had managed to control one of her rages and speak coolly, she was infinitely more formidable than when she made a scene.

There was something, Stephen thought, inhuman about her satisfaction. Perhaps extreme devotion and the purest egoism have exactly the same face. In spite of her withered body she was still infatuated with her husband—what else do you call an insistence on possession which, if it could, would go on beyond the grave until she had absorbed into herself the last grain of his dust?

In spite of his own relief that the American had been chased off, he did not care to sit talking to her.

'If you'll forgive me,' he said, 'I had better see about a cab. It will be difficult to get one, with a fog coming down.'

He went out at once, and had to walk some distance before he found a crawling taxi. When he got back with it Chatteney was waiting impatiently, and stepped in without waiting to be helped.

'The Athenaeum,' Stephen told the driver.

Frowning, he watched the cab turn the corner. He was trying to decide whether or not to go and see his mother: since the evening at the Café Royal—four months ago—he had not been near her. He had given Tarry money to ring him up every week, but it was ten days since her last call and he felt at this moment that what he wanted more than anything was to spend a few minutes with a young perfectly normal human being.

He set off to walk. Near Victoria Station the fog thickened, and when he reached Marion Street it stretched, a dirty grey ceiling, only a yard or so above his head: ragged tentacles from it reached down through the yellowish half-light to wrap themselves round his throat.

A cab passed him slowly, and stopped a short distance from 41A. The first person to step down was a woman who turned and gave her arm to a man to help him steady himself on his feet on the greasy pavement. They were Chatteney and Mrs Duquesne.

Scarcely able to believe what he saw, he drew back against the nearest house and watched them walk slowly, arm in arm, to 41A. They had no need to ring; the front door stood open all day and evening until the restaurant next door closed, to let Kenneth and his friend run to and from the storeroom.

He waited a full two minutes, rigid, stiffening the muscles of his stomach against an impulse to roar with laughter.

When he reached the house and walked into the dark evil-smelling passage, they were nowhere in sight. Running up the first flight of the staircase, he stood for a moment outside the door of the 'studio', and listened. No voices, and not a sound.

Half-way up the second flight, he heard his mother talking in her room, loudly. He hesitated—and realised almost at once that she was talking to herself, as, Tarry had told him, she did almost all the time now. 'Well, not to herself, to people I don't know, and she laughs a lot.'

He went in. She was alone, in her chair: lamplight falling across her face threw into relief one vast white cheek and lock of dyed hair. Staring at him, she said quietly,

'Come in, stranger. What do you want?'

He smiled at her. If he woke her almost childish mischief, she might refuse to tell him anything. At the same time, it was no use pretending with her, she was too shrewd, she knew him too well. He sat down, and said carelessly,

'Two people have just gone into the room downstairs. Did you give them the key to it? Is it safe?'

She chuckled. 'Did you see them?'

'Not distinctly.'

'If you had, you'd know how safe it is. They're my two olds. And if you had taken the trouble to set foot in this house oftener than half a dozen times in the last as many years, you might have run into them any afternoon. They're here three days a week—sometimes four. Once a month an envelope with the rent in it, in notes. Money for jam, my boy; no sheets to wash, no wear and tear. A fire in winter. And all they can do, God help them, is sit there in front of it, talking. An hour. Never more than a couple of hours. On bitter days she'll bring a thermos of coffee, and ask Tarry for cups. Nothing else.'

'Who are they? Do you know?'

'I know her. Years and years ago she came four or five times running to a séance. When she came asking about the room I knew her at once, by her voice. Turns your blood back, that voice.'

'Where is Tarry?' he asked.

'Out at her class,' his mother said with pleased spite. 'You'll have to wait more than an hour if you want to see her. She's only just gone.'

'What class?'

She rolled her eyes up. 'How do I know? Some class she goes to every week.'

He stood up. 'I won't wait.'

She was silent, her mouth drooping, and he felt a brief discomfort. Hardening his heart against her, easily, he went away. A murmur of voices came from the studio as he passed it, nothing he could make sense of. After a moment he heard a low rich laugh, Mary Duquesne's, sliding from one note to another in calm amusement.

Outside, in the empty street, the fog had lifted a little, but the melancholy November dusk had taken its place.

What happens when they leave? he wondered. Does she look for a cab for him? Does he go on to the Athenaeum before coming home?

He was tempted to stay and watch, but decided against it. He would be no wiser. What he ought to do was to think hard and coolly whether there were anything he could do with his discovery. He was torn between amusement, derision, and a pity in which there was very little kindness. There must, surely—without running any risk of betraying the two old creatures—be a way in which he could turn to good use so odd and fascinating a story?

He walked on slowly, frowning.

CHAPTER 14

'NEITHER you nor I, my darling, could say truthfully that we have a soul above comfort—the greatest possible comfort. It so happens that I am richer than you—at this time. I am also older. Don't let's be too precise about that, I don't mind your knowing my exact age, women who knock years off their age—Laura Gide—bore me, but at the moment it's neither here nor there that if I had married at, say, nineteen, you could be my son. I am merely pointing out that nothing gives me so much pleasure—no, that's nonsense—only one thing gives me greater pleasure than to buy you things I should adore to give my son, if I had one.'

Colette Hyde was—she said it so often that it may have been true—devoted to Stephen. She was too intelligent, too shrewd, not to be perfectly aware that the only reason he protested when she gave him an expensive gift was to force her to feel obliged to him for taking it. His discreet gold watch pleased him, so did the Charvet ties, shirts, handkerchiefs. It delighted him to be measured by a Dover Street tailor, and she had been a little disappointed that he needed no guidance from her in choosing clothes.

She had taken a man's dressing-gown from her wardrobe and was holding it out to him.

'Please put this on. You can wear it here.'

'Don't give me any more things,' he said, smiling. 'After all, I'm not your son. I'm ready to prove it—at once.'

'No, no, I want to see if it suits you.... Yes. Perfect. I wish I could have a portrait painted of you. You look ... beautiful.'

He looked at her with a gleam of mockery. 'You have very good taste.'

'Sit down and talk to me,' she said, laughing. 'How are the memoirs? How near the end are you?'

How much of her feeling for him was this famous devotion, and how much a determination not to let go of a line leading to Chatteney and his manuscript? Since the night of Mrs Gide's party, nothing more had been said about taking him into the firm. It would, he knew, be extremely unwise to ask questions or show the slightest anxiety. On the other hand, it could do no harm to let her suspect that he might not be whole-heartedly on her side about publishing the memoirs. He said carelessly,

'The Lord only knows. He's enjoying himself too much making corrections. Last week he had an enormous offer from America and turned it down. But it looks as though the British Museum would have to wait a little time yet for the precious manuscript.'

'My God, it mustn't happen,' she said.

He shrugged. 'He's a stubborn old devil.'

'It would be a crime!'

Sitting down on the floor with his back to her, his head against her knees, he said,

'I believe I ran into your husband yesterday, in Dover Street. It was getting dark and I couldn't be certain, but I think I saw him crossing the street towards Todd's. He didn't notice me.... The day before, when we had that bad fog, I had a much queerer meeting. With a friend of yours.'

'Is it scandalous? Tell me about it.'

'Not only a scandal. Surprising ... I was walking towards Victoria, and I saw your Mrs Duquesne in front of me, walking arm in arm with Chatteney himself.'

'No!'

'Yes.... They went into a house—the sort of house you wouldn't be surprised to find was a respectable brothel, not expensive but discreet. Probably only a boarding-house.'

Mrs Hyde gripped his shoulder. 'My God, Stephen—what did you do?'

'Nothing. What could I do? Follow them in?'

'You could have waited until they came out, and...'

'And tapped them on the arm? My dear girl, think. What would you have done yourself?'

'I suppose—just what you did. Nothing.... But, my darling, it's the most divine story I ever heard. Mary has never, by so much as an eyelash, given away that she sees him. You heard her yourself say she hadn't seen him for fifteen years—not since the case.... Do you suppose it was an accident, they'd just met in the street—and the house might have belonged to someone she knew?'

'No. It wasn't the kind of house where she'd know anyone. And only half an hour or so earlier I'd put him into a taxi in Lowndes Place to go to the Athenaeum. No, no, it was obviously a—a rendezvous.'

She laughed. 'I'm absolutely delighted.'

'Why?'

'Oh, because they've fooled everybody, including his frightful wife. And because—I hope with all my heart—they've been getting some amusement out of it. I adore Mary, I should like to believe she was happy.'

For a moment Stephen said nothing. He had not, when he came, intended to tell Colette. He had given way to the temptation to startle her, and, too, at the back of his mind he had had a vague hope that she would give him useful advice. During the past forty-eight hours he had imagined and rejected a dozen ideas, each less feasible than the last, for making some use of his knowledge. All he had done was to write down every detail he remembered in the loose-leaf book labelled: Notes about H.C. It exasperated him with himself that he had discovered something of the greatest interest to other people and could not profit from it.

Turning his head to look up at Colette, he said slowly,

'No, I wasn't very clever. Perhaps I really ought to have done something more ... enterprising.'

She lifted her eyebrows. 'Enterprising?'

'It seems a shocking waste of an extraordinary coincidence to do nothing with it. Don't you think so?'

'I think,' she said, smiling, 'that young and charming as you are, you ought by now to have realised that you can't burn up everything and everybody to warm your hands.' Her smile became pleasantly mocking. 'Hands I love. Eyes, wilful chin, mouth I love.'

He stood up. 'You exasperate me.'

'Do I?'

'Do get it into your head that, however many years younger I am, you are not my indulgent wise efficient mother.'

He pulled her to her feet and forced her full length on to the bed with a measured brutality and tenderness he knew gave her the greatest pleasure she was capable of feeling. She was not capable of a violent pleasure: nine times out of ten some comment she made showed him that, whatever else in her had been silenced, her mind had not.

Later, lying soothed and drowsy, she said, 'I told you there was one thing that made me happier than giving you the sort of things you ought to have.'

'Do I make you happy?'

An amused smile softened her mouth. 'All the men I have known make love to prove to themselves that they exist. You're not like that. You want power and enjoyment, and you get both out of it. But no more than they did do you want to be loved. Not one of them wanted me to be faithful to him. Or not for long.'

'Why not?'

'My darling, because it would have made him ashamed of his own fickleness. You're just the same. If you thought I was hopelessly in love with you, you'd first resent it, then run for your life.'

Bored, as so often, by her cleverness, he said,

'There must be genuine love in the world somewhere.'

'You wouldn't know what to do with it, my dear.'

In the hall, waiting for the man to bring his overcoat, he noticed for the first time a long nearly invisible crack running diagonally across the large black and white marble tiles of the floor. He was looking at it when Frederick Hyde came in from the street and said affably,

'D'you know how that happened? A land mine came down five hundred yards away when I was standing here, the house didn't even shake, but I watched that crack race across the floor like forked lightning. I ought to have it repaired, but it amuses me—souvenir de la guerre, eh? ... Been seeing Colette? I want to see you myself—did she tell you?'

His pale eyes seemed capable of laying open any depth of flesh to reach a nerve, and the young man felt a tremor of excitement and fear.

'No. She didn't.'

'How are you with Chatteney? Are you, I mean, nearly through?'

With relief he answered, 'If I were allowed to go straight ahead with the typing I could finish in a week. As it is, I copy and re-copy the same chapter, the same page, again and again and again. I can't see why we should ever end. There must come a moment when even he can't change a comma, but God knows when. It's become a bore.'

'Ha, well ... a bore ... yes, I dare say. But you shouldn't

leave until the manuscript is on its way to the Museum—if the old sinner really is determined to cheat us all out of it.... How much of the day d'y'work with him?'

'Now,' Stephen said, 'only in the morning. It tires him.'

He felt a prick of excitement. For a split second he knew what was coming. It came.

'Then there's no reason why you shouldn't work for me the rest of the day,' Hyde said. 'Is there?'

He said calmly, 'None.'

'Well—it may surprise you to know that you can't step into publishing like being measured for a new suit. You need training.... What? No, wait.... I don't mean a start at the trade counter or in the packing room. And I don't, at the moment, want you on the side of the business that supports the firm.' He showed his teeth in what passed with him for good-humour. 'You think, don't you, like everyone else, that best-selling novels do that? You're wrong. If I hadn't the best technical and educational list in the world —yes, in the world—I couldn't afford to publish Master Avens, who sells his thirty thousand copies or Miss Cordelia Brand, who sells half as many again and has given her editor a duodenal ulcer. They're my wife's affair. It amuses her, she does it as well as anyone in London and it gives her the chance to manage Avens and the rest instead of trying and failing to manage me. That's where—if you want to come into the firm—you'll start. I warn you, you'll be managed.'

His malicious inquisitive glance moved from the young man's face over his body and up again, as though he were appraising an animal.

'Well?'

Stephen had the sense that he was hearing and watching himself behave with admirable coolness. He said in a frank voice,

'I'm very lucky to be given this chance.'

'Didn't you expect it?'

'I hoped.'

'Come and see me tomorrow afternoon,' Hyde said curtly, 'at the office. You might as well start at once. What's to-day? Thursday. On Monday, eh?'

'Thank you.'

'So long as you're working half time, a half salary,' Hyde said. 'After that . . . Dugdale, who is in hospital humouring his ulcer, has been with the firm twenty years, and draws two thousand five hundred. You'll be worth—I hope you'll be worth—a third of that for a year, then half, then . . . it depends on yourself.'

'Thank you,' Stephen said again.

He was going to make some modest youthfully impulsive remark when Hyde said genially,

'I believe we share a tailor. Weren't you coming out of Todd's the other afternoon?'

'I was there Tuesday,' Stephen said.

He realised that the fleshy vulpine arrogant man eyeing him with a trace of a smile knew very well that he had been upstairs making love to his wife, and was indifferent and amused.

For no reason he cared to put a finger on, this stung him.

CHAPTER 15

A T his first sight of the young woman with whom he shared a small room in Frederick Hyde's offices in Portland Place, Stephen had taken her to be the editor who was going to train him. She put him right at once, as soon as they were alone.

'Officially, Mr Hind, I'm your assistant. In plain fact I'm your secretary-typist—as soon as you need one. Until then I'll go on helping out Mr Dugdale's secretary—like the rest of us in this firm she's rather driven.'

He picked up, or thought he did, a thread of anger in her voice, a very pleasant voice. Sarah Bernard was a pleasant young woman, good-looking in a fine-featured way, with a quick gaiety and a good-humour that nothing fractured. After two weeks, when he had become lightly and comfortably friendly with her, he asked,

'Why, since you know a great deal more about this business than I do, are you my assistant? I ought to be yours.'

She laughed. 'There are no female heads of department in this office, and never will be. Mrs Hyde's ruling. She has no use for women who might have ideas of their own.... Don't think I'm snarling, she's very clever, very tough, very sensible, knows all there is to know about this side of the firm, and works hard.... I suppose the truth is she can manage men—she's not so certain of being able to manage another intelligent woman.'

'Why do you stay?'

'Because I shouldn't do much better anywhere else,' she said swiftly. 'Not in publishing. A job for a gentleman, yes—perhaps. If he is also an energetic shark. Hardly ever for a woman.' She laughed again. 'I'm perfectly happy.'

'Really?'

'Yes. Don't get a false idea of me. I'd infinitely rather enjoy life than scramble for place. I leave that to you.'

'Is that what you think of me?' he said lightly.

'Why else are you here? This isn't one of those firms—they still exist, I believe—where no one is sacked unless he

129

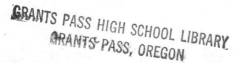

is really an imbecile, and no one is ever bullied or feels he must keep running or drop out.'

He smiled at her as though she were his mistress. 'Tell me about it.'

'About ... ?'

'The firm. Which of them is the boss?'

'He is. Of course. Not that she isn't just as shrewd, just as ruthless, but she hasn't his—oh, call it genius, since that means nothing. This side, hers, the novels and belles-lettres, is the least important, it gratifies her to run it, but ... You know her, don't you? I mean, you knew her before you came in. So you know how clever she is, and as hard as nails, and only likes successful people, and she can be malicious. But she's not a bully. He is. A bully and a brute to work for. But he has the sort of biological energy that spreads to other people, he doesn't *need* to savage his staff, he bullies because he enjoys it.... You'll know you're *in* here when he moves you to his side of the firm. If he does. She'll kick about losing you, but he won't budge and she'll give in.'

'How long have you been here?'

'Long enough to know my place,' she said, smiling.

He looked at her, at a warm curve of cheek, its fine down visible in the light from her desk lamp, at her bent neck, a little thick, but white and smooth: cleverly cut black hair drew to a point in the nape.... Is she a virgin? Almost certainly not. A body as lively as hers must need men.... He felt certain she would enjoy them without feeling any impulse to be clever, and without becoming sentimental.

At this moment he realised that not once in the two weeks he had been here had she allowed him to feel ignorant. So far he had done nothing more exacting than read the firm's forthcoming novels, write amiable descriptions of them for the catalogue, and attend the weekly meeting

130

of directors and editors. At every turn she had prompted him, opened his eyes to the malign touchiness of this colleague and the peculiar vanity of that, warned him of mantraps, and put into his mouth words he could use if, only if, he were called on to open it.

'My dear Sarah,' he said, 'don't imagine I don't know that I'm leaning all my weight on you. I make shameless use of you, and you let me do it. Haven't you any ambition of your own?'

'I told you. To enjoy life. In my own way.'

'Where do you live?'

'In London.'

'Yes, but how? With your family, with friends?'

'You're inquisitive.'

'Yes.' He looked her in the face. 'I like to be able to place the people I like.'

She laughed gently. 'Haven't you placed me yet? I'm a Jewess, my father and mother are orthodox Jews, very strict, very good, the two best people I know, kind, warmhearted, ridiculously generous. I ran away from them to avoid being smothered. You don't know anything about that clutching warmth and solidarity and closeness, there's nothing like it left in the world—the civilised world. No other families.' She hesitated and said in a curious voice. 'I love my parents and I *hate* families.'

'I have nothing that counts as a family.'

'You're very lucky,' she said gaily.

'Are you married?'

'No.' She frowned. 'And that's enough. No more, please.'

'I'm sorry,' he said. 'Don't cut me off, though.'

'No, I won't. You can't do without me—yet.'

'I know that.' He drew his eyebrows into a single black line above narrow eyes and fine aquiline nose: it gave him a diabolical beauty. 'And I need advice at once. Tell me—is

131

it because I'm the innocent new boy that I've been told off to give Dugdale's ulcerous female lunch at Quaglino's?'

'Yes. And because everyone here knows she intends to leave us at the end of her contract. One more book. And no one wants to be in the position—when Tom Dugdale comes out of hospital—of having to say: Cordelia Brand slapped my face and left.'

'Will she slap my face?'

Sarah Bernard looked at him with a very fine, very friendly smile. 'I don't think so. But she'll leave.'

'Why don't you like her?'

'Any *good* female writer—come to that, any good female dancer, singer, painter—who is a success, is either a sacred monster or a bitch. The in-betweens are always defeated. George Eliot and old Compton Burnett are sacred monsters, C. Brand is a bitch. She can't help it. I just happen not to like the combination of sex and God. But it's enormously saleable, and she does it with style. She's no slouch. But—she's a tiger for money. She's being bribed away from us. Mrs Hyde—she hates to be outbid, and she's a bitch herself—would be willing to overpay her to keep her. *He* won't. So you have nothing, but nothing, to play her with.'

'I see,' Stephen said.

'She's not to be seduced by charm. I warn you.'

'Perhaps I could persuade her I have a soul to be saved.'

'Try.' She threw her head back to laugh. He was tempted to run his hand down the strong white throat, to see whether it were as hard and slippery as it looked. 'I'll pray for you.'

Odd, he thought, that novels so remarkably witty and intelligent are being written by a fortyish female turned out by, oh by any expensive Knightsbridge store. Neither their elegance nor their wit went deeper than her agile mind. Already, half-way through the meal, she was telling him, with a fine greedy smile, about her brief love-affair with Chatteney. She had a low penetrating voice; it carried easily to the nearest tables and drew discreetly amused glances.

'That was in 1947. I was twenty-nine. I was overwhelmed by him, y'know, what sensitive young woman wouldn't have been? He was a very great man, and a wonderful charming boyish lover, all in one. He adored me. It never crossed my mind that I could refuse him anything, anything, and I didn't. And then one day—without warning—he broke it off. Y'know, it was becoming too painful for him, he was more than twice my age—he couldn't help comparing himself with the other men I knew, young men. Once, y'know, he said ...'

Throughout the recital, he kept his eyes on her face, with a look in them of eager ingenuous admiration. Her complacency and singular unconscious vulgarity bored him more than it surprised. He began to think that she was manageable, he had only to flatter her with whole-hearted extravagance. A pound, pounds, of the best butter. ...

He was shortly and thoroughly undeceived. The moment, over coffee, when he began talking to her about her work, the fatuous side of her withdrew behind a long-jawed business woman, well aware of her value, and not in the least moved by his charming enthusiasm.

She said frankly, 'I like you, y'know. But I'm not going to sign a contract for less advance than Gregg's are offering. Tell me—why should I? I'm a working woman, I have to live.'

She expected him to plead with her. And she would get an almost sexual satisfaction out of listening to it. He determined to disappoint her.

'Then don't let's discuss it any more,' he said, smiling at

her. 'Since you're leaving us I shall never have the chance to talk to you again, or ask the questions—about your books—I'm burning to ask. I won't waste my chance.'

She was very taken aback. The muscles in her face sagged and she looked old, older than she was. Rallying at once, she said,

'What do you want to know?'

What did he want to know? Nothing. Like Sarah, he disliked her sharp-edged amalgram of adultery, violence, and sensitive moral scruples. He reflected rapidly and said,

'Your cruel streak. Your cruelty to your characters. That poor randy old girl in your last book—and the old woman who gets her throat cut—and the others.'

She smiled sharply. 'You mean that no one, not even the silliest reviewer, will ever write about Miss Brand's well-known compassion. . . . I hope not. Compassion, tolerance—nowadays—means a soft corrupt mess, and wallowing in it like animals. No!'

'Oh, come,' he said, 'you don't mean that.'

'I mean it. Y'know, you, I, are animals yoked to a spirit. One must be reasonably kind to the animal, discipline it kindly, give it nice food and wine'—she had been doing just that, choosing carefully from the more expensive dishes—'and cultivate the spirit by meditation and the contemplation of masterpieces. I belong to a small club which meets every first Thursday for group meditation.'

A very pleasant religion, he thought. 'I'm beginning to understand you—a little. You make me think of a—a religious Voltaire, if you can imagine anything so exciting and alarming.'

She was silent for a moment, twisting together small ugly hands. She said abruptly,

'Don't you agree that I'd be a fool to turn down Gregg's offer?'

'You'd be a fool to take it,' he said calmly.

'Why?'

'They won't sell any more of your novels than we do, they'll merely overpay you for them for a few years.'

Her eyes started at him. 'Surely you ought to be trying to keep me? Why aren't you?'

He shrugged. 'By bribing you? We're not Gregg's, we don't need to do that to get authors on to our list.'

'Tom Dugdale begged me, almost crying, not to leave. So—without tears—did Mrs Hyde.'

He leaned towards her across the table. 'And you thought no better of them for flattering you. You're infinitely too intelligent for me to try to flatter you. I'd rather not try. Then, perhaps, when Gregg is your publisher, you'll let me come and see you now and then as a friend.'

She was silent for so long that he thought he had made another mistake.

'We'll talk about this again,' she said quietly. 'The contract, I mean. I won't decide yet.'

Sarah was right about her, he thought carelessly. She's a bitch and bitches need the whip. But she's also intelligent and hysterically vain and needs to be soothed and reassured.

He looked at her without a smile, and said in a simple voice,

'Make any use of me you like.'

CHAPTER 16

LIVVY's savagely alert friends, Jane and Jane Mary, had invited him to a late night party. Knowing too well what it would be like, a stifling crowd of young men in sweaters or long narrow jackets, and ingenuously raffish young women, bare-shouldered in trousers, in long thick hairy skirts, in tight dresses riding up slender and not so slender thighs, he would have refused if he had not hoped to find Livvy there. Her silence—it was now two months since he had heard from her—irritated him.

Poor in the 'sixties way—that is, they were supported jointly by the state and their professional parents—the two girls shared the top floor of a tall dilapidated house in the wastes of Camden Town. When, a little after ten o'clock, he found the right place, the living-room was buzzing like a wasps' nest with excited voices and rancid with smoke and the smells of gin, scent, and male sweat. The bare floor-boards were far from clean and the feeble lighting came from two naked electric bulbs dangling from a rafter—both girls were conscientious about their status as intellectuals free in spirit and flesh.

Bored, he stared round him looking for Livvy. He caught sight of her at last, at the far end of the room, standing between Jane and two ill-kept beards.

To his astonishment she greeted him with an enthusiasm wildly unlike her usual manner.

'Stephen! Where have you been?'

Something has gone wrong, he thought dryly. The man has broken it off, or they have been quarrelling. Find out if the place is still occupied, temporarily deserted, or what.... His inelegant reflections were cut short by a young woman moving about under a dank cloud of hair, with a tray of glasses and a stone jug: she poured him out what seemed to be gin with a drop of some other liquid, not water.

'Ooh, you're the actor, aren't you?' she said.

'No.'

'I never said he was an actor,' Livvy said sharply.

'I thought you did. Well, it's not of the faintest importance. Here. Let me give you a drink.'

She refilled Livvy's glass and pranced away.

With regret, and very puzzled, he realised that Livvy was rather drunk. Her narrow face, as smooth as a pebble, was flushed, her lips pouting and soft, as though she were on the edge of falling asleep. Jane and the two young men had drifted away, leaving him alone with her. He said quietly,

'Give me that drink. It's lethal, and you've had quite enough.'

Looking at him with a teasing smile, she swallowed it down. 'Where did you get this elder brother tone? It's silly.'

'Silly or not, you really have had enough.'

'Don't be a clot,' she said calmly. 'Hi, you—Michael'—stretching out a thin bare arm, she took his half-empty glass from a boy near her—'my need is greater than yours.'

Stephen let her drink it, then said deliberately and coldly,

'Why are you behaving like a tart? What is the matter?'

She blushed. For a moment she said nothing, and he thought he had struck too hard.

She looked at him with an oddly humble smile.

'I would tell you if there weren't so many people about,' she said under her breath.

'Isn't there anywhere we can go and talk?'

'Perhaps Jane's bedroom ...'

He followed her as she elbowed her way through bedlam, and out on to an uncarpeted landing. She opened the door of a room; it was in darkness, and a grunt of protest came from the formless mass on the bed. Closing the door quickly, she stood, arms hanging.

'I don't know what to do. If it weren't so bitterly cold we could sit outside, on the fire-escape. No one will come there.'

'Right,' he said. Coats had been heaped in a dusty corner of the landing, he picked out two, his own and a woman's long fur coat. 'Where is this fire-escape?'

She took him through the cluttered kitchen, opened a door, and stepped out, apparently on to nothing. His heart missed a beat. Then he was standing with her on the shaky top step of an iron stairway running from top to bottom of the building, with a slip of landing at each of the five storeys. She sat down. After the heat inside, the icy December air stung his nostrils and lungs.

'Won't you be too cold?' he asked.

'No.'

As his eyes became used to the darkness, the black corrugations below them fell apart in irregularly shaped masses separated by ill-lit gullies. In the distance, leaning against a less dark sky, the rows of street-lamps imitated a military cemetery with yellow flickering grave-heads. Exactly facing the house an electric sign, two letters missing, flared and went out, flared and went out, at intervals of a minute. The blinding flash struck the fire-escape immediately above their heads.

'How frightful London is,' Livvy said.

'This part of London.'

'All of it. I should like to live in the remote country and never come here again.'

'Tell me what is wrong.'

'I—I don't know if I can tell you.' She leaned forward, elbow on her knee, head propped on a hand. 'I did drink too many of Jane's unspeakable martinis—my head isn't clear.'

'It doesn't matter. There's no hurry.'

'You're too good-looking,' she said. 'That's why I didn't much like you. I thought you must be conceited.'

Fragments of an adroit reply rushed into his mind; he rejected them and said firmly,

'You had no reason to think that. I didn't think it about you.'

'I know.... No, I oughtn't to be talking,' she mumbled.

He realised that, for the first time, she was laid open to him, no longer the self-possessed young woman able to keep him at a distance by a trick of manner learned at the time she was learning to imitate the inflections of her grandmother's voice. He felt a cool satisfaction and some curiosity.

'Let's suppose I'm your brother,' he said. 'I have a sister who is rather like you. I can easily believe I'm listening to her telling me that she doesn't know what to do next and what do I think she...'

She interrupted him. 'And if she told you she was pregnant?'

Although—more because of Colette's story than because he had thought her likely to make a pitiably commonplace fool of herself—he had half expected it, he was for a moment at a loss. The instant of contemptuous triumph was overlaid at once by a surprising—surprising himself—anger.

'Is that it?' he said. 'Poor Livvy.'

'Oh, don't be sorry for me.' Her voice rose sharply. 'The person to be sorry for is my grandmother.' He heard her catch her breath. 'Oh, what can I do? She's had too many awful disappointments in her life. She'll be ... I don't know ... angry, heartbroken. And she's so *old*.'

'Don't think about that yet,' he said gently. 'Tell me, is she all the family you have? Haven't you anyone else?'

In a steadier voice she told him,

'My mother. But I don't know her. She married again almost at once after my father was killed. An American. I suppose she was thankful to let my grandmother—my great-grandmother—keep me. I've only seen her twice in my life—she lives in California and sends me a dress on my birthday that doesn't fit and I have to give it away.'

'Well, that's no good,' he said. 'We must think again.'

In the darkness she seemed not only slighter but younger, a child talking in a child's light thin voice.

'How old are you?' he asked her.

'Nineteen. Nearly twenty.'

A year younger than Tarry, he thought. 'Listen. There are all sorts of questions I would ask my sister, and you can guess all of them. I don't want to make you feel I'm prying. But tell me anything you can—so that I can at least try to help. I want to, you know.'

'Why should you? I don't know why you should.'

'That doesn't matter. You haven't got anyone else.'

'That's true.'

He waited.

'He's married. There's no faintest chance of a divorce, there never was, he's very fond of his wife, and she'—her voice steadied—'she's a very *good* person. I saw her once, by accident, and I saw then what he meant about her and how it's impossible to hurt her—and there are two sons at school and a daughter who is nearly my age. So you see.'

He saw more in the story than she did. He reflected cynically that a man—of what age? forty-five?—with a kind, faithful, no doubt useful wife he is afraid of hurting, who is in love with a nineteen-year-old girl and takes her to bed with him, is not, however weak or contemptible, too unusual or too inexcusable a character.

He hesitated. 'You don't have to have this child, do you?'

'There was a girl at L.S.E. who had an abortion. I thought it was absolutely loathsome.'

Her young cold frankness disconcerted him. 'Perhaps, but...'

'No.' In a quieter voice she said, 'If that's what you would advise your sister to do, she's not in the least like me.'

'Does he know?'

'No.' She went on fiercely, 'I'm not going to tell him. Don't try to make me. I can't. I can't possibly.'

He now saw that she had been hurt, mortally, in her young decent pride, more deeply in her pride than in anything, however much she was in love with the man. This enraged him again. But only for a minute, because his mind had begun to grope about in the situation for something it could take hold of and turn to some use. Sooner or later this always happened. It was not even deliberate. Years earlier, in a moment of terrible desolation for himself, little Dorrit had said to him, 'Stephen, you can't help using people, can you?' and he had answered sincerely, 'I don't know what you mean.' Nor did he. At certain moments his mind put out antennae which picked up, with a thread of excitement, an idea, a formless possibility, much as the fingers of a sculptor move over a lump of clay he finds under them. He felt the premonitory excitement now. Like the movement, at a great depth, of a distant sea swell. A chance. Perhaps valuable, not to be missed . . . He felt her shiver.

'You're getting cold out here.'

He put an arm round her shoulder to pull the edges of the coat together, and felt her stiffen. At this instant he made his mind up—rather, it was made up for him. He thought swiftly: No, I really am sorry for her, poor little beast.

'There's one other thing you can do,' he said.

'What?'

'You can marry someone else. It's not difficult.'

She shook his arm off. 'No, only impossible. I don't know anyone I could marry ... Which of the idiots in there do you think would do?'

'None of them. But you could fall back on me. I'm not an idiot.' The boldness of what he was doing—jumping in darkness from a height—made him smile: a twitch of the lips.

They were wedged so closely on the narrow staircase that he thought he could feel Livvy's heart knocking at her ribs even through the coat. She was shaking violently, not, he thought, from the cold. Glancing down at them, he saw her hands clenched on a fold of her thin dress.

'You don't want to marry me,' she said. 'I mean—you're not so frightfully keen on me, are you?'

The schoolgirl phrase, the effort she was making to seem sensible and cool, struck him as pathetic—pathetically courageous. Curiously, it made him conscious of areas of inexperience in his own life. He said soberly,

'I like you a lot. I certainly wouldn't want to marry you if I didn't.' The impulse seized him to speak frankly. 'Listen. I'm as alone as you are. I need someone who can help me to get ahead. Keep me from making an ass of myself in all sorts of ways—I mean, partly, women. You would do that. Between us we could think of a way to placate your grandmother. What do you say?'

She fastened on one sentence in his rush of words.

'How d'you mean you're alone?'

Feeling his way again, he said, 'My mother is like yours. I don't like her, and she's not in the least interested in me. Apart from her, there's only my sister, she's quiet and sweet-tempered, and'—he hesitated—'You must meet her, though—some time.'

142

'I should like to,' she said politely, with complete indifference. She was too sunk in her difficulties to feel any interest in his unknown family.

He waited a minute and said,

'I'm not trying to hurry you.'

'No. I know. You're kind.'

It gave him a curious amusement to say, 'Not very, I'm afraid.'

'I couldn't sleep with you, you know,' she said in a voice that surprised him by its harshness. He caught an echo in it of Lady Emily, and grinned sharply to himself. Then thought lucidly: You still have Marion Street in your spine. It gives you a cheap satisfaction to be able to put one across the old woman.

'Of course you couldn't,' he said coolly. 'I don't expect it. But I shouldn't care to make a third. Only vanity—but I should dislike it.'

'I'd loathe it,' she said quickly. 'If you think I'd go on with it, married to you—to anyone—you know nothing about me.' He saw her close her eyes. Opening them, she scowled at him. 'It's finished. I mean that. Can you take my word for it?'

'Yes. Of course.'

Her thin voice went on, almost unemotional. 'I *will* be decent.... No, listen—if you wanted to get rid of me some time, you can divorce me, I should want you to. I'd help you.'

'We needn't talk about that,' Stephen said.

Is it true, he asked himself ironically, that I don't want to sleep with her? Yes, quite true.... The chance he had seized was so utterly unforeseen and full of ambiguities that he could not let himself feel any complacency about it, he must get away and think.

'Oh, I'm cold,' Livvy said suddenly, 'cold, cold, cold.'

He jumped to his feet. 'You've had enough of this, you ought to be in bed. I'll take you home at once. I'll come and see you tomorrow afternoon—where? at the School? Then we can decide—oh, everything.'

Looking down, he had the sense of a black precipice on his left; a single clumsy step and he would be over the edge. He closed his hand over the ice-cold iron rail, which shook.

'Come,' he said urgently.

Livvy stood up. The light from the electric sign swept across her face. She was pale and her eyelids heavy, as though she had been crying in the darkness. But she was dry-eyed.

'I'—her glance moved over his face in a puzzled way— 'thank you, you're very good—I didn't know.'

A genuine pity for her seized him. He said quietly,

'Don't worry. It will be all right. You'll see.'

She turned to go back into the flat. Walking behind her, he drove back a sudden uprush of excitement. I can do anything, he thought, anything. The prick of doubt he felt instantly was nothing like sharp enough to break the skin of a triumph so insolent that instinctively, when he stepped into the lighted kitchen, he passed his hand over his face.

CHAPTER 17

He went to his interview with Lady Emily Grosmont in the same state of rude moral health, certain that he would end by seducing her—a tremor of stage fright when he was waiting for her in the hall of her club, but nothing more serious. The place was empty, gaping with the boredom of

Sunday afternoon. She took him into the ornate morgue where she gave her grotesque tea-parties, to a corner between two pillars, as far as possible from the few persons drinking after-lunch coffee; the room was so vast, so lofty, and so poorly lit by wall lights, that there was as little danger of their being noticed or overheard as if they were sunk in a diving-bell, an image that crossed his mind at the moment an elderly man, bald, with the jaw-line of a hake and light protrusive eyes, drifted past them, yawning.

She did not offer him coffee. 'I must tell you at once that this bitterly disappoints me. It is not what I wanted for my granddaughter—great-granddaughter. Not at all. I don't think it suitable and I don't like it, and it would be quite absurd not to make that clear. I'm sure you understand.'

He lifted to hers a serious glance from narrowly bright eyes. 'Yes, I do understand.'

'My granddaughter'—she paused—'Olivia has always, from the time she was a child, known what she wanted: never cried, never begged for anything, was perfectly good-tempered, and always in the end got her own way. She is exactly like her father, the elder of my grandsons. When I talked to her yesterday—about this—I heard his voice when he was a boy. The same tones, the same accent.'

To Stephen the extraordinary thing was that she acquiesced in her defeat—he had expected anything but this cold acceptance of him. After a moment he thought that it was one of the virtues of her class to know when not to fight in the last ditch. The very room he was sitting in—the ballroom of a great London house, luckier than others in that it had not been torn down, but simply denatured—was an example of it: there had never been and never would be a bloody revolution in England because its rulers knew when to retreat.

'I hope you know what I feel about Olivia,' he said.

145

Her moustached upper lip twitched. 'Your feelings are no doubt all they should be. They don't interest me. Olivia's do.'

'All the same,' he began, 'you ought to realise...'

She interrupted him brutally. 'There are no oughts. Olivia is not twenty, I could insist on your leaving her alone for another fifteen months. If I don't do that, it's because I am a very old woman, I may not live so long, and because, since talking to her, I have no hope she'll change her mind. I know her. I know her very well.... At my age, Mr Hind, months slip past like minutes. I can't have many minutes left.... I have nothing against you personally—if I had you wouldn't be sitting here now. Understand that. What it comes to is this—if Olivia is going to marry you, I'd rather it happened under my eyes than when I'm dead. I think that's reasonable. It's what I've decided.'

Treatment of the sort she was giving him is an hereditary skill and needs long practice. Without losing any of his confidence, Stephen felt at a loss. Where, to warm it, do you grasp an old gargoyle? His mockery of her could not wipe out a perfectly sincere admiration. Gargoyle she might be, but she was not laughable. He said quietly,

'Since you won't let me tell you that I fell in love with your granddaughter the moment I saw her—before I knew who she was—I'll only say that I'm grateful to you, that I know I'm lucky and'—he risked a smile—'I hope to deserve my luck.'

'What do you propose to live on?'

'I have a salary of eight hundred from the publishing firm I work for—Frederick Hyde—and the very small one Sir Henry Chatteney pays me, which will soon stop. In less than a year my salary from Hyde's will be twelve hundred pounds, and after another year or...'

'Wait, please. Olivia has the allowance I make her—five hundred pounds. She has nothing else.'

'She knows how much I have, or how little,' he said calmly, 'and she's willing to make it do until I'm better off. As I shall be.'

'Who are your parents?'

He had prepared for this. 'My father is dead—he was a musician. He died when I was two years old. My mother is a complete invalid. She has to be nursed, and the least excitement, a disturbance of any kind, would probably kill her.'

'But she's not dependent on you?'

'No. She has her own money. An annuity.'

Her glance, a little less impersonal, examined him from head to foot. 'Is there a Spanish strain in your family?'

'No,' he said, smiling at her. 'For a long way back'—as far as my father, he thought derisively—'we are purely English.'

'The upper part of your face,' she said reflectively, 'and your skin.'

He held his head back, to look at her through his thick eyelashes, a look he knew to be troubling. 'I don't think so, Lady Emily. I think your great-great-grandsons will be English.'

She looked through him, not unkindly: she was staring at something too remote to include him.

'Both my sons were killed by the first war; my two grandsons were killed in 1944, in Normandy. Olivia was born that year, three days before her father was killed: he never saw her.'

Stephen leaned forward. 'Try to stretch those minutes to see *his* grandson.'

'Yes,' she said after a moment, 'yes. We'll see.'

It struck him that her extraordinarily ugly and bony

147

figure masked not only a still vigorous mind but a habit of brutality adopted in self-defence, out of love. He believed he had, as it were, turned her flank. It had not been entirely easy, he felt satisfied with himself, and—surprisingly —ready to go on humouring and honeying her for her own sake.

'Did Olivia tell you that she—we—would like to marry as soon as possible—and have Christmas together?'

'Yes. She did. Thinking it over, I see no reason to wait. As you say'—a smile came and went between her small merciless eyes and the line of stiff black hair along her lip—'those few minutes ... You'll be married in Dorset, at King's Stanton, and I'll leave Grosmont House to you for two weeks ... I shall give Olivia as a wedding present five thousand pounds, and you must set up house in London with it—you can take what you want from Grosmont, the house is a great deal too full of everything.... As you see' —the same ironical flicker—'I spent a great part of the night planning. I don't sleep much.'

She stood up. He smiled at her brilliantly, and said,

'Please trust me.'

She shrugged her shoulders. 'You can see that that's precisely what I'm doing.' In a rather gentler voice she went on, 'Which is your club?'

'I haven't a club,' he said coolly, 'I can't afford to have one.'

'I must see about it. A young man should have a club. Not this'—she looked absently round the now empty morgue—'it's convenient, it does very well for an old woman and a certain sort of young man, but you would be better in ... no, I must think about it and talk to my cousin; he'll advise me.'

No, he thought. Nothing he would enjoy more, but a little opposition would be good for her.

'Thank you,' he said, 'but please don't. I would rather wait.'

'Very well.... Good-bye. You can find your way out.'

As she turned away, he saw from her twitching chin that he had surprised her. This sharpened his satisfaction.

He went straight from her to see his mother.

When he came in, Tarry had just finished arranging the old woman's hair across her forehead in damp newly-dyed curls: in her sweater and narrow trousers, with her hands still in rubber gloves, she was an oddly ritual figure. The horror, as he saw it, of her life in this house, servant to their disreputable mother, struck him freshly. He had meant to be tactful. Instead, he said curtly that he was going to be married very shortly, a young woman she had never heard of, Olivia Stanton, and if there was anything she wanted to ask him, 'better ask now, I shan't see you for some time'.

His mother grimaced in a way that deepened the two enormous folds, like the wrinkles on boiled milk, on either side of her cheeks. 'You mean you're not bringing her here?'

'No. I'm not.'

'And why not?'

Standing behind the old woman, peeling the reddened gloves from her hands, his sister shook her head at him. He took no notice. A surge of hate filled him against the squalid heap of flesh he had come from, and he said,

'Ask yourself why I should want anyone to see you and this place.'

She said nothing for a moment, staring at him in a reflective way, as though she were not sure how grievously he had insulted her. If she had meant to reproach him, she changed her mind; a sly bitter smile drew down the ends of her mouth.

149

'Very well.' She closed her eyes. 'If you don't want to tell me about her I don't want to hear. I'm sure you've bettered yourself—it would be like you.'

He was not pleased with himself. With whatever intentions, good or bad, kind or unkind, he came, when he saw her it was always the same; he could not stand far enough away from her to wheedle her or make himself pleasant. I detest her too much, he thought. I'm too near her.

An extraordinary phrase came into his head. He thought: I'm guilty of her.

He jerked his head at Tarry, and she followed him out of the room and upstairs to her cold bedroom.

'You shouldn't talk to her like that,' she said.

'I'm sorry. I didn't mean to annoy her. It happened.'

'Oh, annoy her'—she lifted her hands—'she wasn't annoyed, she was hurt.... Tell me about her—this Olivia.'

He told her as much as he could tell quickly and easily, and went on with the curious anxiety he felt when he was with her in this dark little room where so much of his childhood had passed.

'She's rather like you—not in looks, but her voice, and she's sensible and doesn't fuss. Like you. Let me tell you something—I care far more for you than for her. And don't you forget it.'

'How ridiculous you are,' she said lightly.

'I mean it.'

'If it was true, I shouldn't like it at all, but...'

'The truth is, you're the only creature in the world I feel absolutely safe with. Every time I come back here and remember listening at night to hear if you were crying or if I'd only dreamed it, I think, yes, that was real ... Perhaps I mean safe, or innocent.'

'We can't be innocent as we get older,' she said in a

150

placid voice, 'we begin to think ... I should like to see her. Perhaps you'll send me a photograph of her some time.'

'My love, I'll take you to see her.'

She shook her head. 'No, I don't want to meet her. I'm sure you haven't told her, or her super relations, the truth about us. Oh, I know, I know, it's not on—it would be far too difficult—sometimes when I'm not thinking about our mother and I see her suddenly, she frightens me. And then the *olds* and one thing and another. But it would be just as difficult for me to have to pretend.' She laughed. 'And, you know, Steve, I'm not presentable, I don't know anything about anything, and I haven't any very decent clothes.'

'I can give you some now.'

'No. It isn't clothes—and I have no use for them. It's all the—the necessary lies.'

'You blame me,' he said roughly.

'Oh, no, no. I don't, really I don't.' She smiled very sweetly. 'You know what you want.'

Walking away from the house, he remembered that he had not asked her what was the class she went to every week. Vexed by his carelessness, he pushed her out of his mind and began to think how he could convince Colette, gracefully, that his marriage altered nothing. He did not want to tell her the whole story. Not out of discretion, but —he put it to himself as cynically as possible—he did not want everybody to know he had given his name to a bastard. Decency or vanity? Perhaps, he thought sharply, both. Moreover he did not know how much his position in the firm depended on his relations with her. Perhaps not at all, but...

When he came into her room, the excitement and tension in his nerves turned into a more violent need of her than he had ever felt. It was less need than an atrocious physical impatience, which spread through his body,

151

strangled his voice in his throat, and forced him to stiffen the muscles at the back of his knees to keep upright. The sediment of something calm, reasonable and even cold at the bottom of his mind saved him. To make love to her and *then* tell her would be the clumsiest and most fatuous thing he could do, she would, any woman would resent it, and punish him.... He smiled engagingly at her, kissed her with as much skill as he knew, sat down facing her, and said coolly,

'My dear darling Colette, I've done something I hope you're going to approve. Well, I know you'll approve ... I've asked Livvy Stanton to marry me. What's even more sensible, I've asked for her terrifying grandmother's blessing. And got it. This afternoon.'

Colette sat up. She made no effort to pretend that she was not astounded, and no effort to be adroit. She stared at him.

'Stephen—my God! When did this happen?'

'Two days ago—Friday evening.' He seemed to hesitate, and went on, 'Need I tell you that it's not what you'd call an affair of the heart? She has quarrelled with you-know-who....' Does she know? he wondered. 'She was looking for someone to console her. I certainly wasn't looking for a wife who will be useful to me, but I'm willing to take one as good-natured and pretty as she is. And that's an exact account.'

'You shock me,' she said, smiling.

He touched her bare arm. 'I've never had any use for the novelists' twaddle about being in love with two women at once. It's a physiological impossibility. One or other of the said passions is humbug, deliberate or not.... I dare say I shall get fond of Livvy, she's a nice child, but I'm not in love with her, I have no energy left over for her. You know that better than anyone.'

The frank mockery that came into her smile was not even lightly unkind. 'My dear, that's too bad! Because I have one rule I never break—I break any others cheerfully, but not this one. *No married lovers.* I have never in my life had an affair with a husband. Not, need I say, out of moral scruples, but because it would bore me. Rather like being asked to share a bathroom. No, no, my darling, this finishes it.'

He did not believe her. Pulling her to her feet, he compelled her to take the whole weight and pressure of his body along hers. She pulled herself away, with, he knew it, regret, but very firmly.

'No, no, no rape,' she said. 'Sit down.'

He sat down and put his head in his hands. He was not pretending to frenzy—that was real—but his brain was almost detached.... What do I do now? What can I save? ... Lifting his head, he caught sight of himself in the cheval glass, and was reassured. At least he did not look ridiculous.

Colette was watching him with a warm smile, indulgent, even loving. He swallowed his savage resentment and smiled back at her.

'Are you sure you can live without me?'

'I have every intention of trying. If I told you I had been madly in love with you, it would be a lie. I am extremely fond of you. I shall miss you. I mean I shall miss being made love to by you, you do it so well.... But a rule is a rule. I want us to remain friends. You need friends, you know, my dear, and only women will forgive your appalling egoism—provided you take a minimum of trouble to keep them.... And now I'll tell you something. I guessed a long time ago—in Dax, to be quite honest—that you came from pretty far down the ladder, and I took the trouble to find out a little. I don't suppose I know everything, but I know you haven't a soul or a sou behind you, you went to some wretched school or other, and you've been climbing hard ever since. You want passionately to know the right people, and to have money to spend and all that. No, don't scowl at me. I sympathise—these are the very things I want myself, I enjoy knowing important people, I revel in luxurious houses and hotels and travelling in the greatest comfort, I have absolutely no use for an ascetic life or cheap clothes or high-minded discomfort or a pure soul smelling of poverty—not I ... I'm really not lying—why should I lie?—when I say I'm madly interested in your climb. And very very amused.'

He had had time to become cold all through. 'I may manage to go on climbing, but I shall never get more pleasure from anyone.'

She laughed. 'You're extremely intelligent. But there are any number of intelligent young men about. Your unique talent is for seduction. I'm not talking about your looks—you know all about them. But about your diabolical talent for getting under the skin to the nerves—rather the way a stain spreads. . . . But I warn you, my sweet—don't start seducing out of vanity—either you'll hurt a really innocent woman very badly, or you'll rouse the hatred and resentment of another sort of woman whose own vanity you've damaged. Then, ouf, watch out!'

'Is there anything you don't know about me?' he said dryly.

'A great deal—or I shouldn't have been so astonished about that poor girl, Livvy.'

He ignored this.

Leaning towards him, she stroked his cheek lightly. 'I'm interested and amused, and I like you. That's not the only reason why I want you as a friend.'

'Do I stay in the firm?'

154

'Of course!' She stared at him with genuine amusement. 'How naïve you are still! We took you on your merits—only on your merits. Both Frederick and I think highly of you—you're going to be extremely useful to us.'

His smile couldn't have been more brilliantly youthful and candid. 'I'm glad. I thought you'd decided to get rid of me.'

'Only in one capacity! How many more times must I tell you that I really like you? I like your very peculiar form of honesty. You don't tell *yourself* lies about your ambitions or the unprincipled way you use people. In that way you're honest, and no fool. I don't disapprove of you a bit. I simply move myself out of harm's way.... And now, my darling, I must turn you out. I need a little time to draw breath before dinner.'

He was in no state to go peaceably back to Lowndes Place. The torment of impatience in his nerve-ends and muscles started up again when he was outside in the icy streets. He would have given a fortune to be allowed to stay with her and work off his intolerable relief, humiliation, anger. Even to be able to insult her would have done a little to help him. He was striding aimlessly up Bond Street between the closed shops when he caught sight of Sarah Bernard crossing the road towards him between a double line of cars. She saw him in the same instant, and lifted her hand.

He stood in front of her. 'Where are you off to?' he asked curtly. 'Wherever you're going, don't—have dinner with me instead.'

'Nowhere,' she said, laughing. 'I was going home.'

He turned her round and took her to Scott's to sit at the counter and eat oysters. She was gay, and took the responsibility for the evening entirely on her shoulders, talking without waiting for him to talk to her. She was richly warmly carelessly attractive, and he felt no fear that she would want to burden either of them with fine sentiments. Towards the end of the meal, he said,

'Must you go home?'

'Yes.' She hesitated only long enough to smile at him. 'You can come with me and I'll give you another drink. I live alone.'

She lived, he found, in a minute flat behind the British Museum. He found, too, with the least delay, without having to go through any sentimental hoops, that he had been perfectly right about her; she made love sanely, violently, gaily, with an enjoyment as great as his.

CHAPTER 18

THAT Chatteney did not want to have done with his memoirs was very obvious—and what could be more natural? Why shouldn't he cling to them? Once they are irrevocably out of his hands, thought Stephen, he might as well step into the grave and pull the stone down over himself. Imagine a life with nothing in it except his wife's railing tongue and the afternoons in Marion Street with Mrs Duquesne, an old empty man sitting in his dry bones for an hour beside an old woman who can't now be anything to him but a voice. He needs them as another might need God or a moral passion, to keep his blood moving.

He was not, in any real sense, working on them. Throughout the winter and now the spring—five months— he kept them on his desk, changing a word or a colon, adding a paragraph. Stephen came to the house twice a week, in the morning, and did what recopying there was to do, and listened, without risking comment, to Chatteney speculating about the number of months or years he would be able to keep the manuscript under his hand.

'Mustn't be found dead with it,' he said with a fine smile. 'She would be able to play her last trick on me.'

This morning—Monday, May the 4th—Stephen had spent less than an hour with him. He was on his way out when Lady Chatteney called him into her room. She had been watching for him through an open inch or two of door.

'Tell me how you think my husband is,' she said at once. 'I'm anxious about him.'

She had become more lively as Chatteney dwindled. To-day for some reason she had twisted round her neck, shrivelled to a bundle of cords, what if it were real must be a fabulously valuable necklace of pearls and small emeralds, and painted her mouth thickly with dark nearly violet rouge. In spite of the sun pouring into the room, every window was shut—for Simon's benefit. He had become an invalid dog, old and always ailing, a repulsively misshapen object swaddled in wool. At the sight of the young man, he showed all his decaying teeth in a malevolent sneer, then whimpered pathetically.

'My love, my angel, my child,' Lady Chatteney murmured, stooping over him. 'Where is the pain?'

'He strikes me as very tired,' Stephen said.

'I'm afraid so. I'm afraid I shall soon be alone. My husband has no feeling for him—and very little for anyone else.'

'It was Sir Henry I was talking about.'

She sat up. 'Oh, you think he's tired?' she said quickly. 'He won't see Benham. What am I to do?'

Which obsesses her more? Stephen wondered. To possess him alive, or to possess his memoirs when he is dead?

'He really ought to see his doctor.'

'I know,' she said feverishly, 'I know ... *And the memoirs* ... You're so good, so sensible, I look on you as a dear friend ... Is there nothing we can do about them? I feel that time is getting cruelly short. That is, in this world, and I don't expect to get any great pleasure in the next from their publication—when it happens.'

'We can hope he'll go on revising them'—he had been going to say: until he dies—'for a long time. His mind is still young. And he lives quietly. Does he still go to the Athenaeum?'

'Every day.'

'That's splendid.'

'Don't desert us, will you?' she exclaimed. 'Go on coming here.'

'As long as you need me,' he said gently. *As long as the manuscript remains where I can keep a finger on it.* 'But I shan't be able to come next week or the week after. I have a fortnight's leave due me and we're going abroad.'

'Oh, where?'

'Lugano. Livvy needs a holiday, and later will be too late.'

'Ah, yes'—she smiled, an avidly female smile—'how is the dear girl?'

'Thank you. Very well.'

He left the house with intense relief. Its atmosphere of old age and old scorched ludicrous passions suffocated him. If he were not obeying a precise order from his new employer—'Don't give Chatteney up until the last minute, look on your visits to him as part of your job here'—he would have dropped all such wild hopes as he had of getting the memoirs, and let the old man find another copyist.

It was a clear warm day, stretching itself to infinity

158

under an immense sky not at the moment in use—not an aeroplane, not a cloud. The young leaves of the plane trees blandly promised everything, even a fine summer. He felt an access of gaiety, as wild as his hopes.

In the office that afternoon, Frederick Hyde came in and congratulated him sardonically on his handling of Miss Brand. Smiling, rolling a pale predatory eye, he said,

'Anyone who can bring off the moral seduction of dear Cordelia has earned his stripe. It may not be lasting, but the new agreement on the old terms is signed and delivered, this morning. You're no longer a learner.'

He went out, slamming the door. Looking up from her typewriter, Sarah Bernard said a little dryly,

'What did I tell you? You haven't had to wait a year. But you don't know as much about the slippery side of the business as old Dugdale's little finger. And go carefully with Mrs Hyde. She doesn't love anything or anyone more than getting her own way. Don't think you can risk contradicting her when she's in the wrong—it will be your first mistake. When she needs putting down, her husband will do it—brutally, like the bully he is.'

He stroked the back of her neck. 'When you see me making an indiscreet ass of myself, tell me. I'll take your word for it.'

'Ah,' she sighed, laughing a little, 'you. You have a use for all of us, haven't you?'

He made the answer she expected.

On his way home, he noticed in a little shop full of miscellaneous junk a tiny ivory figure, old yellowed ivory, not much more than an inch high, of a young woman who might be a mediaeval peasant, and might or might not be pregnant. On an impulse he went in to ask the price. It cost more than he expected, but he bought it.

One thing his marriage had done for him was to reveal—

159

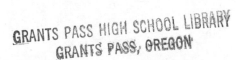

very much as invisible writing shows up when you know the trick—the web of useful cousins in his wife's world: the cousin who has a house to sell cheap, the old cousin who offers to pay school fees, offers a useful loan, offers a job as farm bailiff, apprentice financier, and the rest of it and the rest of it. It was, as they say, a world. On its way out, but not yet entirely gone or toothless.

A cousin by marriage had owned the house Livvy's grandmother bought for her, in a quiet dusty cul-de-sac in Chelsea, a small house, with a minute courtyard in front. Mrs Green, the elderly woman who had been a servant in the family for uncounted years, lived some few streets away, and came in to do the heavier share of Livvy's housework.

When he reached the house, Mrs Green was in the courtyard, bending over the patch of mint she had planted herself. She answered his friendly Good-evening with one a great deal more reserved. He had never managed to make friends with this stupid country-bred good-natured all-but-illiterate old woman; she ironed his shirts, asked about his favourite meals and cooked them, mended his socks, and kept him at a bleakly respectful distance. Her indifferent hostility irritated him.

He found Livvy in the sitting-room, half kneeling in a corner of the sofa, and gave her the tiny figure.

'For you,' he said. 'She reminded me of you.'

Turning it over on the palm of her hand, she said in a strangely absent voice,

'Pretty.'

He watched her moving quickly about the room, clearing the table of papers and books scattered over it: she was still, with a stubbornness that touched and amused him, working through the books she would have been reading had she stayed at the School. She was in the eighth month

160

of her pregnancy, she did not look to him seriously deformed by it; no one, he reflected, would be disbelieving or surprised to be told that she had only reached the sixth. So far as he knew, she had not had to suffer any of the ills pregnant young women are supposed to go through. But in fact, he knew almost as little about her everyday life as if he were not living in the same house with her. She was self-contained and evasive in the way of a good-tempered boy, sheering away from questions. From the very first, it had never been anything but very easy to share a house with her, as easy as if she had been his sister. Perhaps easier. He came and went as he pleased, with no obligation to account for his movements. A sister, Tarry herself, might have felt some curiosity about his habits: might, when he spent the whole night with Sarah, have looked a question. Livvy never did. Now and then he wondered whether she even noticed that he was not always in the kitchen at eight o'clock making his breakfast coffee.

'Our plane tickets have come,' she said suddenly.

'I hope it will be all right,' he said, frowning, 'I hope you really can stand the journey.'

'Of course I can.' She arched her back, smiling. 'I'm terrifically strong, stronger than any of the girls I know.'

Their plan—it was entirely hers—was to spend ten days in Lugano, then travel by the direct Rhine express train to Baden-Baden, arriving there in time for the birth. 'Why Baden?' he had asked when she explained her scheme to him. 'Do you really want your child to be born in Germany?' She shrugged her shoulders. 'But why not? What's wrong with Germany? Since he can't be born in England, Germany is as good as anywhere else. The point is that it's the one country my grandmother will never for any reason on earth come to. She wouldn't come if I died there. She hates it, and Germans—she calls them Huns. So that it will be perfectly safe to write and tell her that I have had a seven-months child.'

'Very clever,' he said.

'Oh, d'you think so?'

Watching her swift neat movements, and thinking about the ingenuity with which she had worked out her scheme, he reflected that she was *not* crafty. Not shrewd and intriguing. With a self-control far older than she was, and with the greatest directness and simplicity, she had set herself to save an old woman pain by deceiving her.

No doubt, too, she hoped to deceive the child's father.

At this moment, he had a maladroit inspiration.

'It was Cadnam-Plessy, wasn't it?'

She turned on him with a flash of rage. 'Don't ask me questions,' she said contemptuously. 'You have no right. And you promised.'

He felt very lightly ashamed, even remorseful. 'I'm sorry, Livvy,' he said gently, 'I really am sorry. Forgive me. I don't know why I said that. I was thinking that you looked much too young and thin for this business.'

To his stupefaction she burst into tears, crying not like a woman, but like a very young child, blindly and hopelessly, streaming tears, and sobs broken by hiccups. He took her in his arms—for the first time—stroked her hair and patted her back as if she were choking. For a minute she allowed him to do it, then drew herself away. Drying her cheeks with the back of both hands, she managed to smile at him.

'Goodness, what an idiot,' she stammered. 'It must be his fault'—she always spoke of the child as 'he': it seemed never to enter her head that she might have a daughter—'I suppose. Do you know, I couldn't understand anything I read this afternoon, not the simplest sentence. You wouldn't think it would have that effect, would you?'

Before he could say anything, she turned and ran out of the room.

CHAPTER 19

H E admitted to himself, painlessly, that there was an absurd side to his happiness. Waking in his bedroom in the Baden-Baden hotel, he lay for some minutes considering it, its three large french windows, its discreet luxury, from white-painted panelling, long wall-glasses, immensely thick carpet, splendid bathroom: he had left the shutters folded back when he got into bed, and the curtains open, and ceiling and one wall rippled with sunlight and the shadows of branches. His senses responded like a cat's to this comfort, exquisite. Absurd to enjoy it so avidly? Perhaps. But he could not imagine a day when he would cease to feel this triumphant energy starting up in his body at the touch of wealth. When he thought of his bedroom in Dax, only one year ago, he felt better than satisfied with himself and his progress.

For some reason, at this moment, the dusty image of little Dorrit, almost weeping with disappointment in him, came into his head, and he laughed aloud.

He got up, shaved, bathed, and then—it was nine o'clock —rang up the clinic. Waiting for an answer, he thought briefly that it was—for Livvy herself—a little sad that he had not thought of her the instant he woke. Someone should have had her in mind. The child might very well have been born during the night, while he slept soundly.

A female voice speaking slow precise English told him,

'No. It is not yet. But all makes well. We shall telephone to you the news when is time. At once.'

Later in the morning—he had stayed in his bedroom with, at last, a feeling that he was involved in this birth. What if it went wrong?—he stepped on to the balcony and stood looking over the gardens of the hotel. Several long chairs, red and yellow, were scattered about the lawns. His room was on the first floor and he could see clearly the details of certain grotesque figures stretched out on them. Immediately below him, an elderly man, half-naked, stomach ballooning upwards against his shorts, feet in leather sandals pointed stiffly left and right, long fleshy lips folded round a cigar, stroked tenderly the hairs of his chest. A young woman, very young and quite lovely, with a slender body and a head of smoothly dressed hair, came out of the hotel, walked past this swollen effigy and laid her hand on a chair standing fifteen or twenty yards away. Instantly, as if he had been stung, the man sat up, pulling the cigar from between his lips, and spoke in a harsh loud voice.

Clearly the young woman did not understand German. She stared at him in dismay, as at something against nature. He began again, in barely intelligible English, his eyes starting, an angry old frog. 'You have the chaise of my...'

Without waiting to hear the rest, Stephen got himself out of the room, down the double flight of shallow stairs and into the garden so rapidly that the German was still in labour.

'You've taken Wotan's wife's chair,' he said, smiling. 'Let me get you another.'

'Oh,' she cried, 'I'm sorry.'

Her voice was singularly clear, its light American accent rounding and defining each separate tone.

'Come at once, politeness won't save you,' Stephen said.

He led her to the other side of the lawn, to a couple of chairs placed under one of the magnificent lime-trees. As she fell into the chair—fell was hardly the word for so practised an action of legs and arms—he took hold of the other.

'Is this by bad luck the chair of your husband, fiancé, brother, aunt?'

'I don't have any of them. Please sit down.'

It was the first time he had had under his eyes an example of that flawless American elegance which makes all others seem the work of an apprentice. From head to small narrow feet each joint, each line, flowed into the next to form a perfect whole: in particular, her legs took away his breath; they were very long, very slender, not a milli-metre too long or too thin, narrowing suavely into ankles of exquisite fragility. A miracle of breeding and rearing, no money spared, no care omitted, no use foreseen.

He drew a careful breath and said,

'Did you know you were in enemy country?'

'I did not,' she said, smiling. 'When you came I was starting to run for my life. I just knew he was insane.... Are you English? Yes, of course you are.'

As well as elegance she had been taught, probably in the cradle, that she had a duty to be agreeably talkative. In the course of talking agreeably she told him that she was here with her father, who was meeting, secretly—hence Baden-Baden and not, as it would otherwise have been, Dort-mund—the head of some great German firm that was mak-ing a new kind of light metal.

'He's buying it or merging with it, or something of the sort,' she said lightly. 'It's terrific, and I know nothing at all about it. He brought me over with him so that he could tell them in Pittsburgh: I'm taking my daughter to Europe....

I hope you're not a spy or a journalist—you don't look in the least like either one.'

'No.' He smiled at her under half-closed eyelids. 'Mine is a genuine holiday—or was until yesterday. Now I'm sitting here waiting for a telephone call from the clinic where my wife is having a baby.'

'Here? In Germany?'

'Two months ahead of time,' he said. Might as well rehearse my lines, he thought coolly. 'We were on our way home.'

She simulated to perfection a well-bred young woman moved to the liveliest interest—or was it genuine? Smiling with wide eyes, she said,

'You must be very very excited. It's a wonderful story. If daddy and I weren't flying back to New York this afternoon, you might allow me to . . .'

She stopped. One of the young clerks from the hotel desk was hurrying towards them. He spoke in German, a sentence of which Stephen understood only the word *telefon*.

'Forgive me, I must go,' he said quickly.

Following the clerk across the grass, he surprised himself by his feeling of tension. After all, I'm fond of the poor child, he thought; I'm responsible for her, I don't want anything to go wrong.

Nothing had gone wrong. The same dehumanised female voice said,

'I shall tell you—you have a son.'

As he came away from the telephone, he caught sight of the American girl crossing the hall as swiftly as her exquisite legs would carry her. She stepped into the lift and was swept off. He felt a pang of disappointment. She could have waited to hear. What a superb show of interest and friendliness these people put on, he said to himself, and totally meaningless.

166

He asked the clerk for her name. Ancel. Fräulein Virginia Ancel.

In the early evening, walking from the hotel to the clinic, he had the impression, at every step, of brushing past the outstretched fingertips of another century: this path following the edge of the narrow river had looked no different to Turgenev when he sauntered along it: except for an air of well-bred shabbiness, of an old actress serenely refusing to notice that she was being neglected, the town itself, at least here, had not changed since that time, there was a light scent of resin and acacia in the air, and the trout nosing into a shallow fall of water below a foot-bridge were the great-great-grandsons of those Turgenev glanced at as he passed. A race of stolid dowdy Germans had taken possession of the paths and the Casino—no other change.

Livvy surprised him by her air of untouched glowing health. He had brought yellow roses; she thanked him and gave them carelessly to the nurse, and asked her—it was more an order—to bring the child to show him. Sitting up against her pillows, she looked very young and triumphant —transfigured by triumph. He had not expected this. It amused him a little, and he felt relieved of any real responsibility for this radiant young woman. He said gently,

'I'm thankful it's safely over, I was very worried.'

She brushed this aside. 'That's kind of you, but there was no need. I told you, I'm very strong.'

When another and older nurse came in carrying the child and said, 'For three minutes, not more. It is the rule,' she seemed to forget that she had wanted him to see it. Looking down at the tiny swaddled body in her arms, she became instantly absorbed and as distant from him as if he were totally a stranger. He glanced at what he could see, a minute face, closed eyes and tightly-folded colourless lips.

'He seems all right,' he murmured.

Without looking up, she said, 'The most remarkable thing is his nose—practically all babies, the nurses say, are born with a shapeless blob, but as you see, his is perfectly formed already.'

It was true. He had her grandmother's equine nose, and at this moment, opening his eyes, he focused on Stephen for an instant a sharp glance alarmingly like Emily Grosmont's. My God, thought Stephen, what a family; even its bastards fall into line.

The nurse came in to take the child and told him that he could stay with his wife another five minutes. Livvy's glance, following her child out of the room, came back to him with a visible effort.

'You've been very patient with me all these months, Stephen. Don't think I'm not grateful. I seem to have been taking your kindness for granted—I don't really, but there's nothing I can say except I hope it hasn't been too bad, I mean you're reasonably happy, aren't you, and doing what you like?'

'We're managing splendidly,' he said lightly.

'Then that's all right.... Remember—you needn't stay married to me a minute after it gets to be a bore, or a hindrance of some sort.'

He bit back an unwise sentence about his having served his purpose, and said, 'Do I bore you?'

'No.' She gave him a frank glance. 'I hardly ever think about you.'

'Well, now you can think about your son,' he said, laughing. 'Do you realise that I shall have to telephone to your grandmother this evening?'

'You'll do it very well,' she said absently.

In effect, he had no need to use any diplomacy. He expected a blast of fury—that a member of her family should

168

have had the disloyalty and bad manners to be born in Germany—or uneasiness about a seven months' birth. What he had never expected was to be treated with warm affection.

'My dear boy, my dear dear Stephen, no, I'm *not* anxious. If you weren't with her I should be, but I have complete confidence in you. I'm delighted you have a son— I should have doubled Livvy's allowance in any case, but for a boy I shall do it with real satisfaction. And tell me, which of you is he like?'

'He's the spit image of you,' Stephen said, 'nose, eyes, even his expression.'

She laughed. It was an extraordinary sound to come from that iron throat—almost a girl's laugh.

'You'll stay until she can leave the clinic.' It was an order, not a question.

'I should like to, of course, but my leave is up tomorrow, I shall have to get back....'

'Nothing of the sort. I forbid it. If you feel embarrassed, I'll go up to town tomorrow and speak to Frederick Hyde. I knew him when he was a little boy, his grandfather was one of my grandfather's agents. There will be no trouble there.'

For a moment after he put the instrument down, her strong arrogant voice went on echoing in the room. Old devil, he thought mockingly. The disrespect was deliberate. He liked her, but arrogant old women—if it is not possible to ignore them—should be mocked.

His reflection in one of the long looking-glasses smiled at him with insolent confidence. Stretching himself, he felt all his muscles as smooth as a young animal's. What a day, what an evening, what warmth, what sun!

He thought devoutly of the dinner he was going downstairs to eat, and with a moment's light regret of Miss Ancel's legs, now at the other side of the world.

CHAPTER 20

THE day after his return to the office, he was summoned to
Mrs Hyde's room. Her secretary was with her when he
came in; she sent the girl off and held out both hands to
him, with a warmly brilliant smile.

'Congratulations, my dear.'

He lifted his eyebrows. 'Thank you. On ... ?'

'On your son, of course. How is Livvy, and where is she?'

'When I left her—sunning herself in the Black Forest.
She was ten days in the clinic, after that I took her to a spa-
hotel in the Forest, to stay a month. I shall have to fly out
there to fetch her—if you'll let me.' He paused, and said, 'I
can't tell you how grateful I am to you for letting me stay
in Baden the extra ten days, her grandmother is capable of
anything.'

She smiled again. 'My dear boy—one's first child! I long
to see it. Which of you is he like?'

'He's very like Lady Emily.'

'How lucky! And how lucky that you were in a civilised
country and not in some barbarous French or Spanish
village. These premature births can be tricky.'

He would not give her the satisfaction of letting her see
that he knew she had guessed the truth. He said calmly,

'Lady Emily doesn't regard Germany as a civilised
country....'

The desk telephone interrupted him. Mrs Hyde
frowned. 'I told them not to put calls through.... Yes, yes,
who...?' Her voice changed. 'Mary. Yes, my darling,
yes ... I'm so sorry ... Are you sure? ... No, that's utterly
unimportant. Get well....' Laying the receiver down, she
said, 'That was Mary Duquesne. She was going to lunch

with me, and she has 'flu—very mildly, she says, but she won't risk infecting me. Mercifully.... Is that still going on—she and old Chatteney?'

'So far as I know.' He knew it was, because, only the evening before, when he telephoned Tarry, he had asked her whether 'the olds' were still coming to the house.

'Poor old things,' Colette Hyde said, smiling. 'What an extraordinary affair. I'm sorry for them.'

'Why?'

'Oh'—she lifted her hands—'to be reduced to meeting each other in some sordid room. A man who has lived *his* life, and had every kind of amusing brilliant affair.... When do you see him next? And what about the memoirs?'

'The day after tomorrow.... You know, you're wasting your pity. He's absolutely certain that he's going to survive as a great writer, greater than any of the other great figures—Churchill!—of his time. Whatever he and his Mary Duquesne talk about, you can be certain it's not her or her feelings.... I've wondered occasionally whether one couldn't get at him through her in some way.' He hesitated, not certain how far he could go. 'If she knew—or if he knew—that they'd been found out....'

'What do you mean, Stephen?'

He made an evasive gesture. 'Once the script of the memoirs has been deposited in the British Museum, nothing can be done. They're out of reach. But until then ... If anyone can persuade him, perhaps she can. If pressed.'

She had not taken her eyes from him as he spoke. For a moment she said nothing. A curious expression, half ironical, half sad, came into her face.

'I'm very glad I knew you a year ago,' she said lightly. 'You've progressed a great deal in worldly experience since Dax, but you're less—oh, not less beautiful, my dear—but

171

less lovable. The'—she laughed—'the madly attractive young man, rather touching with his *airs de loup*, is hardening into a strategist. It doesn't make you less likely to get what you want—on the contrary! But I shouldn't now be so ready to fall into your arms.'

An insolent retort was at the end of his tongue. Prudently he rejected it.

'Then I have every reason to be thankful to Dax.'

She laughed again and said affectionately,

'Go away and go on. I told you—I'm madly interested in your progress.'

Two days later, in the library in Lowndes Place, he copied the last paragraph of the memoirs for the last time. Watching him, Chatteney said idly,

'How many times have you typed that page?'

'I hardly know, sir. Ten? Twenty? Are you sure this is the end?'

'Quite sure. I really can't tell you why I've come to a stop.' He was speaking with indifference and a trace of hauteur. 'The other night—while you were abroad—a spring in my brain suddenly uncoiled. I felt it—and I knew it was the end, I couldn't make any more efforts.' He paused and went on with the same indifference. 'I imagine that dying will be a very similar sensation.'

Stephen chose his words carefully. 'At least you know that you have finished your work. Not like Proust. There's nothing for an editor to clear up.'

'Oh, as to that,' Chatteney said. He shrugged his thin shoulders. 'I have no doubt I might have gone on altering a word and sharpening paragraphs until the last minute. Admirable death-bed scene.... But—for some reason or other—I no longer want to.' A look of almost youthful malice brightened his face. 'It's really vanity, you know,

172

dear boy—I've told you that before. If I dared leave it to someone to hand over to the Museum when I die.... But I don't trust a soul—or, rather, I won't trust a soul with my monument. I want to see with my own eyes that it's safely locked up.' He chuckled. 'We old men—monsters of distrust and duplicity. And conceit.'

When Stephen gave him the finished page he scrutinised it, word by word. 'Not a comma out of place,' he said. He sighed. 'Put the whole manuscript back in the cupboard—I'll deal with it later.... Right. Give me the key.'

He ambled about the room for a moment, stood still, and took from his pocket a creased letter he must have read more than once. He read it through with a slight smile.

Stephen felt irrationally certain that it came from Mrs Duquesne—no doubt sent to the Athenaeum to warn him that she had influenza and couldn't come to Marion Street.

The door opened noisily. Lady Chatteney shuffled into the room, with a massacred face, arms out, like a decrepit Lady Macbeth.

'Simon is gone,' she said. 'I found him dead in his chair, twenty minutes ago, when I came in from the shops. I came in, and called: Simon. No answer. Good, I thought, he's asleep. I wasn't surprised, he sleeps most of the day now. I went down to the kitchen with my parcels. When I came back to my room I looked at him closely, he was lying there, exactly as he always did, his dear head on his paws, but he wasn't breathing. I touched him, he was still warm. He must have died alone, as I was walking home.'

Chatteney was still holding the letter open in his hands. Keeping his eyes on her, he slid it with a deft sideways movement under the sheets of blotting-paper on his table. Then he put his hand on her arm.

173

'My poor Renée,' he said gently, 'this is very sad. Where is he?'

'Still in his chair. What am I to do?'

'I'll come with you.'

Stephen waited a second, then lifted the blotting-paper to get at the letter. It was a single sheet of round large writing, straggling across the page in irregular lines. Without reading farther than *My darling Harry*, he pushed it into his pocket. It can't be left here, he thought; the old boy hasn't an idea how thoroughly she rakes through his desk as soon as he leaves the house.

On his way to the door a second thought halted him. To take it away and give it to Chatteney would be infernally awkward; it exposed him in a very curious light, knowing more than he ought to know. How the devil could he excuse himself for knowing that this letter was what it was?

But there was something more in his mind than genuine indecision—a muted excitement, like the involuntary tremors of an over-alert animal.

Biting his lip, he told himself: No, no, she's in too much of a state to go through her normal routine this afternoon. . . .

Folding the letter back under the blotting-paper, he went downstairs.

Chatteney was standing in a helpless attitude, long arms dangling, with an expression of ironical distaste. His wife had gone on her knees beside the dachshund; she was stroking it, and talking in a harsh tragic voice.

'Dear little Simon, dear dear little fellow. Look, Harry, he hasn't changed. I can't believe he won't be lying beside me this evening, and all the other evenings, watching me; I can't believe I shan't feel his warm soft paw on my face when I wake up in the morning.' A sob choked her. 'He's dead, and all the kindness, all the gentleness, the happiness, the meaning of my life has gone.'

Her husband, Chatteney saw, was completely at a loss and very bored. Now and then, surreptitiously, he glanced at his watch. At last he said,

'Renée, I'm sorry, but I must go.'

'Go? Where are you going?'

'I'm lunching at the Athenaeum—you've forgotten. This ... tragedy has driven it out of your head.'

'Yes, yes, I remember,' she said distractedly. 'Very well, go.'

'Stephen will stay and see to things for you.'

He hurried out of the room and a moment later out of the house. Idiot, thought Stephen, he didn't go back for the letter. . . . More than an hour later, when he was able to leave Simon's heart-broken mistress with the vet, he hesitated for a minute. Should he or should he not run upstairs to the library and remove the letter?

No, he told himself, frowning, no. It's not necessary.

Just as he was leaving her, Lady Chatteney said, 'Don't forget that you're dining with us this evening.'

He had forgotten, and groaned inwardly. 'Surely you don't want me.'

'Yes, yes, you must come. You'll be the greatest comfort I could have.'

More than once during the afternoon, when he remembered Mrs Duquesne's letter lying hidden—as well or as little hidden as a bird in long grass—in Chatteney's room, a gust of excitement sprang up in him. He did not allow himself to be conscious of it for more than a second. Nothing has happened, nothing will happen, nothing can, he thought briefly.

Since he came back from Germany, Sarah had been spending the night with him, leaving the house in the early morning before six. It was not usual for Mrs Green to come in time to prepare his breakfast, but she had done it once and might again.

Looking at the young woman as she cleared her desk, admiring the strong column of her neck—too thick, but a supple warmth between his hands—he thought impatiently that either he would have to do without her tonight or endure the discomfort of the narrow single bed in her flat. A better idea struck him.

'Why don't you have my key and let yourself in after you've had some dinner—there's nothing to eat in the house—and wait for me? I'll get back from the Chatteneys' as early as I can, before ten o'clock at the latest, and find you in bed, like a faithful wife. Will you?'

'Yes, why not?' she said, amused.

'You can leave the front door unlatched.'

He detached the key from his ring and gave it to her. Except for the cleaning women they were alone in the building. He had been working late, to make up for the morning. With a swift movement, he leant his cheek against the side of her throat and kissed the curve of her shoulder, pushing the stuff of her dress out of the way. She turned and held him. There was an ease between them, a complicity of the flesh, he had never known with anyone else. Is she becoming a little too necessary to me, he wondered shortly. And answered himself at once. No, no danger, no one is more necessary than I let them be, nor for a day longer than I choose.

'Very well, then ... until I come.'

He walked to Lowndes Place. It had been one of those rare days when, even in London, June demands its right to freshness and a sky like an opaque bubble. Now, at nearly eight o'clock, the bubble was losing its brilliance and an aeroplane that an hour ago would have been invisible, wiped out by the light, showed up on it like a dark insect. The air was warm and country soft. Walking slowly, he reached the house just as a cab stopped in front of it, and Chatteney began to lower himself from it cautiously. He took the young man's arm to help him balance.

The door opened before he could get his key in the lock. Bruegel looked at them with annoyance darkening her pale eyes.

'You're late, both of you. Weren't you told to be here at seven? If you weren't, it's not my fault, nor my fault that the paprika chicken is in rags. Please be quick now.'

'You're a bully,' Chatteney told her blandly.

He went along to the little cloakroom at the end of the hall, and Bruegel gripped the young man's arm in her hard fingers. In a flattened voice she said,

'Be careful now what you talk about, she's in one of her moods.'

'The dog?'

'I suppose so. Anything that upsets her as badly as that opens up hell, so don't say anything that will remind her she hasn't always been a ruined seventy-odd.'

'What did she do after I left?'

'Cried a bucketful and talked about the child who died. I put her to bed.'

He thought swiftly: She didn't find the letter.

He felt an involuntary stab of disappointment. His genuine admiration for Chatteney, even the sort of affection he felt for him, had its hindside of resentment. The old devil had had everything, every privilege. It would have been enormously—what?—satisfying to see him fall flat on his aristocratic nose.

Satisfying, amusing, exciting—what else?

Chatteney was in high spirits, his eyes very bright, his threadbare face full of mischief. He was talkative.

'At the luncheon today there was one man I haven't seen for more than thirty years. He has been immensely successful in everything he's done—not that he has done anything that will be remembered a month after his obituary in *The Times*, but he has chaired royal commissions, advised on the noblest sorts of project, dined familiarly with the royal family—several royal families—and is now directing I forget what, but it involves millions of dollars and a great deal of rushing across the Atlantic in jet planes. He treated me with such deference, such appalling tact, that I almost begged him to say aloud: My poor fellow, what a mess you've made of your life! I managed to hold my tongue, but when he was leaving, I suppose to climb into a jet, and pressing my hand warmly, I said: D'you remember telling me in 1930 that as soon as you had feathered a modest nest you would devote the rest of your life to—what was it?—some charitable labour? How did it turn out? ... The fellow had the grace to blush.' He cackled delightedly. 'I may have mismanaged my life, but I don't think I'm a humbug.'

His wife, who had made no pretence of eating, opened her mouth for the first time, to say,

'No. Only a sublime egotist.'

Leaning across the table, he touched her hand before, with a start of repugnance, she could pull it back.

'Yes, yes, my poor Renée, you know all about my egotism. But I take comfort—like the Pharisee—from the thought that I could have been worse. I don't mean evil men, Eichmanns and Himmlers, I mean the great and highly respected and totally unforgivable. I might have been a general and in the name of patriotism arranged for young men to butcher each other, or an atomic scientist and held that the freedom of the intellect required me to · invent a method of searing their flesh off a million of my

178

fellow human beings, or a militant atheist. Perhaps you're surprised that a confirmed sceptic—which I am—considers militant atheists as scoundrels? At one time it would have surprised me. But little by little I've come to realise that for all but a handful of highly intelligent people, life has no enduring meaning, none at all—and never can have a meaning. And if you convince these millions of ordinary men and women with their limited minds and decent instincts that there is nothing in front of them but a lifetime of repeating the same actions, office, factory, bed, a few years of not very exciting copulation, and years of making the best of an ageing body, with extinction at the end of it, no chance of a consoling hereafter, why you are an inhuman devil.... You'll notice how modestly I imply that my place is with the highly intelligent handful!'

The overcooked chicken was followed by a savoury. Renée Chatteney touched neither of them. Now and then, jerking her neck like a tethered animal, she moved her dry lips, rehearsing some phrase or other. She's a human crocodile, thought Stephen, a snapper-up of stray limbs. *Why* did he marry her? And why hasn't he left her?

Remembering the letter lying upstairs, he reflected that Chatteney's self-confessed crimes of egotism and vanity had been paid for already. To have been found out now, in this last innocent fugue—no, no, that really would have been devilishly unfair.

His sensations were all the livelier when—in the drawing-room, after Bruegel had set the coffee beside her and gone away—she drew the letter from her faded petit-point bag and held it up for her husband to stare at for a moment before thrusting it back.

'You see it? Yes, you may well open your eyes—*adulterer*!'

179

Chatteney said very quietly,

'Not now, my dear. We have a guest.'

'Stephen is a friend,' she said, 'and I need friends.' She turned to him. 'Eighteen years ago, the writer of this abominable letter gave an undertaking that she would refrain from meddling with my husband. *Shall not at any time hereafter or in any manner directly or indirectly disturb or interfere*—that was the agreement. You don't know her—a loose woman, without a shred of moral sense. She never had any at any time. A slut and a thief....'

'Renée,' her husband said, in the same gentle polite voice.

She made an extraordinary gesture, lifting her hands, fingers curved inwards. 'What else can you call a woman who robs another of a rightful possession, except a thief?'

Chatteney's manner became colder but not less patient. 'You might ask yourself, my dear, what to call a woman who regards her husband as a possession. . . . But don't let's inflict this scene on a third person—it's most discourteous.'

Reluctantly, Stephen got to his feet. As he expected, she said fiercely,

'Don't go away. I want you to stay. I want you to know what my life has been like and what I went through in 1946....'

'No doubt he knows all about it,' Chatteney said.

Stephen looked with grave kindness into her disfigured face. 'No, I know nothing about it. I would stay if there were anything I could do to help you, but... Let me come and see you tomorrow—or send for me when you want to see me.'

Scrabbling in the bag, she took the letter out again and held it under his eyes.

'Read it!'

He allowed his glance to move across the page, trying to give her the impression that he was reading, and Chatteney that he was not. A few phrases caught his eye—
'...*when I see you on Thursday ... no, my dearest, you certainly mustn't run the risk of letting the memoirs fall into Renée's hands ... We might, as you say, have the very end of our lives together, it's possible, but ... Dream dreams, my love, dream of one of those warm nights in Vence ... the scent of musk ...*'

'You see? You see the kind of cheap whore she is?' She put the letter away again. Without a change of expression she began to talk in a loud voice, shockingly high-pitched and raucous. 'I can't bear it, I can't bear the thought of her hands on you. My whole life since I knew you and her has been a hell I didn't deserve. I've been quixotically generous, I forgave you, I forgave everything, all your treacheries. But this—this is too much.'

During the last minute a change had come over Chatteney's face. A look of cruelty, cold, almost impersonal, wiped out its habitual serene courtesy. He said,

'In my experience, the only persons capable of searching blotting-pads for scraps of paper have been charwomen or underpaid clerks. And they at least did not indulge in hysterical scenes.'

He glanced at Stephen, a glance dismissing him in the least amiable way.

Opening the door, Stephen knocked against Bruegel. She was squatting against it, listening. Straightening herself with massive unconcern, she pushed past him into the room and closed the door.

Outside the house, the warm night struck him as deliciously fresh. He was as excited in every sense as if he had been drinking. He felt a twinge of sympathy for Chatteney —none at all for his wife—a very pleasant twinge. The situation was grotesque, not tragic—wildly richly comic. If ever I write about him, he thought lightly.

A part of his mind was beginning to ask coolly whether there were any nearer use for so full-flavoured a story.

Nothing that he could see at this moment. . . .

He had no intention of telling Sarah what had happened —it was too complicated and ticklish an affair to talk over with a young woman for whom, moreover, he had other much more pressing uses.

As he had hoped, she was lying in bed, ready for him. Her bare shoulders and arms gave off the warmth and somewhat pungent scent of a supremely healthy young woman. It exasperated his impatience.

'How horrible to grow old,' he exclaimed.

She was running her hands down the sides of his body, and he saw her smile. 'Do you feel old?'

'No. No, no.'

CHAPTER 21

A T intervals during the morning he tried actively to invent an excuse for calling at Lowndes Place. Not to know what was going on there exasperated him and made him uneasy. Whatever was happening, whether it were much or little, important or wholly unimportant, he wanted to know and have a finger in it. His mind circled round and round the situation, like a dog on a confused scent.

His indecision—he had not been able to think of a discreet reason for telephoning to either husband or wife— was settled by a telephone call from Lady Chatteney asking him to come.

'When?'

'Come this afternoon,' she said. 'Not later than three. I have an appointment at four o'clock.'

Now what? What was she up to? He arrived at a quarter to three, and Bruegel, who was standing in the hall when he let himself in—he had kept his key—told him curtly to go up to the library. He found Chatteney there, at his writing-table, nothing on it, not even the fatal blotting-paper. He might have been sitting there immobile for hours, over-large head sunk between his shoulders, a stone gargoyle. At the sight of the young man, a trace of animation came into his eyes.

'Ah, Stephen, I have something for you to do. I want ...'

A barely audible footstep on the landing. He stopped, listening.

His wife came in briskly. She was dressed to go out, in a long silk coat, black, and a black three-cornered hat, unsuitably rakish.

'I wanted you to come,' she said, without any preliminary greeting, 'to tell you that I am going to start proceedings against the writer of the letter you read yesterday—a Mrs Duquesne. It will be a painful ordeal for me, very painful, but I must at all costs—at any cost to myself—get rid once and for all of a woman who is still, even now, after all these years, determined to get my unfortunate husband into her hands.' Turning on Chatteney she said sarcastically, ' "Have the end of your lives together" is, I think, her charming phrase.'

'Your unfortunate husband ...' Chatteney began. He paused and went on in a dispassionate voice,

'My dear girl—think. How could I go away with her? At my age.' He lifted his hands, and let them fall again on the table. 'One says things ... mere day-dreams. ...'

'A court of law will know where to draw a line between

day-dreams and a breach of the agreement she made. Meeting her, planning to end your days with her ... *Where did you meet?*'

She was controlling herself, but her hands opened and shut on each other like small squamous jaws.

Chatteney looked at them, and looked at her, with an expression between curiosity and disbelief—much, thought Stephen, as he might have glanced at a freak of nature.

'I shall shortly be seventy-six, you are at least seventy-two, Mary must be close on seventy...'

His wife passed her tongue over her lips. 'She was seventy last week.'

'...the whole thing would be absurd, laughable if it were less humiliating—if you weren't determined to humiliate all of us. Are you?'

'I know what I'm doing,' she answered, 'and I know why I'm doing it. My conscience is very clear.'

'You'—he hesitated—'you really are an extraordinary woman. You're going to devastate this poor end of my life —and Mary's and your own—and you don't seem to have the faintest suspicion that you may be behaving foolishly or cruelly. Or that you might in any way at all be at fault.'

'I've been too magnanimous, too trusting,' she said coldly, 'that's my real, my only fault.'

After a moment, Chatteney said,

'You haven't asked this young man's opinion of your plans.'

It caught Stephen unprepared. For a moment, between embarrassment and anger, he felt the blood jerk through his temples. He steadied himself sharply.

Of the two, he thought lucidly, she's the stronger and more dangerous, she won't forgive me if I disappoint her. He ... he expects less—of anyone—and, in the end, cares much less.

184

She was looking at him with serene assurance. 'If you have anything to say, Stephen, say it.'

Deliberately, he gave her the smile he would have given any woman he meant to make love to. Proffered to an old woman, it was faintly impudent, but not the less grave, charming, tender. He bent over her. 'I understand your indignation so well that I needn't say so. And I needn't tell you that, whatever you do, I shall agree that you're justified. But there are two things you may not have thought over long enough—you're much too upright and impulsive and single-minded. The first is that you'll be severely criticised—by people like my grandmother-in-law, who won't see the purity of your motives—something I should hate you to have to face. And then—you've given your life to cherishing your husband's reputation—can you now, for any reason, expose him to'—he seemed to hesitate—'to a shadow on it? . . . Forgive me if I've vexed you.'

She smiled at him. 'Not at all. I know you want to shield me. But'—her smile became blissfully vindictive—'women of Mary Duquesne's sort are through and through rotten. She should be whipped.' She made her voice full and ringing. 'I know her very well, it may be that she's weak rather than wicked, I feel I mustn't shrink from anything that may save her from herself.'

This last phrase struck the young man as wholly devilish. He smelled sulphur.

She looked round her for her gloves. 'I must go now, or I shall be late for my appointment,' she said with energy.

Stephen held the door open for her. As she passed him, she gave him a friendly glance, very slightly condescending. It said: Thanks. I count on you to carry out *my* decisions.

'You did what you could,' Chatteney said coolly, after a moment.

185

'I didn't want to be forbidden the house.'

A gleam of irony came into Chatteney's glance. 'You must have a great deal of success with women.'

'I had none just now,' Stephen said in a frank voice.

Chatteney's wrinkled mask showed no emotion. 'Did you expect to? ... You know, there's something almost pathetic in the way a malignant growth behaves. It's as if a cancerous cell remembered that its job—its perfectly natural job—is to nourish itself, and so it goes on doing it at all costs to the body, quite certain that what it is doing is normal and proper. My wife struggles perpetually to keep up her role as wife, and in the process she destroys me and herself and other people—with the complete certainty that she is right.... Very very queer. And a little sad.'

The mask cracked abruptly. 'But, my God, to have brought this on a person for whom I have the greatest ... affection. It's intolerable, I don't mind being ridiculed and made a fool of myself—that's nonsense, I do mind, but I could stand it easily if she weren't involved.'

Drained of blood, his face alarmed Stephen. Physical and mere mental agony have much the same look, and he asked sharply,

'Are you ill?'

Chatteney leaned forward over the table, gripping the edge.

'Never mind that,' he said irritably.

'Let me get Bruegel ...'

'Certainly not. Don't interfere. Get out.... No, no, wait. I told you I had something for you to do. I want you to go and see Mrs Duquesne—I've written the address down for you'—he straightened himself and felt in his pocket—'Here. Ring her up. Go as soon as you can. Tell her the whole thing ...' Did he know he had groaned? 'My inexcusable carelessness . . . no excuse for bringing her letter into the house. Tell her—warn her . . .'

'You must let me send Bruegel to you,' Stephen said.

'No.' Chatteney waved his arm. 'I don't want her. Don't hang about—go, get on with it.'

CHAPTER 22

H E telephoned to Mrs Duquesne from the office.

'Yes, come at five,' she said, 'I should like to see you.'

She did not ask him why he was inviting himself to call on her; her voice, resonant, careless, accepted him as a close friend.

He was a few minutes late finding the place, a large Victorian house cut up into flats, but not late enough. The woman, as gaunt and ugly as the house, blackbrowed, with cheekbones like spatulas, who admitted him, was a foreigner. She opened the door of the large living-room and said slowly, repeating a lesson,

'Please sit here. Is out.'

Opening the door created a violent draught that blew papers off an ink-splashed table under the open window. 'I'll close it, shall I?' Stephen said.

'Please wait, is out,' the woman repeated in a defensive tone.

She went away, shutting the door. He gathered up pages in Mrs Duquesne's large unformed writing of what he took to be a novel: later he discovered that she made an uncertain income by translating from French and Spanish. The room was very large and high, with a great many untidy bookshelves, and very shabby, very dusty, the pervasive ingrained dust of old woodwork, old carpet, well-worn chair covers. It was also very agreeable, the cocoon of a friendly negligent soul.

At the end of three-quarters of an hour he felt certain he had made a mistake and come at the wrong time or on the wrong day. He was on the point of writing a note—no use to give the foreign woman a message—and letting himself out of the flat when he heard her voice in the hall. She came into the room smiling and pulling off a coat she threw on to a chair.

He looked at her with pleasure and affection, both sincere. Her large opulent body in its loose dress, large hands held out, large face, had an incomparable warmth and good-humour.

'I'm a little late. How nice to see you. Why didn't Pilar give you a drink? I'm so sorry—what would you like? I have sherry and whisky.'

She poured him a large glass of sherry and herself a tumbler of neat whisky, and sat down facing him. Few women of her bulk can afford to loll, but she could, with a mild dignity. She listened attentively while he told her what had happened, quickly and bluntly. He was instinctively sure that bluntness would please her.

Even when she was not smiling, the shape of the lines round her wide mouth, and its curve, gave her face an air of slightly ironical amusement, not unkind.

'I was sure you weren't coming just to see me,' she said. 'But how absurd. How difficult she makes her life—poor Renée. She has always seen herself living a noble life in a pure world, she has never noticed the real world—which is impure and not often noble—or a real human being.' Her voice, with its deep double note, caressed the other woman. 'Poor poor Renée—does she think anyone will take her story seriously?'

188

'She has your letter, Mrs Duquesne.'

She looked at him frankly. 'Ah, yes, the letter . . . I ought not to have written it. But there isn't the slightest chance of his leaving her, not the slightest. That part of it is utterly meaningless.' She half closed her eyes at him, like a mischievous girl. 'It's true, I've tried sometimes—since the case in 1946—to get him to leave her. Not very seriously—I knew it was hopeless. But there are moments when it seems ridiculous to go on as we are, getting older and older . . . So I *have*—in a sense—broken the agreement, and she can tell people I've wickedly injured her.'

Listening to her—to her voice rather than to anything she said—he felt for a moment free of the burden of himself. She was unafraid, uncalculating, as spontaneous as a child, wholly at ease in her ageing heavy body.

'It's beyond me,' he exclaimed. 'Why didn't he leave her?'

'Oh, my dear boy, it's all too involved, it goes too far back, for a simple answer. Nothing to do with men and women is as simple as you—you're too young—think it ought to be. Not that you're stupid. Far from it. Or simple.'

'Has anyone you are talking to a fixed age?' he said. 'You make me feel ten years old one minute and ninety the next —depending on the way you look at me.'

'You know, I'm much too old to choke myself on honey,' she said, amused, 'but I like it.'

He lowered his voice to a tone of calm intimacy. 'I know I oughtn't to ask you—but you're probably the only person in the world who knows the truth about both of them. *Why* did he marry her?'

'Ah! No, of course you shouldn't ask. But perhaps someone, if it's only a clever inquisitive young devil—I believe in the devil—ought to be told the story. We shall all three be dead so soon now, and no one will be able to think about us except as old and used-up, without the energy to behave like idiots.' The expression of smiling meditative irony on her face made it ageless. 'He never intended to marry her. He and I were crazily in love—it was in the war, 1916, I was twenty-two, an unbelievably immature twenty-two, but old enough to want to die when he broke off our engagement to marry Renée. He told me why: it was a shock and an eye-opener and—this is the amusing part—ignorant as I was, I knew exactly how it could have happened. He'd been to a dance where she was. And afterwards he slept with her. She'd been desperately in love with him for a year. A month earlier, when I told her we were engaged, she'd made a frightful scene before forgiving me ... so like her.'

'But...'

She laughed a little. 'But I can't have been half so innocent as I thought I was. As you see. I knew, I knew when he was telling me, that it had been perfectly natural for him to sleep with her, and I didn't dream of hating him for it. Which of them seduced the other seemed unimportant. The only important thing was that she had become pregnant. He *had* to marry her. He knew very well that it was a ruinous thing to do, but he wasn't hard or unkind enough to do anything else. Besides, you know, at that time ... It wasn't like it is now ... Her parents were very strict, her father was a landowner and a J.P., and her mother bred something, I forget what ... bloodhounds ... I didn't think it at the time, but I've thought since that it may have been a trick to get hold of him. And, of course, if it were'—she smiled mischievously—'Renée would find it the easiest thing in the world to convince herself that it was fully justified—I never knew her have any trouble about giving her worst, most selfish actions a crushing air of virtue.'

'My God,' Stephen exclaimed, 'but what a fool to go the length of marrying her.'

She looked at him with lively curiosity. 'What would you have done in his place?'

'Nothing that crippled me fatally.'

'I wonder,' she said lightly. 'He'd have been crippled morally if he had refused to marry her. And—after all, she was going to have his child—I said: Yes, of course you must.'

He let himself say what he really felt. 'You were both cowards, moral cowards. Anyone can make a false step—but he needn't go on to make a worse one, he can turn back, or bolt away to the side. Anything.'

'At whatever cost to other people?'

'I don't believe in self-sacrifice,' he said sharply. 'It's a deadly poison. Look what his sacrifice led to—it ruined his life. And yours.'

She shook her head. 'Ruined? No. No, my dear. Changed it. For the next twenty years he was very happy without me, and immensely successful. He might, if I'd been his wife, you can't be certain, but he might have acted more sensibly after he resigned in 1938. And there would have been no enticement case and no scandal. But probably no monument either!'

'You're arguing after the event,' he retorted. 'It would have taken courage to refuse to commit moral suicide. He hadn't the courage, he preferred to cut his throat.'

She laughed her almost silent laugh, a rich murmur at the base of her throat. 'Give me your glass.' She refilled it, and her own tumbler. 'I made a very happy marriage—less than a year later. I married one of my French cousins—everybody said he was a useless fellow, but we were extremely happy until he died in 1930. I didn't see Harry for

191

a long time. Not until after he resigned. We met that year
—abroad.'

'Will it shock you if I say that his account—in the
memoirs—of his resignation struck me as ... unconvin-
cing.'

She raised her eyebrows. 'I'm not shocked. But very surprised. I think you must be wrong about it.'

'I felt it wasn't the whole story.'

'Let's talk of something else,' she said, smiling. 'Have
you seen any of the photographs of him at that time?'

'No.'

She got up and rummaged at the back of a cupboard full
of books and junk of all kinds. 'This was taken in 1939, in
France.'

Chatteney was sitting on a backless stone bench in the
courtyard of a hotel, leaning slightly backwards, knees
apart, supporting himself on his hands: head thrown back,
eyes more than half covered by his abnormally thick deep
eyelids, arched nose a great deal more fleshy than it was
now, long mouth smiling nearly unnoticeably—a face of
extreme arrogance and sensuality.

'He's still arrogant,' Stephen commented.

'But not ...' she broke off and said mockingly, 'All passion spent, eh?'

'Turned to a pinch of warm dust—or lava.'

'We had eight years. Don't think I'm being sentimental,
but when he was with me he was quite unlike the man his
colleagues and his friends knew. He almost—almost—went
back to being a young man, the enchantingly alive gay
quick-tongued young man he used to be. That pose he had
learned—a parody of his greatness—dropped off, and most
of the vanity ... Until the war we met in France, nowhere
else—he adored France and travelling, and Renée hated
both. We were peacefully and madly happy—for eight

years. It's ironical that the first time we met in France again after the war, one year after, should have been fatal.'

'The enticement case?'

'Yes, of course.' Her deep muted laughter shook her body. 'It ruined him, completely, and it was absurd. Inexcusably absurd. Among other things she accused me of bribing him to leave her—I'd written him that a friend had left me a few hundred pounds and I suggested spending it on a month in France, in Vence. We had our month, but the careless fellow had left letters from me at home, including that one, and another in which I said something about his "unendurable marriage", and Renée found them. . . . She was right to be angry, but not right to make a public laughing-stock of him.'

'She's insane and insanely vindictive,' Stephen said with contempt.

'Poor Renée, no, no, she believed she was saving him from me. She has always been able to believe what she wanted to. The really terrible thing is that she loves him—it's a kind of love you mightn't recognise, and I find horrible, but it *is* love.' She smiled. 'I believe it's a very usual sort—a devouring itch to possess the creature you love. Her whole life with him has been wasted in the struggle. And, poor darling, she never possessed him, he has never given her the illusion of possessing either his heart or his mind. All she has been able to do is destroy him—one part of him.'

'She's a fiend,' Stephen said.

'My dear boy, she was *driven*. She has never been able to control herself and her passions. She expected too much of life. . . . And, don't forget, I had, you know, begged him to leave her. Before 1946 there was still time, we weren't too old. I had no hope he would do it, but'—her smile invited him to mock her silliness—'that didn't prevent my begging him. Oh, not often. I knew he never would leave her, she'd become a habit. He was fond of her, too, in a way—and he enjoyed the orderly comfortable life she gave him. Don't laugh. Comfort is important.'

'Habit and comfort,' Stephen said, 'my God. What a weak creature you make him out to be.'

For the first time she looked at him without kindness. 'Do you know what happened to the child?'

He recalled a violent scene when Renée Chatteney accused her old husband of murdering their child.

'Yes. It died.'

'Is that all you know? Then you know nothing.... They were staying with Renée's parents—he was three years old, a handsome little boy—and she had left him in the garden, playing round Harry's feet. After a time he wandered off, and Harry—he was trying to draft a difficult report for the head of his department—didn't notice. When he realised suddenly that the child wasn't in sight and went in search of him he found him lying in the basin of a fountain—he'd struck his head falling in and drowned in less than a foot of water ... You can imagine for yourself— no devil could have handed Renée a crueller weapon. And she used it. Talk to me of his egoism! It's nothing to hers.'

She stopped abruptly, and began again in her usual voice, slow and caressing. 'I don't blame her, you know.'

Is that true? he wondered. 'All the same I should have left her,' he said. 'I'm still astonished he didn't.'

'Well,' she drawled, 'he's not ruthless. He's self-centred, but he can't stand the sight of suffering. He'd do anything to avoid it—even stay with a wife he didn't much like.... You're too young, my dear boy, and you're a heathen. What you think of as weakness—now and then I thought it, too!—is also a very unfashionable piety. He had his poor reasons for staying with her, habit, comfort and the rest, but only an idiot or a very young man believes they cancel the... the goodness. He married her out of decency and pity, and out of pity and conscience he couldn't leave her, not even after she had ruined him with that ridiculous case.'

She smiled at him with half-closed provocative eyes. 'And after that, too, he had the memoirs to think of. He knew that with her he had an infinitely better chance of finishing them than with me. I'm quite certain that everything in Renée's house is gleaming with furniture cream and virtue. And look at this room'—she waved her arm— 'I'm absolutely helpless, you know. I can't boil an egg for myself! I couldn't have run his house for him. It would have bored me to death to try. And he always—from the beginning—always wanted order, a beautifully-run house, his library—and the rest of it. And—as he grew older— what *could* be more important to him than his monument? After the scandal it was his one last chance to survive as a great man.... Think, my child—what d'you suppose matters to a man of sixty?—he was fifty-eight at the time of the scandal. Do you imagine that his sexual life—*la petite secousse*—is as important to him as his life-work— supposing that he is very intelligent and has a life-work?' She laughed. 'Why even you, young bandit that you are....'

He smiled at her. 'All the same, you met again after 1946. He must have wanted both.'

'Not for years and years,' she said swiftly. 'Not until five or six years ago. He wrote me a tragic letter. It was a mood, only a mood, it would have passed, I knew that, but I suggested meeting him—at a place where we shouldn't be discovered. After that, we met regularly.... As he got older the gap between him and his personage—you know what I

195

mean—widened until he lost himself in it. He was only himself—and safe—when he was with me.'

Stephen was burning to know whether they were able to do anything in the 'studio' but hold hands. Has a man in his seventies erotic impulses, and can he act on them? It was his own infinitely remote old age he wanted to probe. He lacked the insolence.

'He's not safe now,' he said, 'he's humiliated and in despair.'

'About himself?'

'He certainly doesn't enjoy the idea of another scandal!'

'But is she serious?'

'You know her better than I do,' he murmured.

'Yes. Yes, she'll credit herself with the finest motives for causing us all black misery.' She spread her hands. 'But what can I do?'

'If you talked to her... I think that's what he hopes. It would be unpleasant for you.'

'I'll do anything,' she said easily, 'but it might only infuriate her to see me. Let me think it over.'

He got up, reluctantly. 'You must want to get rid of me.'

'I can't ask you to stay,' she said, laughing. 'Pilar is going out, and she has left me what I asked for, a little smoked salmon. Not enough for two people. You must come again —if it wouldn't bore you.'

Looking her in the eyes, he said,

'You don't need an answer, you know I'll come to see you as often as you ask me. You know, too,' he added, smiling at her, 'that I have no morals, no scruples of any sort. I have the appetites of a wolf, I didn't ask to be born with them—and if I'd been born able to satisfy them without making the most of my few assets no one would ever have noticed my want of morals. But there it is—and there I am

I admire you enormously, if you were a young woman I should be madly in love with you. Forgive me for saying so—with all respect.'

She patted his cheek. 'My dear young immoralist, she said warmly, 'I see no reason why you shouldn't be very successful and happy—you're beautiful and intelligent, and quite enough of a hypocrite—so long as you take care to want the right things for your age.'

'What does that mean?'

'A fifty-year-old seducer is only pitiable. By that time you should be wanting—oh, I don't know—perhaps another kind of power.'

'I'll remember that,' he said lightly.

CHAPTER 23

A NOTICE nailed inside the house door ran: This door to be kept closed after six. He was about to slam it behind him when he caught sight of Chatteney's face in the window of the cab slowing towards the kerb. Chatteney saw him at the same moment, and beckoned.

Lady Chatteney was with him. Stepping out as prudently as a cripple, she looked up and down the street of respectable houses with the slightly indecent curiosity of a tourist in a Naples slum.

'You here?' she said to Stephen. 'He sent you, I suppose. Or have you been here before?'

'No,' he said. 'Do you want me to stay with you?'

She looked at him with surprise. 'Of course.'

Insolent old brute, he thought. Chatteney had paid off the taxi, and taken her arm, with formal politeness.

He glanced at the young man. 'Do you know the way?'

'Yes. It's two floors, and there isn't a lift.'

The two double flights of stairs exhausted Chatteney; his face became the colour of clay, and the breath fluttering between his narrowly folded lips was raggedly uneven. His wife did not notice his state. She had eyes only for Mrs Duquesne, whose calm smile when she opened the door of the flat seemed, for less than a moment, to disconcert her. She recovered at once and said in a curt arrogant voice,

'Are you going to let me come in?'

'Certainly,' Mrs Duquense murmured. 'I'm delighted to see you. I haven't seen you for how many years? Eighteen? And that wasn't a very friendly meeting.' She glanced at Chatteney. 'The stairs tired you. Come and sit down.'

Behind their backs she gave Stephen a look of friendly, almost derisive complicity, and shook her head.

Renée Chatteney refused to sit down. She stared round the living-room with the same equivocal curiosity, drawing in her nostrils against the smell of impurity. 'So this is where you live!' She darted across the room and pulled open the door into a bedroom so small that the opened door exposed the whole of it, bed, ugly chest of drawers, curtained recess.

'Is this your bedroom?'

'No,' Mrs Duquesne answered. 'That is where Pilar sleeps—my maid. I sleep here.'

She pointed at the divan: the worn paisley shawl spread across it barely covered what seemed to be army blankets, a coarse grey-brown.

Renée Chatteney's chin worked in a stiff way, like a puppet's. 'So that's where the two of you lay and laughed about your cleverness in making a fool of me. Charming.'

'You're being foolish,' Mrs Duquesne said calmly, 'you

know very well that it wasn't like that. No one ever laughed at you. In any case, this is the first time Harry has been in this room.'

'Rubbish. I don't believe you. Why should I? You were always a liar—since the time you cheated me out of the essay prize. The others didn't know, but *I* knew you'd been to see Mr Grist in his room and wheedled the poor silly fellow into giving it to you.'

'Renée, what a grotesque idea,' Mrs Duquesne murmured, lifting her hands.

'You—you revolt me,' the other woman said. 'So does this room. I could have thrown him out, to live here, in this squalor, instead of spending my heart's blood to make him comfortable—so that he could do his work. Even you won't deny that.'

Chatteney moved in his chair. Stephen saw a look of ironical amusement cross his face, giving it for an instant the baffled air of an old wooden Punchinello. Perhaps the phrase about her heart's blood.

'My dear, I don't deny it, you look after him much better than I could, and always did.' Mrs Duquesne paused and said lightly, 'I'm sure you make him pay for it. How often do you remind him of his sins?'

The atrocious bitterness of Renée Chatteney's voice set Stephen's teeth on edge.

'Don't talk to me like that!'

'Forgive me.'

'You've always had everything—people praising your looks and your voice. And you look years younger than I do. You've been happy, you have three children.' Her eyes started like ferrets from her little head. 'And speaking French like a parrot—I suppose you're proud of doing it. As if it were any credit to you!'

Had the other woman been a sick child, Mrs Duquesne

could not have spoken in a gentler, more indulgent voice. 'We're so old now, so near the end of our lives. Is it really worth being angry with me for the short time left? Can't we finish in peace?'

'That's just what you'd like!' Renée Chatteney stammered. 'All your mean lies and his to be wiped out and forgotten. You've poisoned my days, my nights, and you want me to forgive you because you're too old to do me any more mischief. How vile you are. Oh, how vile.'

'Renée,' Mrs Duquesne said, 'I don't ask you to forgive me, I know you have a right to be angry, I'm only reminding you how few years we shall be alive—three? five? So near the end, my dear. Let's go out quietly.'

For a minute there was silence. Renée's face, shrivelled, pitiably made up, she had been in too much of a hurry to notice that one cheek had been rouged and the other overlooked, changed. Very oddly, as though something, another face—younger? less self-assured?—were trying to insert itself between the furrows. Her thin eyelids fluttered like two rags.

'You never liked me,' she said under her breath. 'You pretended.'

'You know better. I was very fond of you.'

'But you ... Why should I let you off scot free?'

'It's true,' Mrs Duquesne murmured, 'I'd like to save myself from another scandal. But only a little. I'm too indifferent to care very much. The one of us who will suffer is Harry. Do you really want that?'

'I...' Renée Chatteney's glance moved from her husband's face—he might not have been attending, so detached was he, his mouth wearily half-open, lower lip sucked inwards—to the young man's. Stephen looked back at her with a grave smile. Something like a flash of rage widened her eyes. She said violently,

'I suppose *you* admire her, too. And you can't see she's an old slattern.'

'Why,' Mrs Duquesne asked, 'do you want to humiliate an old woman before a young man who hardly knows her?' She stopped, and said quietly, 'My dear dear Renée, don't. You have as little reason to be jealous of me as if I were dead.' A gleam of mischief came into her eyes. 'It's not my fault that I can chatter French, and...'

'I'm not jealous,' Renée said. She thrust her lips forward in a smile. 'One isn't jealous of a sour smell in a room.'

She had gone too far. The blood rose in Mrs Duquesne's broad sallow face, obliterating its good humour and mysterious charm—why should charm survive loss of youth, loss of looks, the coarsening of line and texture?—hardening and ageing it.

'Why have you never forgiven me for the—the comedy that Harry loved me and married you?'

Glancing swiftly at Chatteney, Stephen had the sense that he had been effaced, reduced to a faint pencil mark, by the tension drawing the two women to each other. Does he feel it? Stephen wondered. His eyes were half closed, his face void of any expression but a distant incurious hauteur.

'He was happy with me for more than twenty years until you clawed him again,' Renée Chatteney said. 'And then eight years of deceit and fornication until I found out, and rescued him.'

'Until you'—Mrs Duquesne made a helpless gesture. 'Oh, I give up,' she said in her warmest voice, 'I can't be angry with you, you're impossible.' she stretched her arms out, pleading with voice and soft heavy body. 'There has been nothing in it for so long—only an old man and an old woman sitting talking to each other for an hour or two. Surely you can forgive it?'

'You've proved there's no trusting you! You made a

promise—you were forced to make it, but that's irrelevant, you made it and you've broken it. You can't be trusted. Admit that. Admit that you're dishonest and slippery— worthless.'

'Yes, yes, I admit it,' Mrs Duquesne said.

'And you're smiling about it! It won't do, my girl. I want more than words and sweet smiles.' She smiled herself, a twitch of long violet lips. 'I want you to sign a confession I can show people when I need to.'

'Need?' Mrs Duquesne shook her head slowly. 'No,' she said very gently, 'no, Renée. I'm helplessly in your hands, I know it, and you can punish me for sitting talking to Harry, and I don't mind going on my knees to you this minute and saying: I'm a wicked woman, please forgive me. But I can't stay indefinitely on my knees. And I can't let you run about London showing people some ridiculous document or other.'

'Very well. Just as you please. My lawyer tells me I have a case.'

'But you won't bring it,' Mrs Duquesne murmured.

Renée Chatteney laughed, a sharp sound, like a bone splintering.

'I most certainly shall. Don't make any mistake.'

'Must you make him ridiculous—again?'

'I'm doing it for him—to save him from you.'

During the last three or four minutes of this grotesque duel, the outline of a plan had begun taking shape in Stephen's mind, vague and disjointed, more ferment than plan, intensely exciting. The venom in Renée Chatteney's last words had the effect on it of an acid bath: with a sudden blazing clarity he knew that her hatred of her old friend, stronger than her devotion to her husband, stronger even than her craving to possess him, could be used. He felt himself smiling, and put his hand over his mouth.

In a curious sorrowful voice, Mrs Duquesne said,

'No, it's not simply that you have to see your cruelties as generous and surgical. You're angry because he got up from his knees and was happy with me—now and then.'

Renée Chatteney said,

'If it's the last thing I do, I mean if to do it would kill me, I'm going to make you see what you are.'

A sound made Stephen look at Chatteney. The old man was struggling to stand up.

'Let me help you,' Stephen said, going to him.

Almost inaudibly, Chatteney said,

'Help me to take her away, this is unbearably silly.' He raised his voice. 'Come, we must go,' he said curtly, 'it was no use bringing you here.'

His wife did not move at once. He turned his back on her and walked towards the door. Then she followed him, teetering on her high heels. Holding the door for them, Stephen gave Mrs Duquesne an intimate smile. She did not respond to it, looking through him at heaven knows what remote scene. A flicker of pity moved over the surface of his mind: he saw her lying on her side under the army blankets, her clouded eyes open, staring at—what *do* the old see at night?

Maddened by their slowness, he walked down the stairs a step behind the Chatteneys, she clinging with one emaciated blue-veined hand to the banisters: it was not until they were on the last flight that her husband brought himself to take her arm.

There were no taxis in this lost neighbourhood, and it was ten minutes before Stephen found one and got rid of them. He had a moment of pity for the old man shut up with his worst enemy, then forgot him.

He walked on slowly. A coldly lucid sensation of pleasure had taken the place of his excitement, the mental pleasure of fingering his chances of persuading one of the Furies to eat out of his hand. Renée Chatteney was no fool, not easy to lead and impossible to drive. She had the intransigence of the saints: nothing existed for her, neither pity, tolerance, nor respect for the other person, nothing but what at a given moment she chose to see as her sacred duty. None the less, he felt that he could handle her.

It struck him abruptly that in the last months, beginning perhaps after his first dinner-party with the Hydes, his first insight into that self-assured suavely arrogant world, he had changed radically. The young man wolfishly hungry for a brilliantly sophisticated life lived among the right people had not ceased to exist; he still wanted luxury, money to spend freely, expensive women, travel, but these were no longer all he wanted. Mrs Duquesne was right. What he wanted now was to have securely in his hands the means to compel people. A man like Frederick Hyde was not the sum of what he had, he was what he did, what he had the power to do. The majority of men and women are indifferent to power, real power. The power most of them crave is an illusion, the illusion of happiness. They don't want to have the powers of a god or a dictator.... I do, he thought. I didn't need an old woman to tell me.

He felt a sudden longing to talk to his sister. He had nothing he wanted to say to her. He wanted to hear her speak.

There was a telephone booth at the far end of the street, under a lamp-post. Hurrying to it, he dialled the restaurant next door to 41A, and when Kenneth answered asked him to fetch her to the telephone.

'Do you mind?'

'My dear, of course not,' Kenneth said, 'anything, I'll do anything for you, and for dear Tarry. Trust me.'

Waiting to hear her thin voice, he reflected coldly that

their mother must surely die soon, and release her. He had imagined a great many futures, but none that did not include her.

'Stephen?'

'Is that you, my love? Listen...'

CHAPTER 24

H E did not need to invent an excuse to telephone to Lady Chatteney, she rang him up the next morning a few minutes after he reached his office, and asked him to come and see her. She sounded worse than agitated. 'I need advice, I don't seem able to decide anything, I'm not myself, I must see you.'

I, I, I, he thought mockingly: the truth is you are all too much yourself.

In a comforting voice, he said, 'I'll come this afternoon. Don't do anything, don't fret, everything will be all right.'

'Oh, my dear Stephen, what should I do without you?...'

When he asked Mrs Hyde what, if he could lay hands on them, the firm would pay for Chatteney's memoirs, she looked at him with sceptical curiosity.

'Stephen, what are you up to?'

'Nothing you wouldn't approve. There's a chance, a fifty-fifty chance, of persuading him to publish. It's what his wife wants. Between us, we just might persuade him. But I must know what you would be willing to put down, she's hard-headed and we should be dealing with her, not with him.'

'You mean that you will be dealing with her.... Well, Frederick's not going to be here this week, he's still in

Paris, but we've discussed it several times and I can tell you now that an advance of £7500 would be an arguable figure. They may be worth more—even a great deal more—but that's what we're prepared to offer.'

'I have no idea at all what she expects. And I may be overrating the chances.'

'She's an old woman ...'

'Seventy-two or three.'

Colette Hyde laughed. 'Almost immune to flattery. Even yours, my dear.'

'I should like to land this for you.'

'It would be marvellous. Divine. But let me tell you this —Frederick is pleased with you, and with himself for bringing you into the firm. You don't need to do anything spectacular to establish yourself with him—it's done. If you can get hold of Chatteney's memoirs, it will merely confirm him that he knows how to pick his subordinates.' She laughed again, a little unkindly. 'I'm not sure whether he knows you so well as he thinks he does, there's a great deal *I* don't know about you and I know you far far better than my astute husband. Well, we'll see.'

He said gravely, 'You've been good to me, I'd like to please you.'

'That, my dear, came out of the copy-book.'

He stood up, smiling at her, and thought: She's beginning to show her age. A pity.

He felt gay, confident, and feverishly impatient, but he decided to let the old crocodile wait for him, gnashing her jaws, until four o'clock. As soon as he came into the room he thought that she had reached a pitch of anguished confusion and pity for herself when all he need do was to spread his arms and she would drop into them.

She began talking at once; her mouth opened and poured out her life-story, a torrent of bitterness, rage, self-justification. He had only to listen. He listened. Her capacity for self-deception was heroic; every action she had ever taken, every motive, appeared to her as righteous. She had been terribly wronged and none of it was her fault—except that she ought not to have been so trustful, so quixotically generous and innocent. The whole story could have been squeezed into one sentence: I was good, too good, I was betrayed.... Such an image of herself ought to make her very happy, but she was not happy. Her poor cankered little face was a mask of discontent.

At last she said,

'Haven't I done enough, forgiven them enough?'

'Yes, indeed you have,' he said warmly.

'And yet'—she wrung her hands—'perhaps I ought to make another effort. After all, he's a very old man. Perhaps I ought to drop this case against her. Tell me what *you* think, Stephen. Ought I to call it off? *Tell* me.'

He looked at her with half-closed gleaming eyes. 'It's difficult.... You have every right to punish her....'

'I don't want to punish anyone,' she cried. 'I want to do the right thing... You've seen her—what do you feel about her?'

'May I be frank?'

'Yes, yes.'

'She has a certain loose charm—how to describe it? I don't find her charming, but I can see that to some men she would be immensely attractive.' He smiled. 'Rather like a taste for well-hung grouse.'

She stretched her lips. 'Loose, yes—and not to be trusted.'

'Good heavens, no. But you knew that.'

Huddled in her armchair, she moved restlessly. 'The essential thing is to keep him out of her claws. Nothing else matters.'

'There is one other thing,' he said hesitantly. 'I don't want to alarm you—but d'you suppose there's a danger she might try to get hold of the memoirs? She does some vague literary work—I'm told. It would be a great triumph for her to get her hands on them. Heaven knows what she'd do with them, there are always unscrupulous publishers willing to cheat the ignorant.'

'I hadn't even imagined such a disaster.' Her eyes dilated. 'It would be an unspeakable ... desecration. Horrible. Oh, good God, we must get them into the Museum at once. Tomorrow.'

'Isn't that rather a counsel of despair?'

'But what else can we do?'

He seemed to reflect. 'Might it be an idea.... I'm trying to feel my way ... suppose you were to talk to him again now—he's in a false position and feeling guilty and unhappy—about publishing them? He might—isn't it just possible—be more inclined to listen to you?'

'He has never listened to me about them,' she said violently. 'About other things, yes. But about his work ... I've made great sacrifices for it, and my reward has been to be told nothing, nothing, nothing. What am I to think, except that he knows I should disapprove of them...? My poor boy, you haven't the experience or the background to judge them. *I* am the only person able to judge them and I'm not allowed to set eyes on them.'

Stephen said slowly,

'You were never before in a position to bring pressure to bear on him.'

'That's true! Yes, that's true. Let me think.' She got up, and began to walk about the room, hands pressed to her temples. A tongue of red appeared in both cheeks, licking at the wrinkles. 'If I were to bargain with him.... It's not— you can see for yourself—not a moment to be weak with him. Let me think, let me think.... If I offered to call off the case on condition that he handed the memoirs over to me....' She halted in front of him. 'Stephen. What do you think?'

'You're extraordinary,' he said in a low moved voice. 'I believe I'm intelligent, but—no, I couldn't have cut down to the bone, like that, in one single stroke.'

Pleasure ran across her face like a flame scorching the edges of a crumpled envelope.

'My dear, it's not intelligence. It's long sorrowful experience. My husband has a great intellect, genius, and less ordinary sense than a child of five. That's why her loose charm, as you call it, impressed him.' She struck her hands together. 'Since yesterday afternoon I've been praying for guidance—ought I to go on with the case? I got no answer from our Lord. I realise now that I was praying—one so often does—for the wrong thing, I should just have asked humbly *what* to do.... This is the answer—it won't be easy, but...'

'You have all the courage you need,' he murmured.

'Thank you, thank you, my dear.'

He smiled at her with love. It had been so much easier, he thought coolly, than he expected, that he had very little to congratulate himself on, except his foresight. His mind felt wonderfully lucid. Was this or wasn't it the right moment to talk to her about publishing? Better wait. She hasn't got the manuscript into her claws yet....

'I'm a little sorry that I shall be away for the next three or four days,' he said.

'Oh, no! Where are you going?'

Before he could tell her, the door opened. Chatteney looked at him with surprised displeasure, and said,

'I didn't know you were here.'

'He's here because I invited him,' Renée Chatteney said

dryly. 'I wanted a witness. Listen to me, please—I've come to a decision. I won't proceed with the case—although undoubtedly I could....'

Chatteney interrupted her. 'That's very good of you.'

She went on calmly. 'But on one condition. You'll hand the copy of the memoirs to me, to arrange for them to be published—in a proper form—as and when I decide. On that condition, I pass a sponge over the last eight years of deceit, but on no other.'

Chatteney stared at her in what might be disbelief, or it might be baffled distaste for the naked female.

'Impossible,' he said curtly at last.

'Why impossible?'

He made the gesture of brushing her out of the way. 'I can't hand them to you—or anyone else. You know very well what I intend doing with them.'

She shrugged her shoulders. 'Precisely. If that is what you feel—the case must go on.' Abruptly, she lost her precarious control of herself. 'I've had enough of sacrificing myself to no purpose; I've asked for less and less from you, year after year I've endured, waited, tolerated.... But at last, at last....'

Her voice was strangled by a sob of rage. Chatteney tried to take her hand.

'My poor girl....'

She struck his arm down. 'Don't try to placate me. I'm not your—your concubine.'

'What melodramatic nonsense,' he said. 'There are sillinesses I can't tolerate.'

With a convulsive effort, she recovered her calm. 'After all, I'm asking you to do what's in your best interest—for the sake of your reputation. I've always wanted you to be honoured in your lifetime, not fifty years after we're all dead. The time is now. Now.'

'Perhaps,' he said, 'you are really mad.'

'Is that what you hope?'

'Do you realise what you are asking? Publishing it now —it would have to be cut—mutilated. You wouldn't ask a painter to hack pieces out of his canvas and offer them to the public. Monstrous. Impossible.'

She turned on Stephen. 'You've had the privilege of reading it. I haven't. Would it be necessary to cut it.'

He hesitated. 'I'm not competent to judge.'

He endured the ironical glance Chatteney gave him.

'Of course it would have to be cut,' Chatteney said. 'Horribly mutilated.'

'Perhaps we could take legal advice,' Stephen said, with an air of extreme delicacy. 'That wouldn't commit you, in any way.'

The clay of Chatteney's face looked as though it were being broken up, fissured, from the inside: two fresh lines opened, starting at the flanges of the beaked nose and stretching to the jaw.

'I'd hoped that, when you saw Mary, you would realise that you have no grounds for jealousy.'

His wife lifted her scant colourless eyebrows. 'None?'

He said coldly,

'None that you, with your purely materialist idea of love, would admit as real. But I see, I see at last, that your wish to punish her—for everything, all the harm you've done her, including the minor harm you did in 1946—is the strongest feeling you have.' He paused. 'As hatred is more lasting than love.'

She remained unmoved. 'My poor friend, you're raving.'

He said nothing for a moment. His eyes were half-shut, and he was quite extraordinarily pale, as though his life had retreated to lean against the back of his skull.

'Very well. We'll let a lawyer look at it.'

He stumbled out of the room.

His wife turned to Stephen a face of pure exaltation. 'I think, yes, I think I've saved him.'

For all his own feeling of triumph and excitement, the young man shuddered. He had no taste for executions—and the hangman personified as an honourable sharp-witted intensely emotional old woman a little horrified him. He pulled himself together to listen to her.

'I'm relying on you for advice about publishing. Perhaps not advice, but ... I shall need to know what publishers to speak to about the manuscript, and what to ask for it. The actual sum is not important in itself, but, my father always insisted on this, what you don't pay highly for you don't appreciate. He was talking about pampered workers, but the principle is the same.... What publisher do you consider fit to publish this book?'

'The firm I work for, Frederick Hyde, is very much the best in London,' he said soberly. 'There really is no question.'

She glanced at him with a disconcerting coquetry. 'But you would have to say that!'

'Even if I weren't working for it, I couldn't give you any other advice.'

'Advice? My dear boy, it's not so much advice I want as the facts. How much is this unique book worth? Oh, I know, I know, a great work may not be of the greatest commercial value, but in this case....'

Surprised and irritated, he said, 'You should expect a sum of £5000 or £7500 as an advance against royalties.' Seeing that she did not understand him, he explained what this meant, and added, 'All these business details I can take off your shoulders with Frederick Hyde.'

'If I give the book to them!'

Swallowing his exasperation, he said kindly,

'I'll tell you anything I know about other publishers, but I do give you my word that no other English firm is as solid, as dignified, or richer. This particular manuscript we should send to one of the better-known Q.C.s for his advice, not to a solicitor....'

'Oh—so the publisher arranges that?'

'Of course.'

'You almost persuade me,' she murmured. 'But I must think it over a little.... Where did you say you were going?'

'I've been given time off to fetch my wife back from the Black Forest. I'm flying the day after tomorrow, and I shall bring them back next day—by air.'

'How wonderful for you to have dear Livvy with you again,' she said affectionately, 'and the child. You must be very excited and happy.... We'll talk about this again—as soon as you get back.'

'And decide,' he said gently. 'You won't want to waste time.'

'Yes, yes, and decide.'

CHAPTER 25

THE subtle change in his wife baffled Stephen. Watching her as she made the child ready for bed, he tried to put a finger on it. The barely noticeable changes worked by early childbirth were part of it, but a small part; the new warmth was not physical, it broke through in gestures, as if a hard green skin had begun to ripen.

The day he arrived was intensely hot: at six in the evening, not a breath of air. The small hotel, cut off from the village by an arm of the forest, smelled deliciously of resin. Darkened by its sun-blinds, the bedroom was still very warm, even to the bare floor-boards. A fine sweat came out on Livvy's temples and the nape of her neck as she bent over the child, lifting and turning his little body dexterously in her thin arms: he had been fed and was drowsy, falling asleep as she lowered him into his cot and drew the sheet over him.

'He never cries,' she said. 'All the nurses told me they had never known so good-tempered a baby, he must have been born happy. Look at him.'

Stephen looked. The absurd likeness to his great-great-grandmother had disappeared, but the tiny face was curiously—what was the word?—complete, finished, as though the only change to be expected in it was one of size; the features would not alter. He felt a sudden jealous rage: this scrap of flesh, this bastard, would be given everything, money, position, education, that his putative father had had to sweat, lie, manœuvre, to get a sight of. The anger in his stomach hardened into a simpler one, a mixture of brutality and need. He put his hand on Livvy's shoulder: a hard smooth knob, it fitted neatly into his palm. She moved away a little. Taking her by both arms, he turned her to face him, smiling at her through his eyelashes.

'Livvy, why not pretend, for once, that you like me a little better than you do? It's such a waste of time and your young body, why can't we enjoy what really is extremely pleasant? I don't offend you, do I?'

'Not in the least.'

'Then why...?'

She looked at him frankly. 'You don't attract me. No, I mean I'm not in the least in love with you.'

'Is that necessary?'

'It is for me.'

He noticed the fine powdery down on her cheeks. Moving his hand upwards to her neck, still moist, the hair clinging to it, he held her tightly closed mouth with his. The very thinness and immaturity of her body excited him very strangely, as though he were about to violate a child or his sister. She neither gave way to him nor moved, and he felt another spasm of rage.

'I could force you,' he said.

'You could—but you won't.'

'Why shouldn't I? This isn't a joke.'

She said calmly, 'Because if you did, I should leave you afterwards, and you'd have to live on your salary.'

Stung, he let her go so abruptly that she stumbled back against the cot and turned, catching her breath, to see whether she had disturbed the sleeping child. He had not stirred. Smiling with relief, she said,

'No, don't be a dolt. If you feel I'm being unfair, leave me, I'll take the blame.'

He gave way to a petulant impulse to insult her. 'Unfair? No, I suppose not. Some man or other gets you with child, I agree to take over his leavings so that you can have the brat peacefully—I've no grounds, no legal or any grounds, for complaint. Still, you made use of me.... In fact, my dear girl, you're as hard-mouthed an egoist as your grandmother.'

'Yes.' She had turned pale, but her voice was as cool and off-hand as always. 'Yes, I'm an egoist. So are you. It was because you're selfish, and ambitious and greedy, that I could make use of you. If you'd been innocent or stupid, I couldn't have done it, I'd have been too ashamed.'

'Really?' he said, with an offensive grin.

'You haven't lost by marrying me,' she said quietly. 'We

215

live on my grandmother's money, and the family has been useful to you in other sorts of ways—social ways. And that means something to you.'

He felt a stupefying bitterness—not to do with her directly. With her family, her class. It was one of the rare moments when he allowed himself to reflect that his father had been a servant, a valet, not even a competent one, sickly and already on his way down when he married a robust young woman, a servant herself for a year or two, then almost casually a prostitute before she discovered her very uncommon talents as a medium. That was his family, the part of himself he had to throw out of the window before he could become what he ought to have been born. Without putting his thought into words, he knew that if he could have coaxed or even forced her into sleeping with him, the self-disgust she would feel afterwards would have given him acute satisfaction, the pleasure and satisfaction of tumbling the whole of her arrogant overbred sort. He resented his defeat savagely.

'You,' he said, 'and your bloody-minded grandmother, had everything handed you, free on board; everything I have I've schemed and worked to get, and worked on myself. That's the difference between us.'

'There are other differences....'

'No doubt.'

'... there's the difference that you exploit your cleverness and your looks to make people do what you want. You're a con man. I've watched you at work on my grandmother. She's utterly unlike you, she's as honest as you're dishonest and a liar, and yet you know exactly what to say to her, what she wants to hear you say. You're clever.'

'Thanks.'

Looking at him with direct contempt, she said,

'It would be interesting to know just what you would *not*

216

do to get on. You're not unkind or brutal, you're just, oh, a climbing beast.'

'Of whom you made good use,' he said.

She was silent. They faced each other like two young dogs, quivering with dislike. After a moment, surprising him, she spoke in a calm voice, almost friendly, as though she were making an effort to pull things together between them.

'Yes, I know.... I don't blame you for anything—how could I? You know how to please people—people who are important to you. It's a—a technique, like any other, and much less harmful than some. And you have taste, I mean I notice how fastidious you are, in all sorts of ways I forget about. I suppose you'd call that being—yes—civilised. But your heart—do I mean your heart?—isn't a tenth as clever as you are, it's immature and rather stupid. Perhaps it will grow up some time, but not for me, I'm sure never for me.' She hesitated. 'You've been very kind to me, though, and I'm grateful.'

Her impersonal gentleness infuriated him again. 'My God, I needn't feel sorry for you.'

'Did I ever ask you to feel sorry for me?'

He shrugged. 'Fair enough.'

'You—you offered to do something for me. If it had been out of generosity, I'd have had to refuse. But it was to please yourself—for your benefit.'

An outrageous retort came to the end of his tongue. In the same moment he noticed that she was shaking: a trickle of sweat, starting at the hair line, was making its way down her left cheek, this in spite of the cool breeze which sprang up every evening the instant the sun dropped behind the black wall of trees and was now clattering the blind and blowing the curtains into the room.

'Are you all right?' he asked her.

'Yes, of course.'

217

'Sure?'

'Do go away now,' she said. 'I don't want dinner.'

At the door he turned to glance at her. She was bending over the cot again, oblivious—he might not have been still in the room.

He thought: It can't be left like this.... A hatred as baffled as his sense of humiliation filled him—less for her than for that indestructible old devil, her grandmother.

CHAPTER 26

TELEPHONING to Lady Chatteney the day after he got back, he felt derisively sure that after six days empty of excitement she was waiting impatiently to hand him the memoirs. His confidence lasted until he entered her room, and discovered that she had not been marking time until his return. Far from it. The very day he talked to her she had drawn up for herself a list of half a dozen publishers, rating them by the size of their advertisements in the Sunday newspapers, and asked each of them to make an offer. Five had offered less than £7500. The sixth, a firm as large, rich, solid, as Frederick Hyde's, offered ten thousand pounds—she laid the letter before him with a smile inviting him to praise her acumen. Under its layers of rouge and yellow powder, her face bristled with joy.

He had, at first, the impression that all she wanted was to be reassured that the firm of Frederick Hyde understood what a treasure it was being given. She put him right, quickly. If he could match the offer from X—, well and good, how eagerly she would trust the manuscript to him. If not—'Oh, my dear Stephen, that would be too grievous, I should be so sorry, but you wouldn't, I know you wouldn't, expect me to sacrifice so much money. I know nothing about business but, after all, if X— are making such an offer they must, surely, be the right publishers for the book, and it would be ungracious of me to refuse it.'

No one, he reflected, is more disingenuous or greedier than a woman who *knows nothing about business*: there are no this-worldly checks on her appetite. He said calmly,

'Not at all. Your choice is between a soulless multiple store and, let's say, Fortnum and Mason. And, don't forget, personal devotion counts for a great deal in publishing.' He smiled at her. 'I am talking about my feeling for the memoirs and for you.'

'Yes. Yes'—the glance she gave him was slightly ironic— 'but £2500 is a lot to pay for devotion, don't you think?'

'It's not quite so simple.'

She went on smoothly,

'If you were a member of the family, you would understand at once that I can't let any little personal leaning influence me. This is too important.'

He showed an unmoved face to this too-innocent snub. 'Let me telephone to Mr Hyde. We'll see what he thinks.'

Since the telephone was less than ten yards from the door of the drawing-room, he suffered the double pain of excusing himself to Frederick Hyde in her hearing. As distinctly as he heard it, he saw the furious irritation started up in Hyde by any suspicion that he was being manœuvred—the pulse beating on the top of his naked mottled head, the cruelly stretched lips and rapacious nose. 'What's this, what's this? I was under the impression that you had the old woman in your pocket. We offered a fair price.'

'I know that,' he answered, 'and if you think it would be foolish to go on I'll drop the whole thing. I should be sorry.'

'I take it you've been arguing with her.'

'Yes. Yes, of course.'

There was a silence. He caught the echo of Colette's voice in the room at the other side of the Park and several streets and squares.

'Very well. I'll give you enough rope to hang yourself. Go ahead and do just that.'

He went back to the drawing-room. Looking at him ardently, her mouth avid, Lady Chatteney said quickly,

'I've been thinking, Stephen. If Mr Hyde wants the memoirs, he ought to pay *more* than anyone else, more than X—. That's only justice.'

Exasperation with her turned to hatred, he would joyfully have twisted her scrawny neck until it hung over her shoulder like a chicken's. In a gentle voice he said,

'That isn't possible. Mr Hyde is willing to pay an advance of eight thousand. But—do remember—the more money you take now the less there'll be to come later, and your year's income tax will be very heavy on the larger sum. If you insist on it, I can only leave you to the tender mercies of X— and their somewhat ruthless methods of doing business. It's your decision.'

'Oh, but you'll be there to help me with them,' she cried.

He looked down at her, a long intimate glance, and shook his head. 'That would be unethical, I couldn't interfere in the doings of another firm. Even to help you.'

Her face worked unpleasantly under its fard. 'I thought you would arrange everything for me.'

'With Frederick Hyde, yes. Of course.'

She put her bony little hand on his. 'But, Stephen, I need you,' she said, suffocated.

'Yes, I think you do,' he said tenderly. 'But if you take the book to one of our rivals, I can't do anything for you—for all my devotion.'

After a moment, pulling down the ends of her mouth, she said,

'Very well. I must let you have it.'

He felt a mad rush of relief and triumph, and had the self-control to hide it. He said coldly,

'You're sure? This is the moment to decide—you mustn't change your mind again, you know.'

His coldness had the effect he counted on. 'I know, I know,' she said almost humbly. 'I do want you to have it.'

She hurried on stiff legs to the Chinese cabinet where she kept a collection of family photographs and ostrich feathers from her mother's hats, and came back carrying the heavy typescript across her arms like a child.

'One other question,' he said. 'Have you read it?'

An acid jet of excitement dilated her eyes. 'Not yet. I thought ... there really will have to be cuts, won't there?'

'Quite certainly.'

'Very well. Let your Q.C.—you did say you would employ Counsel, didn't you?—read it first. I will go through it last of all. The final judgement. I'm not interested in libel —that's your business. My interest, my duty, my supreme happiness, is to see that nothing he has written can damage him. *I* know what image of him ought to be left in people's memories. Perhaps I shan't want to remove more than a few passages, I'm not a prude.... In short, my dear boy, you know what I shall look for.'

Stephen felt a brief searing regret. As they stood now, the memoirs had the sovereign truthfulness, the beautiful hard precision of a great sculptor's most nearly flawless work. To mutilate it by shearing off a finger's breadth was scandalous, a stupid crime—of which he would be guiltier than anyone.

He felt something like stupefaction.... Have I become a scoundrel?

221

He scowled. No, I'm exaggerating, he thought dryly.

The lawyer spent two and a half weeks on the script. In the meantime the scent of carrion reached New York and Paris, and three well-reputed vultures cabled offers. Her new feeling of power gave Renée Chatteney an erotic pleasure. She wanted to prolong the orgasm, and behaved with them like an experienced female Don Juan.

A Sunday newspaper, the staidest in London, made an offer for serial rights. She was madly pleased and excited. But here Chatteney dug his heels in. He had not, he said, agreed to degrade himself and his work below a certain point. She made a list of very eminent and respectable statesmen and generals whose memoirs had been sold in Fleet Street, and showed it to him with triumph. He tore it up.

'They may enjoy lapping from gutters,' he said. 'I don't.'

She did not accept this, but for the moment she let it lie, very much in the spirit of a gourmet who knows better than to stuff himself full at one meal.

At last the lawyer delivered, in seven superb folio pages, a list of the cuts which would have to be made: these ranged from single phrases and names to passages of several hundred words.

Handing this document to Stephen, Frederick Hyde said genially,

'You had better take this to Chatteney yourself, with the manuscript. You may be able to comfort him. Take the agreement with you. If he swallows all the cuts, ask him to sign it. It won't surprise me if he shies—in that case I can only leave him to you and his old devil of a wife to argue with him. Point out—to her—that we have agreed to pay eight thousand pounds on delivery of the revised script.

Not until then.' He laughed unkindly. 'You look as though you had stomach-ache. Have you?'

'It's not going to be pleasant,' Stephen said.

Hyde rolled his thin lips. 'What murder is?'

It was Bruegel who answered the telephone when he rang up to say he was coming, and she was on watch in the hall to catch him. Glaring, she asked,

'What's going on between you and her and him? Can't you let him live his life out in peace? He's *ill* with mortification—dying from the heart out. She doesn't see it, she loves him so much she could eat him, and that's what she's doing, but you. ... Listen, you'll live another fifty years—at least—can't you leave him be? You make me mad. If I had a son as beautiful as you, I'd strangle him. You—you Turk.'

He laughed at her. 'What d'you want me to do?'

'Leave him to die his own death. Not one you've pushed him into.' She sighed. 'She's out. Go and talk to him. He knows you're here.'

When he came into the library, Chatteney looked at him from his writing-table with what might have been curiosity. Since the moment when his former secretary had become part of a benevolent conspiracy against him—with the greatest difficulty, and from a habit of politeness too ingrained in him to be wiped out, he was allowing himself to believe that his wife thought she was acting in his best interests—he had adopted towards the young man a manner so suavely and impenetrably friendly that it would not have given foothold to a caterpillar.

'Ah, Stephen,' he said, 'come in, come in. What have you brought?'

In three weeks he had aged immeasurably, and not in any impressive way. He had dwindled, the fingers holding a pen he laid down trembled continuously, his large head

223

shook a little on its insignificant neck, his eyes were very nearly extinct. As Bruegel said, he was dying from the heart out—without even the strength to hasten the process.

Stephen laid the typescript in front of him. 'This.'

Chatteney began turning the pages. After a time he said in a curious voice,

'There are no marks on it.'

'Of course not,' Stephen said gently. 'No one would dare mark it.' He hesitated. 'What we ought to do, sir, is to have a copy made that you can work over. This—the complete perfect copy—can still go to the British Museum.'

'Still,' Chatteney echoed. He laughed shortly. 'No doubt you think that ought to satisfy me. D'you imagine that to know it exists, out of sight, will make me indifferent to the caricature you're going to send out? Of course you don't. You're not an ass.'

'Not a caricature, sir. One or two blank pages and some missing names and sentences won't weaken the effect of the book, it's too overwhelming.'

'Effect, effect,' Chatteney said, with contempt. 'You're talking like a faker or a bad actor. Or like my poor wife, who believes she has a divine right to use any means to, as she says, lift me up in the sight of all men.... I wrote this book for my own pleasure. Try to imagine that you have spent a quarter of a century, longer, on creating a—call it a cathedral, a use of the allotted space which entirely satisfies you, and as soon as it is finished the officials move in and block up a window here and tear down a nave there. No, no—for all your intelligence—you're a limited fellow, I can't make you understand.'

He passed a hand over his face. As if he had pulled away a skin, what appeared when he dropped his hand was a naked grief, an agony of the flayed bone.

'I'm sorry,' he said, simply. 'I dare say there's a great deal of vanity, *amour propre*, in my... disappointment. I had, you know, a high opinion of myself.'

His wife came in briskly. To see them together was a lesson in the vivifying effect of being given the chance to play—even cruelly—with power. She was as thin as he was, an affair of skin and bone supporting a silk dress, a petticoat and a pair of stays, but she crackled with energy. A cancer of joy was at work in her. She looked years younger.

With an instinct to distract her from laying hands on the manuscript under Chatteney's eyes, Stephen gave her the agreement to read, and the lawyer's list of cuts. She read the first carefully, and asked a shrewd question before saying,

'It seems perfectly fair.' Spreading it in front of her husband, she said smiling, 'I'm sure you can sign it.'

Without a word, without glancing at it, Chatteney picked up his pen and looked on the last page for the place to write his name.

'Just one moment,' Stephen said. 'Forgive me'—he pressed a finger on one of the clauses—'you'll notice that this is a promise to pay the advance, eight thousand pounds, on delivery of the *revised* script. If you're willing to make the revisions—you haven't even looked at them—or let us make them....'

'Surely anyone can make them...' Renée Chatteney began.

Chatteney silenced her by lifting one of his delicate hands. 'I've thought about it already,' he said calmly. 'I'll do the cutting myself. Of course.' He glanced at the young man. A rictus of laughter crossed his face. 'Don't be alarmed, I shan't evade any of them—in any case you'll go over it.... It will take me a few days to read it through, then I'll get to work.'

'Would you,' Stephen asked, 'like me to come here for part of the day? I could arrange to do that.'

The glance Chatteney turned on him was without a flicker of interest or kindness.

'No.'

He pushed the signed agreement across the table.

Folding it, Stephen turned to go. A sense of anti-climax pricked him. Chatteney's voice halted him in the doorway.

'You might post this letter for me.' He held it out. 'It's that American chap. Foster. Hudson Foster. Extraordinary passion Americans have for surnames. He's over here again, for some weeks, and he wants to call. I can't bother with him. I've told him so.'

CHAPTER 27

HE dropped the letter to Foster in the post-box at the corner of Lowndes Place, imagining with acute pleasure the American's disappointment when he read it, and took a cab back to the office with the precious agreement. Hyde looked it over, studied the signature, and said curtly,

'The old fellow's tired.'

Expecting congratulations, Stephen waited.

'Well. Let's hope. I'll feel safe when the manuscript is in my hands again. Until then...'

'Chatteney is hardly the man to play any tricks.'

'My good Hind, you don't know writers yet. Habbakuks, every man jack of them, *capable de tout.*'

He jerked his massively bald head, dismissing the young man.

Such bland indifference to his adroitness exasperated

Stephen. He was further exasperated, when he went home, to find Livvy's grandmother in the living-room, worshipping, with Livvy, at the shrine. The infant's basket had been lifted on to the table so that she had not to stoop to bring her face, as covered with ruts and cavities as a relief map, parchment stretched over prominent bones, near it. To look at their three heads close together was an hallucinating experience, they were separate editions of the same face, the one skeletal, on the verge of disintegrating, Livvy's fresh and singularly smooth, its features fined down to a touching delicacy, the child's a scrap of unblemished flesh with the Grosmont beak standing out above the short pouting lips. A gust of jeering laughter rose in Stephen's midriff. To think of the son of a servant and a tart leaving his coarse thumb-mark on a family so insolently satisfied with itself.

'You can't detect any likeness to me, can you?' he said amiably. 'I suppose that was too much to expect.'

Livvy gave him a brief sideways glance, devoid of expression.

'Perhaps his eyelashes,' Lady Emily said kindly. She straightened herself and prepared to leave. 'I've decided,' she told Stephen, 'that Olivia must bring the child to King's Stanton for two or three months. London in summer is no place for a young child.'

'A number of children seem able to stand it,' he said, hoping to annoy her.

'They'll travel down to Dorset with me tomorrow,' Lady Emily said.

When he returned to the sitting-room after seeing the relentless old image out, Livvy said abruptly,

'I want to talk to you.'

'Must you?'

She flushed at his tone, but went on without hardening

her voice. 'I want to apologise for things I said to you that evening in the hotel. I had no right to criticise you—and no right at all to talk about your egoism. When I think of what I did...' She hesitated briefly. 'It's true I wasn't in my right mind, I'd thought about things—thinking about my grandmother's life being ruined—until I was half an idiot. One plan I had was to ask her for money to spend a year at an American university; she would have given it to me, too, and then written to the families of every American she got to know when her husband was in Washington, to look after me. I couldn't think of a single country I could reasonably go to where she wouldn't be able to rake up some splendid acquaintance. There was nowhere I could hide myself to have the child—and then, what could I do with it when I'd had it? I was out of my mind. I snatched at you like a drowning man grabbing the rope they throw him. Talk of egoists—I didn't give you a thought ... I'm not trying to excuse myself.'

He felt an impulse to make her excuses for her. 'You were very young when you got into it.'

She said vehemently,

'That's all bull. People talk as if anyone under twenty-five is a half-wit who doesn't know what he's doing. I knew perfectly well what I was doing when I began sleeping with —with Nicholas's father. I decided I had the right to do it—all that cheap sentimental twaddle about being free to enjoy oneself. If life means anything at all...'

She stopped short, scowling. 'No, no more bull. All I do now is to keep my face in the light—if you know what I mean—not use people the way I made use of you.'

A genuine pity for her seized him. Why? Certainly she did not pity herself, and she was anything but unhappy. Perhaps her so strange likeness, not a physical likeness except that both were thin, delicate-boned, sensible, to Tarry,

228

perhaps only that, although her bones might be as old as the hills, her voice and gestures were those of a schoolgirl.

'Yes, all right,' he said. 'I asked to be used. And you were defending yourself—and that...' he glanced at the sleeping child. 'The way I use people is rather different.'

She gave him one of her cool direct looks. 'No, I was unjust. You *are* kind, it's one of the more unlikely things about you. I mean how can anyone so really ruthless, so greedy, be—when it doesn't harm you—so genuinely kind. I don't understand it—but why should I?' She touched him lightly. 'I'm sorry.'

'Oh, you can say what you like.' He smiled at her. 'You know nearly everything about me.'

'I doubt that.'

He had never—even when he was with his sister—felt that there was anything to explain, far less excuse, about his ambitions. He knew, too, that very probably he would regret frankness. But something like a rage of honesty and loneliness filled him.

'You were saying about your rights to enjoy yourself... I haven't, I never had, any doubt at all that I was absolutely right to use any means at hand to get out of the obscene poverty I was born into. Always, since I was nine or ten I've always known what I had to do, I've made my way up foothold by foothold since then. Marrying you was a long step forward... I didn't ask to be born where I was and to have to kick my way through a society which looks down on the poor and weak, and respects and rewards the clever and predatory and successfully ambitious....'

'Stephen, I...'

He swept her aside. 'This is *true*. To pretend that the world isn't like this is either cowardice, or bad faith, or hypocrisy, or comforting oneself for having failed. Or if the well-off talk about unselfishness and simplicity, it's an

229

attempt to keep the outsider where he belongs—out. What's more, the things I want are all decent—order, poise, comfort, beauty and the rest of it. To have to lie to get them doesn't make them less decent.'

Something sprang between them, a friendliness as brittle and short-lived as a blade of grass.

'We're both pretty fine egoists,' Livvy said.

'I don't think it matters all that.'

'Listen—and don't be angry. I know you're only at the beginning of your triumphs. You'll go on and on. Remember what I said—when you want a divorce I'll do exactly what you tell me.'

'My dear girl,' he said, smiling, 'you may beat me to it.'

She moved her thin shoulders. 'Oh, I shan't want to marry again ... Deserve it or not, I had two years of complete happiness with a man I could respect and—what do I mean?—rejoice in. He knew infinitely more than I do about everything and he made everything come alive for me. In a way I was unlucky to have it all so soon, it has spoiled me for anything easier or duller. But'—she threw a swift glance behind her—'I got a supremely good thing out of it.'

'You're talking as if you were an old woman. At least twenty-two!'

'Well'—she yawned—'I suppose there are miracles, but I'm not looking for one.'

Surprising him, she kissed his cheek lightly. He returned her kiss as briefly and coolly. Their moment of nakedness to each other made the idea of love-making impossible or extremely unlikely. And in fact she was not the kind of young woman he really wanted to take to bed.

CHAPTER 28

H E had given Sarah dinner in Chelsea and persuaded her to come back with him to the house. She was reluctant. It was one thing, she said absurdly, to sleep with him in his house when Livvy was out of the country, and quite— another and uncomfortable when she was less than three hours away in Dorset.

'I never thought of you as squeamish before,' he mocked her, 'an illogical irrational female.'

She retorted sharply, but gave in to him.

As he opened the front door, the telephone at the end of the passage was ringing, but it stopped before he reached it.

'Who rings you up at night?' Sarah asked.

'No one. Probably a wrong number. If it's anything serious, they'll try again.'

Still uneasy, she made him switch the line through to the second telephone in his bedroom. A quarter of an hour later it rang again. Vexed, he did not move. He went on stroking her body, from shoulder to thigh, pausing at the hard points of her breasts and a faint crease in the smoothly rounded belly.

'Aren't you going to answer it?' she murmured.

'No.'

But he felt her stiffen, and in the same instant it struck him that the caller might be Tarry. Lying across her, he lifted the receiver, Renée Chatteney's voice penetrated his brain like a rusted knife, unbearably grating.

'Stephen! At last. This is the fourth time I've tried to get you. Do you know where he is?'

Taken aback, he said, 'Where is who?'

'You must come,' she said feverishly, 'you must, I can't be alone, I don't know what to do about it. Ought I to tell the police or ...'

'Who is she?' Sarah demanded.

He held the receiver to her ear, she listened for a minute and drew back, twisting her face. 'My God, what a voice.'

'...had been working so hard for three days reading through the script that when he said he would go to the Athenaeum I said: Yes, do go, it will rest you. At nearly seven when he hadn't come home I rang up, and they said he wasn't in the club, he had not been there at all. I tried to speak to you, then I went to see *her*, at her flat, I was certain he must be there, but she said she hadn't seen or heard from him since that evening—you remember. It may be a lie, probably is a lie, I am surrounded by liars, but he was not there then, I searched the place, and I ...'

As he listened, barely attending, half disinclined to take her seriously, the story was too grotesque, he went on stroking and playing with Sarah's body. Suddenly, she whimpered like a young animal and pushed his hand away. 'No, I can't bear it.'

'You must come here,' Renée Chatteney repeated.

'Very well,' he said, 'I'll come.'

He hung up. Beside him, Sarah was trembling violently. 'Are you going?'

'Not yet,' he said.

When he left the house it was after eleven o'clock, and he had to walk half the distance to Lowndes Place before he came on a cruising taxi. At the moment when it appeared at the end of the street, he was on the point of turning back; he was furiously impatient, furiously resenting the ruin of his night and the time he would have to spend with a neurotic old woman who might just as well have waited for the morning since she had had to wait until now. Nothing serious had happened to Chatteney, he was too well-known to be lying in a casualty ward, un-identified. Probably—likeliest of all explanations—unable to stand a moment longer her inquisitive satisfied glances, he had taken refuge with a friend. He still had friends. In the morning, ashamed of his escapade, he would return and listen, patiently, to her railing sarcasms.

Get the names of his friends, he thought, and persuade her to wait until breakfast time before ringing them up.

She was in her bedroom, not a large room, prowling be-tween the curtained window and the bed, watched by an expressionless Bruegel. Simon's empty basket was in her way, and each time as she stepped round it she half closed her eyes in a grimace of anguish.

'If you hadn't come I was going to ring the police,' she said.

'I've told her she'd be a fool to do it,' Bruegel said calmly. 'He's quietly asleep in bed, he'll creep back to-morrow and say he's sorry.... One crazy fool in a family is enough.'

Renée Chatteney stood still, pressing her nails into her temples. 'He never did such a thing before.'

'Nor will again, if you let him be, poor soul.'

'Had he been working hard on the memoirs?' Stephen asked.

He wanted to conjure into her obsessed mind the image of an overwrought old man trying to get out of her emotional clutch for a few hours, but before he could go on, she let out a wail that set his teeth on edge.

'But what has he done with them? Oh, my God, Stephen, what can he have done?'

He stared at her, feeling his heart slip slowly towards the pit of his stomach. The room was overwarm and airless, and a trickle of sweat started under his armpits. If the old man had taken the manuscript with him ... She must have told me during one of the moments when I wasn't listening to her, he thought.

'When did you find out that he ...'

She cut him short. 'I told you. Surely I told you. It was when I came back from her flat, I went straight up to the library, I thought he might have left something there, a message, and I'd overlooked it. I looked in the cupboard first—he used to keep it locked, but it was open and there was nothing in it except books, no manuscript; then I looked in the drawers of the writing-table and on the bookshelves. And then in his bedroom. I looked everywhere, every place he might have put it. I called Bruegel and she looked, we searched every room in the house. I couldn't believe it. And that's not all ...'

She sat down on the edge of the bed and began to cry in an ugly way, large tears spouting off the sides of her nose on to her hands. Stephen glanced at the Austrian, who nodded and said in a flat voice,

'It's true. It's not in the house.'

With an effort, Renée Chatteney controlled herself. 'Not all. Look—that was in a drawer of the table.'

She pointed at her bed, at a scatter of paper lying there. He walked across the room to examine it, and found himself staring at the torn fragments of the agreement, Chatteney's own copy, signed by Frederick Hyde. Posted to him yesterday, it had only been in his possession for a few hours before he destroyed it.

'You see?' she said. 'He isn't just staying out for the night. But what is he doing?' Her foot knocked against the basket. 'Oh, Simon, Simon! You were the only living thing who loved me, the one creature I could trust.'

Stephen was seized by repugnance for her stubborn

wallowing in disaster and self-pity. He forced himself to speak gently,

'You must go to bed and try to sleep. There's nothing we can do tonight. Ringing the police would mean reporters on the doorstep and the whole story in the newspapers. Tomorrow we'll ring up the people he may have gone to...'

'I feel ill,' she said feebly.

She collapsed against the end of the bed, her head dangling over one shoulder. What natural colour they still had drained from her cheeks, leaving two dark blotches, her veined eyelids fluttered and closed. She had not fainted. As Bruegel took hold of her and laid her flat, she said in the same dying voice, 'My heart, Bruegel—get Benham.'

Scowling at the young man, Bruegel said under her breath,

'She really has a bit of a heart, y'know. And I've run out of her capsules, I meant to get some.' She was patting the old woman's twitching body with the impersonal gesture of a groom flattering a nervous horse. 'Now, now, be quiet, you're all right.'

'Who is Benham?' asked Stephen. 'I forget.'

'Their doctor. We'd better get him.'

'It's after one o'clock.'

Bruegel shrugged. 'He's well paid for it. I'll talk to him.'

She went out and Stephen heard her lift the receiver and begin dialling. He looked at the woman on the bed. In spite of her grey skin and drawn lips, he did not believe she was in any danger. She is enjoying herself, he thought.

Opening her eyes, Renée Chatteney murmured,

'Stephen, I want you to tell him—and tell her—that I forgive them both. Tell them not to let the thought of the agony they caused me poison their lives, they must try to forgive themselves for it—as I forgive them.' She breathed

235

with seeming difficulty. 'Tell them not to remember how wretched they made me. Tell them to do their best to forget me. Will you do that?'

You're over-acting badly, he thought. 'Yes.'

She closed her eyes again, holding a hand out. He took it with repulsion, and held it until Bruegel came back to the room and gestured him out of the way. Impossible to tell from her expression, when she bent over the bed, whether she were bored or disgusted—he thought both.

'Shall I go?' he whispered.

'Stay until Benham comes.'

The irritable conviction seized him at this moment that Sarah had not kept her promise to wait for him. He went out into the hall and telephoned to her. There was no answer: he listened, without hope, until the operator said: 'There's no reply from the number,' then hung up, raging against the old comedian in the bedroom.

The doctor, a young-elderly man wearing a dinner jacket, arrived as he was putting back the receiver. With barely a glance at the young man he handed him a hat and a silk scarf, breathing over him the smell of fine brandy. He went directly to the bedroom, and left the door ajar, and Stephen heard him talking to his patient in a smilingly easy voice, as to a child or an idiot. He expected to hear her pour out the whole unhappy story, but all she said, in a nearly inaudible voice, was,

'I'm alone, my husband has left the house.'

'I'm going to give you an injection,' the doctor said soothingly. 'You'll sleep.' He spoke in another, almost brutal voice. 'Undress her, please, you.'

Twenty minutes later he left again, seen off by Bruegel, who handed him reverently the hat and scarf Stephen had dropped on a chair. Shutting the door on him, she turned with a frightful grimace.

'Phew, he stinks,' she said dryly. 'Never mind, he's settled her ... You're not going, are you? Stop the night here—what's left of it. You can lie down on your old bed. Look at you, you're half asleep.'

It was true. Fatigue felled him as she spoke, with a blow on the back of his skull: when he had climbed to the top of the house, to the hot unaired attic room, he swayed forward in a block on to the bed and slept before he could disentangle his fingers from the knot of his tie—a sweet dreamless sleep.

Coming in briskly at eight o'clock with coffee for him, Bruegel said,

'She's all right—and talking about the police again. But she'll wait a bit longer.' A curious look, half pitying, half derisive, came over her broad placid face with its airs of a saintly bully. 'My God, the damage people do when they don't know enough to make sensible use of their wickedness. Greedy handsome young devils like you—who are wicked on their own behalf—don't create a tenth of the ruin she does, poor wretch. I don't know how responsible *you* are for destroying the last dregs of his pleasure in living, but she actually doesn't know what she's done. And has been doing all her life without knowing it. I'm alone, I'm alone, she says, and by God she is—walled up inside her wickedness like a nun in a cell.... Where d'you suppose he is?'

He smiled at her sweetly. 'My dear Bruegel, how do I know? He might be anywhere ...'

He stopped. You unspeakable fool, he thought, where *would* he go?'

CHAPTER 29

STANDING outside the door of the 'studio' he listened for a moment before going in.

He had not put so much as his head in this room since he was a child, and he had kept from that one glimpse of it a confused sombre memory of walls covered by some sort of red hangings and stretching away on all sides into a dark vapour. That must have been in the days when it was used for the weekly séances as well as by persons whose needs were served better here than by a hotel or a less intimate bawdy-house. He looked round it now with avid curiosity, his widened nostrils picking up the smell of dust and dry rot and some other, faintly disagreeable. Grotesquely over-furnished, it contained everything that, given a free hand, a prosperous hard-working Edwardian whore might have chosen: the prevailing colour was still claret-red, an immensely thick carpet of the sort his mother called Turkey, damask curtains embroidered in tarnished gold thread with storks and water-lilies, monstrous cushions of faded crimson velvet, a Spanish shawl draping the couch, statuettes of nymphs and a turbanned negro, a foam of voile round the legs of small tables—and the wide double bed.

He walked towards it. An eiderdown and blankets had been pushed against the wall: Chatteney was lying under a sheet, his body outlined by it in all its skinny disgrace, naked except for his shirt. His eyes were open and alive; for the rest he might be already dead.

Stephen stood still and let his mother elbow him out of her way. She was in the highest spirits, her eyes excited and malicious. Bending over Chatteney, she spoke in a cajoling voice.

'Hey, little old uncle, how d'you feel this morning? Better, eh?' She touched his forehead. 'You're cooler. The doc'll be here again soon. Poor old fellow, poor old baby.'

Chatteney smiled, a polite twitch of his colourless lips.

'When did he come here?' Stephen asked.

'Yesterday afternoon,' his mother said. She straightened up and gave him an inquisitive look. 'Who told you he was here?'

'I know him,' Stephen said shortly.

'He told me his name—Chattner. Something of that. Means nothing in my young life.' She dropped her voice. 'I'd like him out of here, though. I'd sooner he died somewhere else than on me.'

At this moment he noticed that something, during the more than half a year since he had been to see her, had happened to her face; one side of her mouth, the left, was pulled far down, and her left eyelid drooped heavily: it disfigured her in a very odd way, lewd rather than ugly. Turning from her, he moved to the side of the bed, and asked gently,

'How are you, sir?'

Chatteney looked at him with a pale gleam in his eyes, a gleam the colour of chalk. 'Thank you.'

Does he even remember who I am? Stephen wondered. 'Why did you come here? We've been abominably anxious.'

Chatteney made an obvious effort to speak in a stronger voice. 'Quite unnecessary. I didn't intend to stay long.'

'But no one knew where you were.'

'Ah, yes. I didn't think. One can't think of everything.'

Stephen hesitated. Looking closely round the room, he saw Chatteney's underclothes folded neatly on one of the swollen armchairs, and his small black shoes under

239

another, but no package, nothing that could be the manuscript. There were several places in the room where it could be hidden, a hanging closet, the drawers of a chiffonier in fake ebony, a faked Jacobean chest. In a deferential voice he asked,

'Where are the memoirs?'

Chatteney did not answer at once. Very slowly, he drew his arm from beneath the sheet and pointed to the fireplace, an elaborate affair of moulded iron, with five bars.

'There.'

For a moment, Stephen did not understand. Walking over to the fireplace he saw that the grate was more than three-quarters full of burned paper, layers of grey charred ash. He touched it. A few flakes rose lightly and settled into a pinch of dust. Disbelief, despair, fury, followed each other in him with sickening violence. He strode back to the bed and shouted,

'Burned—you've burned it?'

Incredibly, the aristocratic old urchin in the bed laughed. 'It looks like it, doesn't it?'

'You...' The extravagance and unspeakable frivolity of the act outraged him; the whole of his mean anxious childhood rose in him against a man capable of throwing away a valuable object as carelessly as he might let a penny roll into a drain. A current of hate prickled at the ends of his fingers, they itched to take Chatteney by his shoulders and shake the remnants of his safe pampered eminent life out of him.

'Of all the senseless tricks—as senseless and farcical as pushing the Duquesne's letter under your blotter and leaving it there ... you must be mad....'

With a spurt of energy Chatteney said,

'Oh, you saw me put it there? Was it you who took it?'

Out of the side of his eye Stephen caught sight of his

240

mother, watching him with an indecent amusement. He controlled himself to say,

'No. I didn't. I left it there.'

'I see. Yes, I see,' Chatteney murmured. 'Well—it's not of the slightest importance.' He looked full at the young man, a long steady look. 'My dear fellow, I suppose you've been trying for a long time to get hold of my memoirs. It doesn't matter. It's only natural that you should be ambitious and unscrupulous—you're young.... The passions of the young don't interest me, except as a spectacle....' His face softened a little. 'At some time or another you may begin to feel that you've behaved towards me with—what shall I say?—a certain lack of elegance. If that happens, remind yourself that I wasn't in the least disturbed.'

He was speaking with the greatest delicacy. Deliberately sceptical, Stephen thought: How he enjoys seeing himself in a superb pose. Even now.

Tarry's clear voice outside the door. 'Yes, go in, doctor.'

A plump middle-aged Indian inserted himself into the room prudently. His smiling glance slid from face to face as though it were oiled, and he held in front of him a pair of singularly beautiful hands with long pointed dirty nails. My God, this won't do, Stephen thought. He left the room and ran upstairs, catching his sister as she went into her bedroom. She turned and clung to him with a desperate eagerness, not like her.

'The poor man, Stephen!'

He kissed her. 'Where the devil did you unearth that seedy object?'

'Who? The doctor? He's not a bad man. He and mummy talk about religion together—well, you know, Krishna and reincarnation and that. It's a sort of religion. ... The old gentleman felt so ill yesterday that...'

He interrupted her. 'Don't you know who he is? Of

course you don't. But if he dies here, there'll be a mob of reporters round and oh, my God...'

With acid despair, he saw the façade he had built up between himself and 41A Marion Street crumble into dust, exposing him to the malice of, among others, the guests round Mrs Gide's dinner-table. That, and the loss of the memoirs and the brutal sarcasms he could expect from Frederick Hyde, ran together into a hard weight in his stomach. It would be a relief to vomit.

'Did you see them burning papers in the studio?'

'No. Not actually. When I was helping her to get him into bed, I noticed that the grate was full of warm ash. Afterwards, before the doctor came, she was turning her little finger in it and laughing.'

'What they burned was a manuscript worth thousands of pounds. She wouldn't know that.'

Her eyebrows flew up. 'Does it matter—to you?'

'Terribly. I'd got it for Hyde—you won't understand, but it's a really frightful knock for me.'

He was sitting on the edge of her bed; she put her arms round him and stroked his face with short rough fingers. Pressing his forehead against the bony salt-cellars at the base of her throat, he muttered,

'My love, how much longer are you going to have to pig it in this house?'

She freed herself. 'Who knows?' she said lightly.

'What's wrong with her face?'

'She had another slight stroke—I didn't tell you, it was when you were in Baden-Baden. It's very queer, but she's far more active and restless than before she had it. She's even been out alone. It does this to some people, the doctor said, and he said...'

'How I wish it had killed her,' he interrupted.

'Hush...'

They heard the Indian's soft blurred voice on the staircase, and a minute later their mother's heavy footsteps coming up to her room.

'I must go,' Tarry said, 'she'll be shouting for me.'

Glancing at his watch, he saw that it was after ten o'clock; he ought to be in his room at the office. Kenneth's restaurant was shuttered and bolted and he had to walk along the street to a kiosk to telephone to Colette Hyde. In his exasperated state her voice started in him something of the excitement he had felt when she rang him up for the first time—not a great deal more than a year ago—and invited him to come to dinner: the sexual excitement of gambling on his talent for seduction, in all senses of the word. He began to be ironically amused by his danger. A half-insolent confidence brushed him; he told her easily that he was having trouble with the Chatteneys and would ring her up again later.

'Are you with them now?' she asked.

'Yes.'

'Is it serious?'

'Too damned serious to talk about on the telephone.'

'All right,' she said calmly. 'Don't worry. I'll wait for you to tell me.'

He went back to the house, reaching it as a car drew up at the restaurant and Kenneth leaned out, beaming lovingly. 'My dear, you look wonderful.'

His mother was standing, frowning and pulling at her contorted mouth, in the studio.

'The old fellow's on his way,' she said. Her frown became a scowl. 'Doc says it's a matter of a few hours, and he's coming back.... Get me my hat, Tarry, I'm going out for a few minutes.'

'Oh, no,' the girl said nervously. 'Where are you going?'

'An errand.'

243

'Let me do it for you.'

'Mind you own business, my girl. And you'—she scowled at her son—'go and sit with him till I get back. If you know what we'd best do, you can tell me then.'

Chatteney seemed to have sunk lower into the bed. He turned his eyes slowly when the young man came into the room, but did not speak. His magnificent head seemed moulded in a friable clay, brittle and lightless. It lay on the pillow as if it had rolled there from a collapsed building. For the first time Stephen felt an acute responsibility. What in God's name to do now? Fetch his wife? Benham?

With something like irritation he blurted,

'You can't stay here, in this place. Why the devil did you come here?'

Startled by his voice, Chatteney frowned. 'Why not?' he murmured.

A saving thought jumped into his mind. 'Would you like me to get Mrs Duquesne?'

The look in Chatteney's eyes was almost one of boredom. 'Don't trouble.'

Hurrying out of the room, he sent Tarry to fetch her. 'Ken's car is outside. Get him to take you there, and bring her back. He doesn't seem to want her, but I do. Hurry.' He watched her go, quick and supple in washed-out narrow jeans, and went back to watch the old man *on his way*.

During the few minutes he had been out of the room Chatteney had covered quite a stretch of it; the glance he focused on Stephen came from the other side of an immense distance, a desert that was swallowing up his lifetime of passionate enjoyment of the good, the beautiful and the rational, and it mattered less than nothing to him that it ended in this whorish room. Possibly he did not see the room. Possibly the noise of traffic in Marion Street was a line of Verdi or cock-crow in a French village.

Impatience made Stephen yawn. He began to walk about the room, threading his way among the suffocating press of furniture. At last he heard sounds inside the house. Opening the door, he saw Mrs Duquesne coming rapidly up the stairs in her heavy soft-footed way. He spoke to her. Without answering, she pushed him aside and went into the room. Bending over Chatteney she said in a warm smooth voice,

'Well, my dear?'

The effort he had to make to attend to her was very obvious. 'Immensely kind of you to come.'

'My darling, as if I wouldn't come ... I love you very much.'

He closed his eyes for a moment. When he opened them he was looking not at her, but directly in front of him, a cold unwavering glance. Mrs Dusquesne said gently,

'How I shall miss you.'

'The fact is,' he said in an impersonal voice, 'I don't at all want to go, I've had a splendid time, and done a great deal of what I intended doing. But of course one never lives long enough to finish.'

For a blinding instant, Stephen saw the event taking place in the seedy baldachined bed—saw it, that is, in its flayed reality. The polite stoicism Chatteney was holding round him did not blunt for him in any degree the knowledge that he was being forced to go, to lose, not any person, not the woman close to him at this moment, but the use of his senses and brain; he was walking to the edge of the precipice with eyes open, knowing that he was being pushed towards it mercilessly—but walking.

Under her breath Mrs Duquesne called him by a name Stephen did not catch.

It brought Chatteney's glance back from an infinitely

distant horizon to move civilly from one to the other face turned to him.

'Well, good-bye,' he said. 'I—I—I . . .'

His expression became ironic, then contemptuously resigned and indifferent, and did not change again.

The young man stepped back to leave Mrs Duquesne as nearly alone as possible. Nothing left, he thought, nothing at all, of all he had. So what? So get everything within reach and cram it into stomach and brain while you can. . . .

Turning, Mrs Duquesne showed him a tranquil face of grief. She would feel it indecent to cry in front of anyone, he thought, stranger or friend.

'Well,' she murmured, 'it was kind of you to send for me.'

'He died easily.'

She looked at him as though he amused her. 'But who dies easily? Except a very young child. . . . Tell me, how did you know he was here?'

He gave her a charming smile. 'This house is my mother's. That's all.'

'Oh, I see,' she said placidly, 'well, I've known your mother a long time, she's a very remarkable woman, I'm very fond of her. Where is she? She'll tell us what to do. Ah!'

She turned as the door opened. His mother came in, nodded at her, and went straight to the bed, where she pressed her hand firmly over Chatteney's eyes to close them.

'Seems I can't turn my back for half an hour,' she said. 'A mercy you were here. He was in too big a hurry; I was going to send for you.'

'Your son did that,' Mrs Duquesne said.

'I'm surprised he knew enough to do it. But I know nothing about him, I'm not on his visiting list. . . . Excuse me, you're not interested in ... Poor old fellow, you'll miss him, after so long.'

'Yes,' Mrs Duquesne said. She went on with a sudden hard anger, 'There never was anyone like him.'

She began to walk out of the room, but stopped before she reached the door and looked at Stephen with a polite smile.

'My dear boy,' she said, 'I'm forgetting everything. Forgive me. Do you want me to help you? ... His wife must be told—before anyone. At once. Would you like me to tell her I think I could do it more easily than you.' She came back to take his mother's hand and press it. 'You'll look after him for a few hours until we can arrange to move him,' she said warmly. 'He'll be safe with you.'

Outside the house she stood for a moment, with closed eyes, gripping Stephen's arm.

'I'm all right,' she said at last. 'Forgive me.'

'Why didn't you wait upstairs until I could get a cab?'

'I wanted to get out.'

Still holding his arm, she walked quickly. He was struck by the delicious warmth of the street; the sky was a hard clear blue and the August sun softened the disgrace of shabby houses. An insolent energy filled him.

In the cab she asked, 'Does she—Renée—know about that house, or about your mother?'

'No.... This morning she wanted to go to the police. I persuaded her not to do it until I had been to two or three places where he might have spent the night.'

'I see. Well, I must do the best I can.'

What she did was to walk into the room where Renée Chatteney was waiting, quivering like a lean dark moth, in a corner of the sofa, hold out both large hands, and say in her scandalously beautiful voice,

'My poor Renée, he's dead.'

247

With a cry, Renée Chatteney stood up and fell into her arms. The two ageing women clung together as clumsily as schoolgirls, rocking from side to side, making in their throats sounds that might as easily have been laughter as grief. After a time, Mrs Duquesne said tenderly,

'Let me tell you about it.'

She drew the other woman to sit beside her on the sofa, and with exquisite care told her that he died 'in the house of a very old friend, my dear, an obscure friend of mine, the house where we sat and talked—only talked, you can believe me. He would rather not have met me in that way, in that uncomfortable place, but I insisted. You'll be able to forgive him, and you must try to forgive me. After all, you were his wife, he depended on you for everything, I had very little of him, nothing you need—now—grudge me. Do you believe that?'

'It was all your fault, wasn't it?'

'Entirely my fault.'

'You see, I was right, all along.'

'You have always been right.'

'You made me terribly unhappy,' Renée Chatteney said, 'I didn't deserve it.'

'But you forgive me, don't you?' her friend murmured.

Surprisingly, Renée Chatteney smiled with a certain mockery. 'Yes, why not? You can't do me any more harm.' She looked at Stephen and said brusquely, 'Go and see Benham, and tell him to arrange to fetch Sir Henry's body here. At once. After that you can inform *The Times* and the B.B.C.'

Vexed by her tone, he said, 'I must tell you one thing before I go. He destroyed the memoirs—burned them.'

She looked at him with a grimace of despair and horror. Tears formed in her eyes and rolled gracelessly down her face, the first she had shed. Satisfied with his vengeance, he

248

went off, leaving her to Mary Duquesne's limitless tact—limitless because it was not subject to *amour propre* or any poor-spirited respect for the truth.

As he ran about town on his errands, he tried to stiffen himself for the coming interview with Frederick Hyde, knowing that he would have to endure one of the atrocious fits of anger that were the terror not only of Hyde's subordinates. He invented and discarded a dozen ways of telling the story, to make his own part in it less inadequate and feeble, and in the end told it without any skill at all.

Hyde listened calmly and said,

'You did all you could, no one can cope with downright lunacy.'

Extremely astonished, he realised, abruptly, that Hyde's bad temper was a pure self-indulgence; he shouted and browbeat to stimulate himself, as other men take to alcohol. When there was absolutely nothing to be done, no remedy, he behaved himself. He was that rarest of animals, a rational bully.

In future I shall know how to handle him, he thought.

He was withdrawing when Hyde said curtly,

'I've come to the conclusion that you're wasted on the frivolous side of this firm. On Monday you'll move over to my side. Understand?'

'Thank you.'

'Is that all you have to say?'

'I'm delighted.'

'You should be,' Hyde growled. 'I'm taking you seriously.'

Curious to see whether the eminent doctor had done as he was told, he went back to Lowndes Place in the early evening. Opening the door to him, Bruegel said,

'Yes. He's in his own room—since three o'clock. And

she's still here, thanks to God. Go in and see them, they've been laughing like idiots.'

As he opened the door, Renée Chatteney was saying gaily, 'You were such a marvellous dancer—do you remember?'

Seated on the arm of a chair, holding a glass of sherry, she was looking down admiringly at her friend's legs, crossed at the ankles: however shapeless they must be above the knee, below it they were still thin and shapely. Mrs Duquesne smiled slightly. She nodded at the young man.

'Old women remember,' she murmured.

In the few hours since he had seen her, Renée Chatteney had cast a skin. The new one was not less haggard and discoloured, but it had been brushed over by a sort of innocence; she looked younger than her friend, as though something joyful had happened to her.

As indeed, he thought, it had. The long dreadful fight to possess Chatteney was at an end, she could turn her memory of him any way she pleased, rearrange it, dispose of every fragment, make it at last, at last, her inalienable property, to the smallest grain of dust. She would mourn him, certainly, but behind her mourning, sincere, there would always be this monstrous happiness. Which she would hide. As Mrs Duquesne, behind her warm and exquisite politeness, would hide a regret beyond comfort.

'I came,' he said, 'to ask if there is anything more I can do.'

'Thank you, no,' Renée Chatteney said. 'My solicitor has taken charge of everything—the funeral, the journalists . . .'

She was interrupted by Bruegel, who came in holding out a visiting card. 'This has just been left. He heard on the six o'clock news.'

Renée Chatteney peered at it with a certain distaste.

'Surely he doesn't expect me to see him—now? These people have no respect for grief.' She passed the card to Mrs Duquesne. 'An American. He wanted to buy the memoirs, but alas, alas, Harry refused to let them go out of the country. You know how obstinate he could be.... Send him off, Bruegel.'

'He's not here,' Bruegel said, 'he handed it to me and left.'

Stephen followed her out of the room. She was leaning against the wall near the door, shaking silently with what, after a moment, he realised was laughter. Without troubling to lower her voice, she said,

'Do you know what she said when they let her go upstairs to look at him—I mean the first thing? She said, "If he had thought of anyone except himself all his life he wouldn't be lying here now...." She was being herself for the last time. If you ask me, my boy, she's going to live a long happy life without uttering another sincere word. And don't think I'm not fond of her. A softer type would have lost heart and stopped clawing him. Not she. She's tough. That's how I like a woman to be. Long-living and tougher than any man ever can be. A question of bowels.'

CHAPTER 30

At the moment when Chatteney's body began to slide out of sight towards the furnace, Stephen was seized by one of the liveliest movements of happiness he had ever had. It sprang from the contrast he felt suddenly between an extinct brain and old withered flesh and his own: he felt it in every nerve and cell of his supple healthy intact body, a sensual pleasure and a pleasure of the spirit—whatever that is. My real life is only beginning, he thought.

He had taken a seat at the very back of the chapel, in the same row of chairs as Mrs Duquesne; she was wearing one of her long shapeless dresses and had tied a black lace scarf round her head to do duty for the hat she did not possess.

Leaving the chapel on the arm of a retired ambassador, Lady Chatteney passed within inches of her friend without a flicker of recognition in the single glance she gave her. Outside, in the warmth, she stood for a minute beside the opulent spread of wreaths on the flagstones and offered her hand to be pressed by an under-secretary of State and a former Foreign Secretary before allowing herself to be led away.

Stephen stopped to look at the wreaths. His eye was caught by the writing on one of the cards—*Faithful after death, Violet Gladys Hind*. Would anyone but his mother use so meaningless a phrase and add to it her ridiculous Christian names? Turning, he saw Mrs Duquesne moving slowly away alone, and ran after her.

'Let me get you a cab,' he said.

'That's very kind,' she answered. 'It would be kinder still if you came with me. I'll give you a drink, I want one myself.'

Watching her as she moved about her dusty amiable room, he reflected that he could speak about Chatteney without being afraid that she would burst into tears of self-pity. She had adored him, she was grieving, but she would not dream of inflicting her grief on another person. She had too much delicacy and contempt.

'Did you notice,' she said smiling, 'that the average age of the people in the chapel was at least sixty, and they were nearly all terribly distinguished? Hardly one of them has taken any notice of him for years and years. But they all came to his funeral.'

'A question of manners. And he'd be indifferent, he wouldn't care if they came or stayed away.'

She looked into her glass of whisky. 'I'm not so sure. He talked to me, and no doubt to you, of the pleasure of living an obscure life, away from intrigues and dinner-parties. It was less than half true. He really suffered when he lost his last chance—after 1946—of remaining in the great world. Poor man'—in her mouth it was a caress—'he was very bitter.'

'Was he bitter in 1938, when he resigned?'

'Ah,' she murmured, 'he had other reasons for bitterness then. Purely personal ones.'

'I knew it,' Stephen said with energy. 'There was a crack in the memoirs there. I could feel the draught.'

She laughed at him. 'You're a clever boy, my dear, very very clever. The whole story is finer and more human than the noble version—and *I* think better worth remembering, because it's part of him, not of his monument.... He'd been in Paris for several years—without Renée. She'd tried living there, and hated it so much that she went back to London.'

She paused, and went on in a voice of smiling mockery. 'Do you know why she loathes France? Only because she can't speak French, and she imagined that the people she was forced to meet, the French politicians, writers, countesses and the rest, looked down on her. Perhaps they did! The French are very apt to think that theirs is the one and only civilised language.... Rather than make the best of it, she left him alone there. That pleased him enormously, he adored the life he lived in Paris as a bachelor. Before 1938 he had a mistress, a beautiful twenty-year-old Greek—she was a typist in the Greek legation. He was very happy. Then in August 1938 he was summoned to London and told they were sending him to Stockholm as ambassador.

Renée of course was delighted—the Swedes all speak superb English! He, poor darling, couldn't bear the thought of official life in Stockholm with Renée—or of losing his young mistress.' Her voice hovered between laughter and a serene tenderness. 'He was nearly fifty, it was his last wild snatch at his own youth—you ought to be able to understand it.'

'I do,' he said, 'but ...'

'But what?'

'But, my God, all the eloquence I typed and re-typed—his principles, his aristocratic contempt for the Chamberlains and Simons and Hoares and Dawsons, the obtuse self-satisfied self-righteous middle-class *canaille* who knew nothing about Europe, and were too ignorant and gutless to try to stop Hitler balling it up—and not a hint of the sentimental story at the back of it!'

'Indignant virtue doesn't suit you,' she mocked.

'I may have no morals, and still find certain sorts of *literary* dishonesty revolting.'

She looked him up and down. 'I believe you are genuinely disappointed,' she said in a warm voice. 'That's very engaging—really engaging, not the charming clever fellow you put on every morning when you wake up. But you're being stupid, my dear. He detested the policy of the government and worked heroically against it. I dare say he would have resigned in any case. The thought of losing his Greek girl tipped a balance that might—how can you be sure with him?—with anyone?—have come down on the side of ambition and his career. He was very ambitious. . . . But all the generous reasons he gave for resigning were *true*. They weren't the whole truth—and he was far too lucid not to know it. But he wasn't telling lies. That's much too simple!' She made a wide movement of her hands. 'In the memoirs he was creating something, a portrait of what

254

a statesman ought to be. A little what a Frenchman means by *gloire*—to be *seen* to do what is right and noble and uncompromising. Don't you understand?'

He understood perfectly. It was, in different terms, only what he had once said to that pompous ass, Duffy Avens. But out of malice he said,

'All the same, he was lying.'

'I don't agree. I'm certain that when he looked back he couldn't believe that a... a mere love-affair had been so overwhelmingly important; he felt sincerely that nothing had counted except his disgust with Munich.' She smiled teasingly. 'The Jesuits call that *diriger l'intention*. They mean that an action can be justified by interpreting its motives in the best possible light.'

'Why not speak English and call it hypocrisy!'

'You know more about men and women than that,' she said ironically.

'Well—what happened?'

'Ah! ... Without a word to him, his exquisite girl went back to Athens—the very week he resigned. He told Renée that a month or two in Greece would help him start his memoirs, he frightened her off going with him, easily, by telling her about the discomfort of Greek inns and the atrocious food, and flew to Athens—and found his young woman married. He ran away at once—to Vence. He had no idea I was living there. We met in the street. We hadn't met since his marriage—more than twenty years. He told me about the Greek girl. Of course. And...'

She lifted her hands in a light gesture and smiled at him, a smile inviting him to imagine for himself a love on one side all warmth and indulgence, on the other an egotistical passion which slowly, over years, became an ageing man's need of warmth and unexacting carelessly poured-out kindness.

He felt a familiar resentment. Why should the old hedonist have had everything?

'He was a great man,' he said, 'and a great poseur.'

'An actor? Perhaps. But it was always himself he acted.... And he could laugh at himself—even though he was shockingly arrogant and shockingly easily bored. He did foolish and unkind things out of his horror of being bored.... And—oh, my dear boy, how impossible it is to tell the truth about anyone, even a man you love with your heart and soul. He wasn't interested in other people. There was even a cruel streak in him ...' She hesitated, and said quickly and softly,

'You saw it when he was dying—that terrible indifference.'

If he had wanted at this moment to be sincere, Stephen would have said brutally that a disinterested man is a freak. Any normal man acts with an eye on himself. Even if he seems disinterested in the sense of sacrificing his own interests, look a little closer and you'll see what his interest is—to be morally comfortable or to live up to the flattering idea other people have always had of him. Only the dead can be disinterested.... He said,

'How could a dying man be interested in anyone except himself?'

She smiled indulgently, her utterly immoral indulgence. 'Oh, you egotists!'

'Egotist or not, he loved you.'

'Oh, yes ... I wasn't the only one. He had love-affairs after Vence—in London during the war—and when he was sent on a mission to New York. He would have been astonished if I had been hurt or vexed by them. And I wasn't. I didn't grudge them to him, I couldn't.'

She narrowed her eyes at him, making him think of a large cat whose feline nature has been deliciously warmed and humanised. 'Great men are often greedy. No, no, don't mock. You're abominably greedy—and you make good use of women, which he never did.'

'He had no need to,' Stephen said, with barely suppressed rage.

She only laughed at him. 'Besides—those episodes had nothing to do with love. He wasn't able to be faithful, but he was not, not, a *coureur des femmes*, it was much simpler —he needed a sort of warmth only women could give him —and he hated being alone.'

'But you ...'

She cut him short almost roughly. 'I didn't want him to consider me or do anything for me. I was with him when I could be—we never met in London, only abroad. We were happy.'

She was silent, looking absently at her hands. Then she said, with an ingenuous malice,

'The only episode which was fairly serious was with a terrible woman who wrote, Cordelia Brand. It ended badly —she made him read the manuscript of one of her novels and ordered him to write a preface for it. It was an ineffably vulgar novel about a gentleman who knew everything about wine and had love-affairs. Poor Harry! ... That was a year after the scandal. He wrote to me about it—he was appalled. He broke with her, of course. It was the only thing he could do!'

'Did he write to you often?' Stephen asked sharply.

'Yes. During the twelve years after the case, when we didn't meet, he wrote at least once a fortnight, hundreds of letters ... marvellous letters.'

'Can you make a volume of them? Or let me do it?'

'Oh, I destroyed them,' she said carelessly.

'All of them? My God, how could you?'

'I kept one.... You know, my dear boy, I regret now,

257

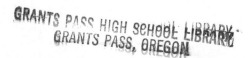

terribly, that for all those years I kept the ridiculous legal promise I'd made. When we met again he was seventy and I was sixty-four. We had five, nearly six years. I feel now that he needed me very badly, I was a fool to keep my promise.' She hesitated and went on in her deepest, most seductive voice. 'Now I'll tell you something. I saw him once after the day he and Renée came here, and tried to persuade him to let her have her case and come to France with me. He had more than paid his debt to her.'

'And he wouldn't?'

'He was too tired,' she said sorrowfully, 'too old, too broken by what she was doing to his monument.'

'I shan't pity him too much,' Stephen said, 'he had you.'

She shook a little with her throaty laughter. 'How absurd.... Would you like to see the letter I did keep—if I can find it?'

'Very much.'

She got up, with surprising lightness, and began to rummage in the drawers of her desk, scattering papers and letters. 'No ... no ... ah, here we are.' Glancing at it as she handed it to him, she said easily, 'He speaks in it about something that happened in France—which meant a great deal to him. But I don't remember it, I must have been thinking about something else at the time.'

It was dated June 1956. The first paragraph was about his memoirs, he had been writing about de Gaulle, 'that past-master of highminded confidence tricks...': the sentence broke off there, he left it hanging and began abruptly: 'Mary, you and I have never made-believe, never duped or been duped by each other. You know everything about me, I have never had to hide anything from you, or deny any even of my most foolish actions.... Even at the beginning my love for women ran at a depth below physical curiosity. Is that why it hasn't changed or aged? You

258

know how, when I was young, I never questioned for an instant that I had the right to every sort of personal and passionate experience, my intellect and my senses were wound up to such a pitch, a hair-spring, that everything I touched, saw, thought, gave me some form of pleasure, or with equal intensity pain. I can't put my finger on the moment when the spring began to unwind, and I caught my first glimpse of the condition I have reached now, of almost total detachment. Except for you, my life has become a spectacle, an inexplicable and often absurd interval between two moments of extreme violence, one I have forgotten and one I can't imagine. Looking back over it, it seems to me that although I wanted power and to be famous—yes, yes, I am vain, or I was—the thing I most wanted was not to be alone with myself. Now, except for you, I am alone and it is not so terrible.

'I remember one moment vividly—so overwhelming at the time that certainly you felt it, too. It was the spring of 1939 when we stayed in Béziers; we'd driven to the Hérault gorge, and we stood looking at that clear cold green water running between the rocks, and for a moment without beginning or end I had a sense of, I can only call it absolute meaning, absolute happiness. Yes, yes, you remember it.

'At worst—my worst—I have never been satisfied with myself. In spite of my vanity—never. And I have never despaired. I don't now, even if the dry solitude I live in away from you is a foretaste of the nothing we come to.

'Should it surprise me that I still love you, *éperdument*, a desperate love, outside of all sensuality—all animal sense, at least,—and therefore indestructible? If I could see you again I would tell you, again, what I love in you. And now good night, my warm kind love.'

Folding the pages to give them back to her, Stephen said,

'You destroyed all the others. Why did you keep this?'

'For one sentence.'

'Which?'

She smiled slowly and provocatively. 'If you knew that, you would know too much. . . . And now, my dear boy, I must send you away, I have another visitor coming any minute—only business. Talking to you is pleasure.'

'May I come again?' he asked.

'Whenever you like.'

CHAPTER 31

WHEN he had gone Mrs Duquesne stood for a moment, thinking about him with absent-minded friendliness. She liked him: his good looks and well-rehearsed natural charm amused her. She had an ambiguous sympathy for him as a heartless ambitious devil—his taste for luxury was foolish, but the rage, the insolence, the savage appetite, the wild beast he kept in his lean belly pleased her in a young man.

Let's hope he isn't called to account too soon, she thought lightly, dismissing him.

She heard the door-bell, and Pilar shuffling across the landing in her canvas slippers like a slug afraid to lose touch with the ground, to admit the visitor.

Mr Hudson Foster was precisely as Chatteney had described him to her, a fine figure of a Victorian, well-built, sedately well-dressed, and tranquilly, without knowing it—since his position was unassailable—self-assured. In his polite glance at her, and in the very brief glance he gave her room with its bookshelves and untidy rows of books in

French and Spanish, she caught a gleam of surprise, instantly snuffed out.

What sort of louche creature was he expecting? she thought, amused.

'It was unpardonable to ask you to see me immediately after the sad occasion, but, as I wrote you, I am flying back tomorrow, a week sooner than I intended.' He paused and said with discreet emphasis, 'As you will appreciate, I want to get the manuscript of the memoirs into safety as quickly as possible.'

She made the effort not to show any emotion. 'The memoirs?'

'Ah, you didn't know! I wondered.... They were mailed to me—I received them the day after his death. They had been mailed, I saw from the postmark, in south-west London.'

A suffocating joy filled her. 'Were you expecting them?'

He hesitated. 'No. But I had a thread of hope—a letter Sir Henry wrote me allowed me to think that all might not be lost.'

'When was that?'

'Rather more than a week ago.'

After a moment she said, 'I was told they had been burned.'

The grate full of paper ash. It could have been the ash of newspapers, of anything...

'One or two questions of fact are troubling me—which I hope you can answer,' Hudson Foster said. 'Do you know whether any money had been paid over by an English publisher?'

'No. None.'

'You are sure of that?'

'Quite sure. His wife, Renée, told me that a contract had been signed, and a copy of it given to him. He destroyed it.

I believe that the publisher has already destroyed his own copy, he told her he would.'

Mr Foster nodded, a slow regal movement of his head. 'That tallies with what Sir Henry's second letter—accompanying the manuscript—led me to expect.... Very satisfactory.... Now I must tell you what I propose to do.' His voice took on an added weight of authority and assurance. 'I look on it as a privilege and a duty—one I should be ashamed to evade—to do exactly what the author of the memoirs wished. I shall lock them away in the manuscript room of the Hudson Foundation to remain out of sight and reach for at least fifty years, perhaps longer. I shall consult only the Foundation's lawyers, who happen to be my brother and two nephews.'

'How very fortunate,' Mrs Duquesne murmured.

'Very ... In the course of nature it is my nephews or their heirs who will complete and implement what I now regard as my trust.' He paused, and went on calmly, 'We can let the future take care of itself. Since no money is involved, the legal position, whatever, in view of the letter giving me full and practically unconditional possession of the memoirs that may be—his confidence in me touches me deeply—is at least fairly unencumbered. In fifty or sixty years the people concerned now will all be dead, the work will be beyond fear of libel, and can be presented for what it is—great literature.'

Mrs Duquesne looked at him with the wicked admiration she felt for any man or woman who has no doubt, not the very faintest, that he is guided in all his decisions by an infallible judge, a private indwelling Omniscient.

'It is a heavy responsibility,' she said. 'He was lucky to be able to count on your courage.'

With a touch of reproof he said, 'Mrs Duquesne, I am saving these memoirs for the world. That scarcely needs courage, it needs the will and the means—and in my position I possess both. Morally I am doing the right thing, and materially I am able to do it. Sir Henry was not making a mistake—I think I may say that.'

'You may indeed,' she said in her deepest voice.

'I am gratified by your approval,' he said warmly.

She smiled at him. 'You should be gratified by knowing that your name will be part of literary history, always.'

'That consideration has not weighed with me,' he said suavely.

A gleam at the back of his fine eyes gave him the lie, but she was sure he did not know it. She felt a brief amused fondness for him. Why shouldn't he, if it helped him to live, purify his motives? ... With a light grief she reflected that Harry would have been delighted by this encounter between old corrupt Europe in her person and the new morality of America, the bland certainty of being right (and righteous) that goes with power—a sort of innocence.

'Would you like to read the memoirs?' he said suddenly. 'I could, yes, stay over a few days. You can read them in my hotel, Brown's Hotel—I have a sitting-room.'

'That's kind of you. No.'

'As you wish.'

Regretting that she had offended him, she said gently, 'I had a great part of them read to me—almost all.'

With intolerable sharpness, she saw the grotesque room in Marion Street and almost heard his voice. Almost, but not quite: the first thing to vanish for ever is the voice, not to be heard again even in sleep.

Curiosity got the better of Mr Foster's discretion. 'Indeed? But surely...'

He meant: Surely you were under an obligation not to see him? Mrs Duquesne looked at him without kindness.

'You were quite right to learn everything about me before coming. Perhaps we might leave it.'

Mr Foster bent his head. There was a brief silence. He succeeded in giving it a little of the solemnity of an armistice.

'One more point—of some importance. In his second letter, Sir Henry instructed me to pay to you the sum I originally offered him for the memoirs—fifty thousand dollars. This of course I shall do, at once. I have an arrangement by which I can draw on funds held in London, and if you will give me the name of your bank....'

She interrupted him. 'Don't be angry,' she said carelessly, 'but I must refuse any money. I don't want it.'

'But you are putting me in an intolerable position,' he said with energy. 'It is the condition attached to my keeping the memoirs, the only one—apart from the instruction to put them away for at least fifty years. You must let me do as I'm told. Otherwise...'

'Otherwise you won't have kept all the conditions?' she said, smiling. 'I'm sure you want to behave as legally as possible in the circumstances—peculiar. But it's ridiculous. And—do forgive me—I won't take the money.'

'A sum of fifty thousand dollars was earmarked for the Chatteney memoirs. I must use it.'

'That concerns only you,' Mrs Duquesne said. 'I'm not interested.'

'Perhaps,' he said stiffly, 'you haven't understood. I must insist on your accepting.'

'You—insist?' Mrs Duquesne said.

'I should have used some other word, but...'

'But I have refused the money,' she said, 'you mustn't argue with me.'

He took his snub finely. 'Forgive me.'

'Let me think,' she murmured. 'Yes, I have an idea. A

264

splendid idea.' Her face creased with pleasure in her own ingenuity. 'Renée Chatteney is going to sell his books. Why shouldn't you buy them from her for fifty thousand dollars and present them to some university in your country as the Chatteney library?' She went on almost slyly, 'You must feel that his wife has some right to the money.'

'Is she left badly off?'

'No. Not at all badly. She's moving into a small flat...' with Bruegel, and her memories, such little room as these will take up, she thought coldly—'and she has been offered eight or nine times what she paid for her house. But people who are well-off can always do with a little more.'

Mr Foster looked at her with something between liking and exasperation.

'I know when I'm defeated,' he said. 'It's a good suggestion. Thank you.' He paused. 'There is one other thing...'

'Oh, what?'

'Nothing that will vex you. I must have something—a letter from you, saying that you refused the money, and that—yes—you approve fully all I am doing. If you like, I can draft it for you.'

'Do that,' she said, with indifference. 'Let me have your draft, I'll copy it and sign it.'

He stood up, and looked round the room, this time openly. He seemed reluctant to go away. 'Tell me—I have read the memoirs, they are I think unique in our time—the superb skill with which he has embodied his judgement of an age in a framework of his own character and conduct. A very great book ... but is it true?'

Perhaps, she thought with anguish, this is the last time I shall be able to speak for you, my darling.

'I think they are his effort to understand himself and his violent contradictions—and in doing it he re-creates himself

265

with the conscientiousness of a great artist. So that it's partly an apologia pro vita sua, concerned to establish his motives.' She hesitated. Would an American understand *gloire*? No. 'In part what you are seeing is the way an unusually intelligent Englishman, of a very old family—that has a certain relevance—behaved in various situations, political, social'—she smiled at him—'personally, with women and other men. He took part in a great many what you would call historic occasions, and after 1938 he had a great many disappointments, and he reworked them into an admirable *récit,* classically lucid and subtle.... I think that, at the end, he became this personage who saw so clearly, penetrated so far and cruelly into himself and the society we are living in—a person of great quality, without a mean lie in him. You could say that he used himself as a great sculptor uses his clay or stone, to make a work of art.'

'Thank you,' Mr Foster said.

' "*Il veut être lucide, et dans ses plus grandes désordres il s'observe et se raille.*" '

She saw from the slightly blank expression of Mr Foster's face that he had not understood the words. No matter.

As he left he said,

'I fear that I shall not be able to come back next month for the Memorial Service. Mrs Duquesne, I shall be with you in thought. With *you.*'

Alone, she closed the door of the living-room against Pilar and her supper tray. Her face became a mask of grief superimposed on laughter, laughter slipping from under grief; her mouth opened, the mouth of a carelessly magnificent clown. Crying and smiling at once, it said,

'Oh, my love, my love, you cheated us all.'

CHAPTER 32

Two days before the Memorial Service for Chatteney, his sister telephoned to Stephen and asked him, a thing she rarely did, to come to see them.

'Why, is she ill?' he asked.

'No.' Her voice dragged a little. 'But she's found out, I don't know how, perhaps Kenneth told her, where you're working and she says if you don't turn up this evening she'll come to your office tomorrow. I think you'd better come. She's frightfully restless.'

His mother's restlessness, he found, took the form of walking about her room, clashing curtain rings on the brass pole, misplacing chairs and ornaments. She had become enormously heavy again, her cheeks, two pouches of white lard, shook as she moved, drawing behind her a wake of strong coarse scent. She had drenched herself with it, even to the swathes of vermilion hair across her forehead.

'So you've come,' she said. 'I wanted to ask you to do something for me. God knows I don't often, do I?'

'What is it?'

'I want to go to his Memorial Service. You're going, I suppose. Well, I'm coming with you. I've known him longer than you—although I hadn't a dog's idea who or what he was—and I shan't have another chance to go to a Memorial Service'—she giggled—'not even as a corpse.'

The thought of showing himself, to Colette Hyde and anyone else who knew him, with this grotesque object, appalled him. He said curtly,

'I shan't be going.'

There was room in her face for two or three emotions to play across it at once—annoyance, disbelief, disappointment. Her drooping eyelid distorted the smile she turned on him into an incipient leer; it started in him something like the sick horror he had felt as a child when he caught sight of her in a spasm of *possession*.

'You mean you don't want to take me,' she said, pouting, 'oh, come off it, I can't get there by myself and Tarry's no use getting me on and off buses, be a good boy and fetch me.' A gleam came into her eyes, below the film of grease covering the eyeball. 'I know something about the old fellow no one else knows. If you'll take me to his service I'll tell you. There now!'

He shrugged his shoulders. He had no desire to be told some squalid little detail, real or invented, about 'the olds'. (Very far back in his mind a tiny distinct image flipped over like a fish.... *Do as I tell you and I'll give you something—What?—A puppy*. Trembling with happiness he waited for his reward and after a day or two she gave him a snapshot of a dog torn out of the newspaper.... His despair, a child's incurable despair, started up her rich jeering laughter: as if the past were a long narrow corridor, it echoed back from the far end.)

'My dear mother, I'm not going.' He added unwisely, 'And I wouldn't take you if I were.'

This infuriated her. She began to scold like a fishwife, in a shrill harsh voice, and when she saw that he was turning to go away she lifted the hideous ornament she was fingering, a heavy brass gargoyle, and tried to bring it down on his skull: he dodged aside and she swung it along the chimneypiece, shattering one after another the row of Delft figures, then dropped it and threw herself at him, clawing him. The overpowering scent, and the smell of her clothes, disgusted him. He tried to free himself, dragging

268

her, holding on to his coat, across the floor. Suddenly she collapsed.

His sister ran into the room as she fell, falling in an indecent mass. 'I could hear her upstairs,' she said, 'what's happening, what have you done to her?'

'Nothing.'

Together they bent over the mound of disordered garments and flesh. 'Don't try to lift her,' Tarry said. 'I'll get the doctor.'

She had gone before he could protest and say: 'I'll go. Alone, he forced himself to look at his mother's face more closely; it was dead except for the bubble of air forming between her lips, and a gleam—anger?—at the bottom of half-open eyes. After a moment he thought that this gleam was focused on him and that it was malice.

The door opened sharply and he moved away, and watched the Indian kneel gracefully on the floor, his delicate unclean fingers pulling at the front of her dress, moving, palping the layers of flesh, lifting an eyelid. After a few minutes, rolling at Tarry a soft prune of an eye, he said,

'A day or two, a few hours.'

Is that true? Stephen wondered. A feathery excitement moved in his body, swelling and hardening.

After the abominable effort of helping the Indian, who was surprisingly strong, to lift her on to her bed, he would have gone away if he had been able to bring himself to leave Tarry. Her coolness—she refused the Indian's offer to send in some Mrs Nightingale he offered her—hurt him. How at her age had she learned it—and why, he asked himself savagely, have I left her to learn it here? Later, she sent him off to eat dinner in Kenneth's restaurant. When he came back she said in a sensible voice,

'You might just as well go to bed. I've made the bed up in your room.'

'What are you going to do?'

'Sit up, of course.'

'Then I'll sit with you.'

'There's no need.'

He kissed her, running a hand up her thin arm, feeling the sharp bone of the elbow, and down over her narrow flat hip. Without glancing at the figure in the bed—while he was in the restaurant Tarry had somehow got it into nightclothes—he made himself comfortable in an armchair. Too comfortable. In the middle of a half-formed thought —*The sooner she goes the better*—he fell asleep.

His sister's hand on his woke him.

'She's gone, Stephen.'

Standing by the bed, he touched her forehead, reluctantly. It was still warm. A shudder of panic ran through him—panic or the tearing out of a single nerve? Whatever the disturbance was, it did not last. Filled with relief, drawing a great breath of it, he looked at Tarry. She was white and tearless. Fatigue, dulling her skin and reddening her eyelids, made her look plain.

'What time is it?' he asked.

'Nearly three.'

'What are we going to do?'

'Wait. All we can do. I'll get old Mrs Nightingale when it's light enough, she's been before—a sort of nurse—she'll help me.' She smiled at him under her heavy lids with heartbreaking insouciance. 'Now you really might as well go and lie down. I'll sleep here.'

Lying outside the bed-clothes, he slept soundly and woke with a feeling of ease and freshness. For less than a second he had been a child waking up in the familiar dingy bed and listening intently to hear whether the child in the next room was awake and calling out. In the street a boy passed, whistling, and he heard the click of letter-boxes as he

270

pushed through a newspaper—exactly as it had always been. Nothing and everything had changed. He sat up, smiling triumphantly. Now, he said to himself, now at last, at last.... He could hardly wait.

The bathroom with its worn-out linoleum—his foot remembered the holes—and ill-tempered geyser was on the floor below, between the kitchen and his mother's room: he heard voices, Tarry's and a voice like a street musician's flute, coming from this room. A little bundle of the clothes Tarry had been wearing the evening before was lying in a corner of the bathroom; he looked at them with a wry smile, they might belong to any schoolboy. Has she nothing else at all? he wondered.

As he left the bathroom she was coming out of his mother's room, and he caught a glimpse through the half-opened door of a bustling old woman, folded sheets, a bowl of water on the floor—obscure images of death. Tarry smiled at him. She must have slept, if only for a few hours —colour had come back to her cheeks and brightness, gaiety, to her narrow eyes.

'Don't you want breakfast?' she said. 'I do. I'll bring it up to your room. Everything's all right, Mrs Nightingale is here.'

She came into his room with a tray she set down between them on the bed—there was no table and only one chair. He had opened the little window, and she stood at it for a moment, smiling and stretching her arms.

'It's going to be a fine day, Stephen.'

She sat down again, crossing thin legs. Jerking his head at them, he said,

'Haven't you any garments but those absurd trousers?'

'Not any thin ones,' she said carelessly.

'Time you had. . . . I'll give you some money, and as soon as you can get out for a few hours you must go to a decent

271

shop and buy what you like. And is there any reason why you shouldn't come home with me now? Can't this Nightingale female stay here—I mean for a few days until...? Livvy will be away for another month, that gives us plenty of time to find you a room near. I've been thinking'—he could not help laughing—'plans, Tarry, plans, plans, a secretarial school, perhaps, if you like, and then...'

His sister interrupted him lightly. 'She's made a will.'

'But had she anything to leave?'

'Well, no money. We live—lived—on the rent Kenneth paid for the storeroom, nothing grand, and then the studio. I never knew how much that was.' She frowned. 'Never mind. And then the annuity left her, that very rich old girl she used to give messages to from her son after he was killed. That was years ago, when she was still—you know.... It wasn't very much, but it came regularly.'

'Do you believe she got messages?' he asked lightly.

She hesitated. 'Yes.' She added hurriedly, 'But I don't know where from, who—what kind of beings sent them.'

'Forget it.... Where is this will?'

'In her wardrobe.... And there's this house, about another fifteen years' lease—she explained it all to me. She's left it to you. Nothing to me.'

He looked at her in disbelief. 'Why to me? Was she off her head?'

'Oh, no. You were the son.' She gave a dry little laugh. 'She used to say: If I knew who your father was I might try to get something for you from there.... But she didn't know.'

'It doesn't matter about the will,' he said. 'You can have all there is. Of course.'

'I knew you'd say that,' she said smiling at him, 'but...'

He cut her short. 'Listen, my darling. You needn't think about anything. And you needn't think that you're going

272

to have nothing of your own. When you're trained—I'll pay for that, of course—I'll find a place for you in Hyde's. You know, I'm well in there already, and I'm sure, quite sure, that in time I shall do very well indeed, and be well off. And you, you won't have a dull life, I've made friends, and you'll like Livvy when you see her, and ...'

'No.'

'What d'you mean no?' he said gaily. 'Don't you want to be a secretary You needn't be. What would you rather do, what would you like? I'll help you to do anything, anything you say.'

She looked at him, a clear very bright look. He noticed that her hands were trembling a little. 'Perhaps you won't like this. I've become a Catholic, I mean I've been received —exactly two months ago, the day I was twenty-two.'

He was startled. And for a moment sharply vexed. 'But why didn't you tell me?'

'You weren't here.'

'You could have told me you were going to.... How long has this been going on? Why the devil didn't you tell me about it?'

'Don't be angry.' She touched his arm. 'I'm sorry if I've disappointed you. I didn't think you'd mind terribly.'

'I don't.'

'I wanted something'—she frowned, like a child with too few words to explain itself to adults—'something fixed and decent—and hard.'

'Couldn't you have waited a bit? You knew I'd give you a safe decent life the minute I had the chance.'

As he said it, he felt guilty. Poor Tarry, poor child, she might have had to wait years. He thought sharply: I could have come here oftener. To see what she was up to.

'Yes, I know,' she said. A very strange expression crossed her face, something like scorn, a youthful loving scorn. 'I

273

knew you would be terribly generous and give me things, but they mightn't have been any use to me. You always wanted to be—well, what Kenneth calls you, a man of means.... How's our fabulously beautiful man of means? he says when I see him.'

'Blast Kenneth,' he said, grinning. He had recovered his coolness and good-humour. 'My dear little love. It doesn't matter, nothing matters. Just tell me what you'd like to happen to you now, what you want to do, and I'll help you.'

'Of course I've got to be trained.'

'Yes, of course. But what for? What's in your mind?'

He was beginning to be amused. What future had she been dreaming for herself? Nothing, he was certain, high-flying, but at that it might be intellectually out of her reach.

She said quietly, 'I'm going to train as a medical nun—you know, to work abroad.'

'You.... Are you crazy?' He stood up with such violence that she only just caught the tray before it could slide to the floor. 'What did you say?'

Now that it was out she was no longer afraid. She said cheerfully,

'It won't cost anything. I mean—they'll be pleased if I have a little money—if you're really going to give me the money from this house. And of course there are a few things I need, but it might be better if you waited, I...'

'You must be ill,' he interrupted. 'Ill or off your head.

'You're angry. Don't be. I knew you wouldn't like it, but it's the thing I want. I've thought it over for months, and talked to more than one person who knows. I'm not making a mistake. Do believe me. I really know what I'm doing.'

'That's more than I can believe.' He forced himself to

speak calmly. 'You've had such a life with her, the old devil, that you're afraid. Afraid of being free, afraid to be happy. Afraid to be who you *are*. You a nun! My God, what a lie.'

He leaned over and touched her breasts with his fingers, blindly. They were small and hard: the absurd thought struck him that she had green blood in her veins. She drew back without a sign that she minded the gesture or had even noticed it.

'And you,' she said, with her sweet smile, 'when you make yourself charming to people, to get what you want out of them, isn't that lies?'

'I don't deceive myself—which is what you're doing.

'Oh,' she said swiftly, 'but that sort of telling the truth is a fearful lie. You're saying: I don't care what harm I do other people or what lies I tell them, I don't lie to myself, so really I'm honest, not a liar or a hypocrite.... A sincere liar—that's awful, worse than just ordinary lies.'

'Where did you get this nauseating rubbish? From some priest.'

'You talk about my being afraid to be who I am, but you, my dear—all things to all people—who are you?'

'God help me,' he said, 'only an utter dolt or a mindless fanatic is the same to everybody. Do I want to spend my life pretending to be a respectful employee with no—never mind, never mind, I can't talk to you.'

She stood up, pushing the tray into safety against the wall. Her eyes, more green than grey this morning, had the mischief as well as the wariness of a sensible child, used to looking after itself.

'No, never mind,' she said. She stroked his cheek lightly. 'Do you remember that night when we decided to run away? I was about five, so you must have been eight or nine. But when we got downstairs into the street it was raining cats and dogs and I had only a thin coat, and after a few steps we were both soaked to the skin, so we crept back upstairs to your room, we didn't even bother to undo the parcel to get at our pyjamas but tore our wet clothes off and got into your bed and lay there naked and shivering, and I cried and you sat up in bed in the icy cold and nursed me until I dropped asleep. Do you remember it?'

'Well?'

'You weren't trying to seem anything then. You didn't want to be liked, or loved, you were ... loving.'

'So what?' he said bitterly. 'We're not children.'

'Poor Stephen, I wish I wasn't such a disappointment to you,' she said very gently. 'But, you know, I might have disappointed you anyhow, I'm not intelligent and I didn't learn much at school.'

Rage and grief clawed at him at the same time. He tried to imagine her slender legs and quick narrow body inside the shapeless garments of a nun.

'To choose to commit suicide,' he stuttered, 'to mutilate yourself, turn your back on life before you've even tried living, why, why?'

She laughed a little, wrinkling her nose. 'Why are you so sure that I'm not doing the very thing I was meant to do? I might, you know, by choosing to turn my back—as you say—be choosing myself.'

'That's nonsense,' he said wearily. 'Some damned priest has got hold of you.'

'No, no, you're wrong, I had to look for one, and he wasn't easy with me, I can tell you. For ages he seemed only trying to beat me off, he said if I was only afraid of being like my mother I was being driven by selfish fear and egoism, and ...'

He interrupted her. 'Egoism! Didn't you think about me at all when you were making your revolting plans?'

'Yes, yes, many many times.'

'Then for God's sake, why?'

She said slowly, 'I wouldn't be any good even to you as a . . . a drifter, an imposter. I had to go my own way. Can't you see? *You* ought to be able to see that.'

He felt that all the blood in his body was concentrated behind his eyes and in his wrists: seizing her by the shoulders he shook her, then crushed her against himself so violently that she gasped, 'No, Stephen,' and struggled to get away from him. He let her go.

'You can't go,' he said, staring, 'I need you too much.'

She gave him a clear frowning look. 'Well, you shouldn't. You shouldn't mind all that much. It's not right.'

He closed his lips together against a groan of laughter started in him by the childish phrase. She was there, within a few inches of him, the one creature he loved more than he loved himself, and completely out of his reach. He was unspeakably humiliated, unspeakably defeated and in pain.

'I shan't see you,' he said. *'Don't go, Tarry.'*

'I'll always be thinking of you,' she said in a young smiling inexorable voice.

'You'll'—anger seized him again—'why don't you say you'll pray to your bloody God for me?'

Very lightly, she brushed her hard square-tipped little fingers across his mouth, then picked the tray up and left him.

CHAPTER 33

A s a spectacle the Memorial Service was noticeably more
impressive, more of a success, than the cremation. It had
drawn a larger . number of personages—much larger.
(Advice to the celebrated, thought Stephen: Never die
during the summer vacation.) They were all here, from the
French ambassador to the famous aged poet who seemed
to be kept going on Old English hormones. Cordelia
Brand, in black, had come, doubtless meaning to enrich
her autobiography with a moving delicately salacious passage on Chatteney's elderly passion for her. Looking round
the great church, Stephen felt sure that many of these
eminent and near-eminent men and women were attending their own memorial: as they knelt, stood, went
through the motions of prayer, their thoughts formed a
vapour round their heads like the breath of an animal in
frost: How long before they come here for me? What
when I am the absence, the nothing, they are supposed to
be thinking about on their knees?

He himself had not given Chatteney a whole thought.
The mere act of seating himself here, with nothing to
occupy him beyond the need to make the same gestures as
the rest of the congregation, brought him sharply face to
face with his defeat. Yesterday, when he was working, and
at night—he had spent it with Sarah, a highly successful,
highly efficient night—he had had no difficulty in keeping
his mind off Tarry. She returned now, smiling, a ghost in
close-fitting jeans, out of place here. His anger and helpless
grief pricked him. The idea that for the next few weeks—
how many?—he would have to see and talk to her, about
their mother's funeral, her will, her own intolerably imbecile

future, exasperated him. Until they were over he could not even begin the process of pushing her to the back of his mind. To become a shadow, then nothing.

This can't go on, he thought abruptly: I can't afford regrets.

He forced himself to think coldly. So far—apart from Tarry—he had had no failures. He was burrowing his way every week more securely into a society of rich secure people; he was not safe yet, but he had come, in a surprisingly short time, a long way from the obscure secretly ambitious tutor and secretary with his two good suits and half-dozen shirts. Farther still from 41A Marion Street. He had made no irrevocable mistake, fumbled none of the chances offered him. Nor, when the next chance offered itself, would he fumble that. He was—what was the precise word?—*available*. Splendidly available, free of all tiresome obligations—Livvy was in no way an obligation—sensually happy to use himself and his talents (including his talent for seduction) to the limit. To have started from Marion Street, and at twenty-six to have got as far as he had ... and without having had to injure, betray, or maliciously deprive man or woman.... On the contrary; by marrying Livvy he had done her a service. Chatteney? The incident of the letter? I might, perhaps, have acted differently, he thought lightly, but it was, admit it, extremely tricky. On the whole I have been lucky in that I have never—so far— had to destroy anybody's happiness to secure my own. If ... oh, wait until it happens.

Kneeling—because his neighbours on either side had knelt—he had a moment of acute excitement. Given the chance, he thought, I shall reach a point when Frederick Hyde will want to tie me safely to the firm, or, if that door fails to open, I shall find another that will. *I'm on my way....* His mother's voice speaking about Chatteney....

Abruptly he decided to employ a solicitor to deal with her will and with all Tarry's needs. And not to attend the funeral. In that way, he need not see her again.

It was brutal, but her desertion of him, her selfishness, justified it.

Without looking closely, he was conscious of a crack opening in him, opened by her short fingers. It was nothing he could not close, provided he were quick and brutal enough.

For the last time—and let it be the last, he thought savagely—he allowed her to stand and smile at him from narrowly bright eyes under surprised eyebrows, hands in her pockets. Then he dismissed her.

Outside, on the steps of St Paul's, he stood a minute to watch the play of feeling across the faces of the mummers as they slipped from under the great weight of stone: solemnity, indifference, self-consciousness, curiosity, even gaiety. They came out like bats into the light and the honey-coloured September sun.

Mrs Duquesne came out slowly. Her eyes, empty of thought, searched the ground under her feet. Whatever she sought was more remote than any living distance. Hesitating at the edge of the steps, she lifted her hand to her forehead before walking blindly and rapidly down. Stephen started forward. He checked himself. Let her go, he thought briefly: what more can she do for me?

He saw Cordelia Brand emerge and look about her for some friend (or some enemy) to pay for her taxi, and fled.

Towards six o'clock that evening he was crossing the entrance hall of Claridge's after an hour spent making himself agreeable to a foreign publisher not important enough to force Colette Hyde to bestir herself.

Sauntering ahead of him, he saw a pair of legs that were

surely unmatched on either side of the Atlantic. He walked past them, turned, and faced Miss Virginia Ancel.

'It's you—we always meet in hotels,' she said gaily.

'Twice in three months,' he said. 'It's pitiable.'

The sensation was perfectly familiar, a wordless certainty, neither wholly serious nor wholly pleasant, that he was face to face with a moment of crisis—like the split second the soloist lives through before bringing bow and strings into touch—and a familiar sense of detachment as though he were standing at his own elbow, watching his gestures, overhearing himself. He knew very well what to say and how to glance at her as he said it. But—for the first time—he felt not so much confident of success as unspeakably committed to it.

'Last time I ran away.'

'Yes. Why?'

'I was afraid you were being called to get bad news. Terrible of me. But I don't like being told that something sad has happened. It bores me and I don't want to know. I'm very sorry.'

'But you're perfectly right,' he said. 'Why should you allow yourself to be bored or harrowed? Absurd.... What are you doing here?'

'This minute? When I saw you I was wondering what to do for a quarter of an hour before going to meet my mother and bring her back here, she's visiting a friend in— would you believe it?—Whitehall. She collects important Englishmen.'

He listened to this nonsense with pleasure. American voices, even the most carefully nurtured, have not yet been devitalised, flattened, purged of colour and resonance, as have most educated English voices.

'You have time to drink a martini.'

'Thank you.'

Facing him in a low chair, she crossed her legs: above the knee they were as prodigiously flawless as between it and the ankle. Her seemingly fragile bones were probably made of one of the new metals, extremely light and extremely hard, invented by her father's scientists. There was more than a spice of menace in a creature at once so fine, elegant, and steeled against unwanted feelings. It excited and in the same moment steadied him. He had none of the advantages over her he had over a woman twice his age or over a young woman without family or standing of any sort, like Sarah.

'I don't know your name!'

'Stephen. Stephen Hind. I know yours, I asked one of the hotel clerks in Baden.... What is your father buying here?'

'Nothing, he didn't come. This is a genuine holiday. Mamma and I have been staying with my sister in Italy, her husband is an Italian, the Marchese del Grianta, my father was furious when she married him and won't see the poor man, he's terribly sweet, he breeds horses, but he's useless as a son-in-law, quite useless. Poor daddy, he did so want a son, and all he got is two dumb girls.'

His smiling glance took in another detail: the line of her jaw, from the tip of a small ear to the point of her chin, was a surprisingly long one; yet, seen in full, her face was narrow, on a long slender neck.

'I don't think you know what you're saying.'

'I do so. And the worst—for daddy—is that he believes I might be intelligent if only I would try. When I use a little bit of my allowance to buy stock, I always make money. Always. That infuriates him, he would far sooner I lost the lot. But, you know, it interests me to play the market, I like risks. But not to do it the whole time—there are too many things I enjoy doing.'

'Such as?'

'Oh, travel, music, I adore Verdi, don't you, and Britten, and I like dancing, I can dance until breakfast without a stop, and I like to ski, ride, swim. Oh, scores of things.' She glanced at the gold wafer dangling from the lapel of her dress. 'Mercy, the time! I must fly.'

Stephen stood up. 'Before you go tell me how I can see you without waiting to run across you in a hotel in Rome or Berlin.'

'Are you ... you wouldn't dine with us this evening? No, of course you can't, your wife....'

His voice carried a fine overtone of ironical gaiety. 'I haven't a wife. No sooner were we back from Germany than she went off to stay with her grandmother—great-grandmother—in the country.'

'But ... But how dull!'

'For her? Not at all. She's living in the house she lived in until she married, in great comfort—a great deal happier and more comfortable than she is in London.'

'But ...'—she hesitated long enough to give a sudden effect of intimacy to the words—'how could she bear to leave you?'

'Almost every Englishwoman—didn't you know?—prefers her son to her husband.' He gave her through his lashes one of the long sincere glances which had never yet failed him. 'My private belief is that most of them marry because it's the easiest way to acquire a son.'

She met his look with the utmost steadiness. 'No, I don't believe that. No one you had married would feel that.'

The tension between them made it difficult to breathe. He held her glance until she turned away her head.

'I really must go.'

'Did you, or did you not, ask me to dinner?' he said.

283

She laughed under her breath. 'I asked you. You'll come, won't you? Here. Eight o'clock.'

'But your mother ...'

'My mother will be delighted.'

'You're very kind.'

The line drawn by her body as she stepped into the taxi had been taught and practised; she backed in, folding her legs in last, in a single unbroken movement. As the cab drew away along Brook Street, she waved to him, smiling.

He saw the next step he would take clearly, so clearly, with such intense almost impersonal excitement, that he knew there was not the smallest danger he would miss it.